I0739335

MARY CRANE

AND A

POMPEY HOLLOW BOOK CLUB SEANCE WITH SHERLOCK!

~BOOK 3~

A NOVEL

FIRST EDITION

JEROME MARK ANTIL

Copyright © 2015 Jerome Mark Antil - Dallas TX
All rights reserved.

ISBN-13: 978-0-9893044-5-0 (HC)
ISBN-13: 978-0-9893044-6-7 (TPB)
ISBN: 0989304469

**Library of Congress Control
Number: 2014922610**

SCENE: RURAL AMERICA
TIME: SIXTY YEARS AGO
(CENTRAL NEW YORK FAMILY FARM COUNTRY)

Historical references offered by:
Fabius Historical Society; New Woodstock Historical Society; Cincinnatus
Historical Society; Binghamton Township Historical Society;
NY Historical Society; Onondaga County Historical Society
Bi-Plane flight and radio instructions: Robert Penoyer
Wing and wind for flight instructions: Peter Sealey
British slang Coach – Maurice C. de Montfalcon

INTRODUCING
Para_coustics_© Sound & Effects _by_ Little York Books

_All characters appearing in this
work are fictitious. Any resemblance
to real persons, living or dead, is purely
coincidental._

Cover Illustration: Jessica Clark
Interior Illustrations: Marina Giraud
Para_coustics_ sound dubbing – Don Canterbury PRIZM

PRINTED IN AMERICA

ALSO BY
JEROME MARK ANTIL

HANDBOOK FOR WEEKEND DADS
...and anytime grandparents.
Little York Books - ISBN: 978-0-9893044-0-5 (TPB)

THE POMPEY HOLLOW BOOK CLUB
Little York Books - ISBN: 978-0-9847187-4-0 (TPB)

AVENTURAS DE PASCUA DEL CLUB DE LECTURA POMPEY HOLLOW
Little York Books - ISBN: 978-0-9847187-7-1 (Ebook)

THE LONG STEM IS IN THE LOBBY
Little York Books - ISBN: 978-0-9847187-6-4 (HC)

THE BOOK OF CHARLIE
- Spirit of the Pompey Hollow Book Club
Little York Books - ISBN: 978-0-9893044-3-6 (TPB)

ABOUT THE VOICES

I remember vocal inflections of an upstate New Yorker in the 1940's and 1950's being similar to English speaking Canadians. In individual discourse, however, I often found rural dialects could vary from farm to farm. An elderly individual, as an example, living alone in the country, with no electricity– thus no radio to listen to or neighbors to converse with might manage with vocabularies or dialects from immigrant parents, their one room schoolhouse days, or picking up words and phrases while serving in the armed services in 1916's WWI. Some country folk in the period of my youth lived much of their lives without dialogue or reading materials – alone and in silence. A character in this story is just such a gentleman, someone I looked up to and admired. He was a person with fractured grammar who, to this young lad, offered more wisdom and insight than many of those better read and more fortunate in station. Author

HAVE YOU MET MARY CRANE?

It was the Easter in 1949 after they'd saved the rabbits from becoming livestock and rabbit stew suppers - when her friends decided to create a name for their new club of valor.

Barber stepped up on the cemetery stone, raised his arm in the air and declared:

"Ain't a mom in the county would stop us from going to a club meeting - even on a school night - if we called ourselves the Pompey Hollow Book Club."

"Well, we might stop saying ain't," Mary suggested.

Mary was made president.

That was four years ago.

Now Mary's fourteen.

TABLE OF CONTENTS

For

"Mickey and Moose"
Captain Donald G. Lederman...
...the B17 Crew
and his Mary.

A Novel series inspired by

Ike's D-Day invasion…

General Dwight D. Eisenhower
Five Star General

Supreme Commander-in-Chief
Allied Expeditionary Force
European Theater of Operations
1943-1945

…our childhood hero.

READER WARNING

By reading this book you may learn what American rural life was like in the shadows of WWII around 1953. My friends and I got to live it.

If you weren't there, enjoy our innocence, foibles.

If you were, enjoy the memories.

Author

A WORD FROM CHARLIE PITTS

It's fun now, bein' a guardian angel and all – knowin' I can be as smart as I want or need to be at any given time. I can give young readers the colloquial flavor of this period of time in rural America, without giving them a completely wrong impression of proper English.

This 'optional extra' for angels, came with the wings.

~ Ole Charlie, Guardian Angel

CHAPTER ONE

BOYS WILL
BE BOYS

First time he ever laid eyes on the naked lady calendar, Jerry stepped on a cat.

These types of bolts out of the blue happened without warnin' to young teen boys in 1953, and to cats of any age.

Guardian angels like ole Charlie here knew these sorts of things. We called them curveballs from Lucifer.

Spellbound to near stupor, he stood starin', forgettin' what he was even doin' in the coffee diner's kitchen.

In her full glory the lady was, just as naked as a jaybird - and at eye level, to boot. Magnetic blue eyes following his the way those calendar-girl-eyes have of doing - salacious being the word for them.

That's biblically speaking, of course.

The cat's yowlin' and cobra-like hiss kept him from going into a spell he mightn't have broken soon enough to finish running his errand for Big Mike.

While the lad gathered himself, the cat eyeballed a rip in the screen door as opportunity the second Jerry might be considerate enough to lift his foot…chances being better in the streets – one would think - was on this cat's mind.

Backing into a butcher block table, Jerry stumbled off the tail… and with a hiss, the cat parted company…

It was Saturday morning around nine thirty.

As he typically did when he rode to Homer with Big Mike on Saturdays, Jerry had walked over and picked up the bakery's mail from the Post Office across the street. Ever since he was nine, being trusted with the box key and bakery mail, running that errand made him feel important. And now, being thirteen and a freshman, before delivering the mail out behind the alley to Big Mike's office on the second floor, he'd take the time to sit in Leonard's Coffee Shop with his routine of hot chocolate and glazed donut, passing time with the comics in the Cortland Standard.

Glancing up at the wall clock hanging above two toasters and a stainless steel bowl of slick, soft butter, he saw it was later than he usually delivered the mail.

Little Orphan Annie was cumbersome having more adult dialog in it than he was accustomed. It required thought, almost like a schoolbook, at too early an hour for a Saturday.

Pressed for time, he grabbed up the mail and took a short cut through Leonard's coffee shop kitchen which led to the back ally of the bakery.

That explains everything up to now, exceptin' perhaps why a 1952 Marilyn Monroe calendar was still hangin' on the wall, it being autumn 1953.

It was this particular November Saturday morning that would begin a week-long odyssey of a kind that could earn guardian angels like ole Charlie here their keep, even extra feathers. It's a story long since a legend in the Crown, but one that needs to be retold now, for the great-grandchildren.

To know how to find the Crown you need to get a map and draw a line from Big Mike's place on Cardner Road all the way up to Cazenovia, then one back down to Delphi Falls, then up to Pompey Center, down to Fabius, up to Pompey, back down to Apulia Station, up to Lafayette and then down to Tully. From Tully draw a line clear across just past Gooseville Corners, down to Cardner Road and that will be the Crown. Weren't much more than sixty farms in it back then.

This is its tale exactly how it began back in 1953.

It was just days after Halloween, a few weeks before Thanksgiving.

The air was crisp, I do remember that. The leaves on the trees were bursts of reds and yellows and breathtaking as far as you could see.

Not making it easy for me, Jerry began making inquiries. Questions his seeing the calendar had churned up.

Problem was he was askin' the wrong people so naturally he was getting the wrong answers. He first talked to his brother, Dick - known to be a scoundrel at the drop of a hat. Jerry went next to Duba – Dick's friend - another rascal of repute, ready to cloud a victim's innocence at a moment's notice.

Both were older by enough years to stir a pot like this to boiling. Good young men, mind you, but scamps given the slightest opportunity to take sport in a lad's naiveté. They'd bellow, bantering foolishness, strutting about waving their arms like Gospel preachers. Why they was making up yarns so bold and audacious to an innocent mind they might as well have been painting vulgar pictures with a floor mop! They were jubilant in their illustrations of seamy illusions of purposes meant for certain of nature's parts in God's creation. They would elaborate so, pausing only to watch the lad scratch his head and squirm.

Any guardian angel worth a salt knows to come up with a path to alternatives, keeping moral perspective intact. If we've done our job proper, a lad could reflect on his past to find his future paths.

It's called character.

Jerry and his friends in the Pompey Hollow Book Club were in their awkward stages of development, but they had a healthy respect for womanhood.

If you haven't met them you should:

Jerry, Holbrook, Barber, Bases, Randy, and Mayor.

Jerry, the lad who stepped on the cat, is a one-time city boy from Cortland who inspired the club's beginnings soon after he moved to Delphi Falls back in 1949. He created a reputation early on after walking behind the working end of Farmer Parker's horse-drawn manure-spreader-wagon piled high, steaming and operating at full crank. That situation speaks volumes about the boy.

Holbrook is Jerry's best friend. Poor as a church mouse, the boy couldn't see the side of a barn without his thick glasses. He worked after school to buy his family a water heater. He gets Jerry's lunch quarter every day so he can get a square meal in the school cafeteria. (Weren't his idea. Jerry makes him take it, - said it was what best friends do. Jerry always considers it an even-up trade for Holbrook's sack lunch, which was usually a sugar or ketchup sandwich, for appearances sake, made by his momma, who had seventeen young'uns to feed.)

Barber, this boy has worked his daddy's farm since the day he could walk. Ain't all that much bigger now but he liked to talk, so Mary Crane, the club president made him the club's meeting-caller.

There's Bases – he does nothing without a baseball glove on his hand, eating included. He fetches foul balls outta the creek for a dime apiece at Sunday games in the stone quarry.

Randy is a good friend to all. His daddy, Mr. Vaas drives the milk can hauler from barns to dairy before sunup and could often be seen hauling a load of kids to the picture show or to club meetings in between his stops at farms.

Then there is Mayor. They all call Bobby Penoyer, 'Mayor'. (Seems everyone just reckoned he'd grow up to be mayor – so 'Mayor' stuck.)

Why the whole lot of them had such a healthy respect for womanhood they even elected Mary Crane to lead them since back when they were nine. It was round about the same time ole Charlie here passed on and became their Guardian Angel.

Now in their teens - thirteen to fifteen - and having started high school, I won't lie. The boys have been known to pass the time playing pitch and guessing who in their ninth grade might have started wearing brassieres - but as God is my judge – and He is - not a one of them would think of making sport disrespecting their mothers, sisters or friends – or women in general.

These lads were now of an age when kissing a girl was beyond phenomena. It was generally considered a natural pastime, like baseball, if the occasion would arise. Holding hands at the picture show was another. Those recreations and spin-the-bottle at birthday or square dance socials were pretty much accepted as polite and respectful expressions of affection. Their fathers were excellent male role models for the most part. The brave young men in uniform who came home from the War throughout the 1940s also made lasting impressions on how important a family was to a person...

...and Jerry and his friends saw a lot of young men returning home from that War, living during the whole War-torn 1940s as they had.

Take it from me; there were only two kinds of teenagers beginning their coming of age in 1953. There were those who admitted having a curiosity about Nature's ways, and there were the liars.

Ole Charlie here was confident in the wholesomeness of those under my wing.

For the time being though, especially this single moment of this particular week, I had good reason to want to manoeuver around this interruption by a curiosity that started - shall we say, with Jerry stepping on a cat?

I'd do my best to get him through the gum-flappin' foolishness of Dick and Duba's braggadocios.

Struttin' around like peacocks, stompin' and scuffing in the crackling fallen autumn leaves, they even went out of their way to tell the lad they were going to the New York State Fair in Syracuse on Friday and sneaking under the big canvas tent on the Midway. They plan to sit in front row seats and watch the breath-taking - 'Hoochie Coochie' - all-girl peep show – starring the Beauteous Bombshells from Paris Review, like the poster promised.

"Why would we waste a State Fair day off from school gawking at a stupid wall calendar when we can see the real thing live and in person?" Dick said.

"Insalubrious," shouted Duba, pointing a Latin textbook in the air, trying to wrap depravity with a cellophane intellect.

"Shut up!" blurted Jerry – defending his first calendar girl.

"A bevy of them - ladies from the world over!" Duba affirmed, attempting to tantalize the boy.

"A plethora. A virtual harem," Dick reaffirmed.

"That means, a bunch," offered Duba.

Dick and Duba would punctuate inappropriate innuendo with a devilish snort or snicker, sometimes choking on their own cigarette smoke in guffaw. They'd boast as though each had been around the block a few times with girls.

Ole Charlie here knew better – the two sixteen-year-old braggarts knew more about gettin' their faces slapped and eyes blackened than they did about worldly wilds they were going on about. They were putting on a big show in front of an innocent kid, sure enough. All talk.

Innocence oft-times sees through these moments. It's a blessing. I would handle these matters in due course. When the time was right and the moon was full, I'd maybe call on a few of my angel friends (like angel Arnold) for some help. Might even have another Guardian Angel Congress on Big Mike's barn-garage roof to conjure with and collaborate on the calendar situation.

There were bigger needs this Saturday morning, though, important needs my flock weren't aware of.

Seems it was early this morning that Farmer Parker, across the road from Jerry's house got terrible laid up reaching too far off a tall ladder trying to rehang the hay-fork-lift up top of his hayloft cupola. A flock of pigeons fluttering from a rafter spooked him causing him to lose his footing.

If you'll recall, the Pompey Hollow Book Club borrowed his hay-fork-lift to hoist Minneapolis Moline Conway and the two girls with the polio and in leg braces up top of the pine tree on Halloween, the night they caught the Nazi crooks.

Not needing it until today, Farmer Parker let the hay-fork-lift set in his barn until this morning. His rubber boot slipped on a rung - but he caught himself - wrenching his back doing it. Ailing so, Dr. Brudny came in from Fabius shakin' a finger at Farmer Parker for trying to climb such a tall ladder at his age - ordering him three days bed rest.

"Mrs. Parker, make him lay still and get this here liniment applied - like it or not - every few hours," instructed the doctor.

The doctor even warned her she would have to make him rest - called him an ornery ole coot.

Well, pained as he was, Farmer Parker was still a-grinnin' and snickerin' a mite into his pillow. Had been since the night he helped the Pompey Hollow Book Club run those Nazi POW escapees off to their just desserts- making him feel young and alive again.

Problem here in the Crown is 'bed and rest' were two words which didn't often appear together in a farmer's daylight vocabulary. Least not in 1953, they didn't. They couldn't - cows had to be milked twice a day – before sunup and after sundown. The sun was good but couldn't take a chance on rain coming. The cut hay on top of the hill looking down over the cemetery had to be barn lofted before rain came and tainted it in the field leaching out its nutrition.

Thinking all what had to be done and nobody to do it was when Mrs. Parker set her coffee cup and saucer down, and picked the wall telephone earpiece from its cradle. She cranked the handle and asked Myrtie, the operator, if she would kindly get Missus, across the way on the wire. She then proceeded to tell Missus their woes, holding back the weepy tears of despair in her tone.

Mrs. Parker was a strong woman. Farm women were - like the Knockout roses behind her porch she raised mainly on supper dishwater. She just needed a good ear for now and maybe some ideas – some time to think.

"Fay doesn't cotton to being laid up," she said, "worse - he says he won't be still. He's determined to work the farm."

"No husband does," said Missus. "Like to stay put, I mean. They're all such boys when they're sick."

"I'm afraid he'll hurt himself permanently," said Mrs. Parker. "Without this farm, I don't know what we would do."

"Now don't you worry, dear," Missus said. "There're plenty of friends around to help. Let me find my boys and I'll call you back. No need to fret. Sit by the phone."

Before hanging up, Mrs. Parker added, "He's worried because the almanac says a rough winter is coming soon."

Missus walked through the house looking for either Jerry or Dick. Their brother, Gourmet Mike was away at college, in Syracuse. This being a Saturday neither were to be found. No telling where they were off to but, in her mind, Dick was most likely with Duba under the hood of a car somewhere. Jerry, she thought, was probably back from his Saturday morning trip to the bakery with Big Mike and up under the second falls with Holbrook or plinking cans with the 22, or above it watching beavers build a dam for winter.

Not certain, Missus picked up the phone.

"Myrtie, can you connect me with the Barbers, please?"

"Are you looking for your boys, Missus?"

"Desperately! The Parkers need help."

"I've heard," said Myrtie.

"I need to find either one of the boys."

Now, if any one person could thread a needle of where every living soul was in what Jerry and his club called "the Crown" in 1953, it was, Myrtie, the rural telephone operator out of New Woodstock. From her second floor walk-up telephone exchange board Myrtie could smell a trail of anyone who's picked up a telephone better than a bloodhound. She's even been known to help the club solve a crime or two by using her talent for listening.

"Missus, I know for certain Dick called for Duba this morning to meet him in Manlius for something or other, it seems to me it was about getting car parts – a spark plug or something," said Myrtie.

Myrtie spared Missus from what else she had learned listening in on Dick and Duba's conversation. She overheard their going on about wondering if they'd get seen by any teachers or caught by any parents when they go onto the Midway at the State Fair and sneak into the 'girlie-girlie' show tent this coming Friday. The lads were discussing such detail like which of them was going to lift the tent flap first so the other could crawl under to see if the coast was clear.

"They were both going to drive and meet up in Manlius," Myrtie said. "I think Jerry is at Barbers helping shovel manure into the honey wagon. Big Mike dropped him there not long ago.

According to Tommy Kellish this morning up on Berry Road, Holbrook isn't working at the Tully bakery today and is being dropped off at Barbers as soon as Mr. Holbrook comes home from the railroad and can drive him. He would have walked but he had to hang out some wash on the clothesline for his mother. They're all going to a picture show in Cazenovia. "Stalag 17" is playing, I do believe. It's a War movie - a true story. Jerry with the money Mr. Barber pays him for shovelling manure."

Myrtie took a deep breath.

Young Bobby answered, "Hello?"

"Here you go, Missus, good luck," interrupted Myrtie. "If I hear anymore, I'll ring you up."

"Hello, this is Missus. I'm looking for Dale. To whom am I speaking, please?"

"Hi Missus, this is Bobby. Dale's out in the barn, with Jerry."

"Why, Bobby, it's good to hear your voice. Hello. How's your daddy?"

"Daddy's good. They're putting up silage."

"Tell him hello for us. Sweetheart, would you please run out and get Jerry and put him on the phone for me?"

"Hold on, I'll go get him."

"Thank you, dear."

While she waited Missus thought of Mrs. Parker's plight, of Farmer Parker, a farmer with no hired help, in need of a helping hand. She knew Jerry and others would be there for him.

She thought back to the time (not that long ago) her Big Mike was taken away from them for a year with tuberculosis. TB was the fear of the land. Still was in 1953.

It happened on a winter day. The sun was out but it was well below zero, cold enough to bind up your nostrils. Dick and Jerry had stepped off the school bus and saw a car they didn't recognize start driving toward them from the house...crunching down the ice crusted snowy drive...they could tell by the stature of the silhouette they were able to make out that Big Mike was in the backseat, a passenger. A medical aide in a white uniform was driving and what appeared to be a hospital nurse was sitting on the passenger side of the front seat.

Big Mike's tests had come in positive for TB, and they were afraid the boys could be infected so they drove on. The car didn't stop or even so much as slow down for the boys to get a look.

The two could see Big Mike turn around in the backseat and wave a gentle, sad wave. He was weeping, and neither of them knew why or where he was going. They stood and watched (out of love and respect, in case he was still watching them), until the car had turned down Cardner Road.

Thinking back to that day Missus remembered that Jerry started to cry. Like he cried when Ole Charlie here died and became their guardian angel. Their dad had never left the family like this before and neither of the boys had any idea why—or why he didn't stop to talk. It was all kept from them until now. She watched them running as fast as they could into the house to find her standing in the book den, staring out the front window with tears in her eyes.

That's how Jerry and Dick learned their dad, Big Mike, had tuberculosis…and…and that they wouldn't be able to see him at all for an entire year he would be in a "sanitarium"…

Hearing sounds of footsteps coming through the earpiece, Missus started, sitting up straight.

He and his brother Dick took charge and ran the house all while their dad was away. Jerry wouldn't let his friend Farmer Parker down, she thought; it wasn't in his nature.

"Hello?"

"Jerry, Farmer Parker is hurt, and needs help."

Click

It wasn't but forty-five minutes when Jerry, Barber and Bases were standing on the grey back porch talking with Mrs. Parker about all there was to get done. It wasn't another hour when

Randy's pap, Carl Vaas, was droppin' Randy, Holbrook, Mary Crane, and the Mayor off to help.

Things was about to happen.

The Pompey Hollow Book Club was about to get 'er done for Farmer Parker.

A week you won't soon be forgetting, I'm telling you.

A friend was in need.

*Big Mike's and Missus house and waterfalls
across from Farmer Parkers*

CHAPTER TWO

LIFT THAT CAN, TOTE THAT PAIL

For a Border Collie, Buddy was gettin' on in years. 'Bout blind with cataracts, but he surely knew Farmer Parker's young friend by scent and gentle manner. He missed Jerry but hadn't stepped off the back porch to run greet him if ever he walked by like in the old days for more than a year. Wouldn't leave the lad's side on the porch...

Jerry steered the book club with a jerking head motion down toward the barn. The old dog lumbered off the porch and followed alongside nudgin' against the lad's leg from time to time as if it was his compass.

Doc and Mrs. Webb turned onto the drive and stepped out of his jeep. Catching Jerry and Mary's eye, Doc waved a big thumbs-up at the group, clasping his hands together and wriggling them up over his head like a winning boxer in congratulations for the club's running off the Nazi crooks.

"Bully for you!" he shouted.

The Halloween event was still the talk in the Crown and promising to be for some time to come.

"We have potato salad," said Mrs. Webb. "Hope you like mustard. We also have some pickled beets and a dish of apple-crumb-bake as well."

"Bless my soul," said Mrs. Parker from the porch. "Will you be taking a jar of my butter pickles back with you? I was hoping to enter them at the Fair but now I don't know. I have plenty, please take a jar home."

"We will and thank you. The apple-crumb is from the Butlers – best in the county - and the pickled beets are the Chubbs," said Mrs. Webb.

"…more is coming," said Doc. "Now if you or Fay don't like apple-crumb declare now and I will personally volunteer to take it off your hands."

"Oh, Doc - now hush!" chided Mrs. Webb.

"You concentrate on getting that old fuddy-duddy back on his feet, Mrs. P. Let your friends keep you out of the kitchen a spell," said Doc.

Jerry, Buddy and the others stepped around to the side of the barn. By the time they'd slid the door open and found the light switches, three more cars had dropped off food dishes, baked goods wrapped in wax paper, and well wishes, before heading back home to their own chores. Big Mike even stopped and asked Mrs. Parker to pass the word to all the helpers in the barn that he was making spaghetti tonight for whenever they were done. They would hold supper for them all. (He didn't know Missus had already suggested it to the lad when she walked a basket of Moore's farm apples over to Mrs. Parker).

As club president, Mary took charge.

"Tell us what to do, Jerry," she said, just that easy. "You know the place better than any of us and you've talked with Mrs. Parker. Tell us what to do."

Jerry bent down and scratched under Buddy's collar letting the dog know he was a remembered friend, and they all appreciated him being there. He knelt and moved a pail from off the concrete ledge Buddy was used to sleeping on while Farmer Parker milked. He lifted the dog onto it and let him "nest-sniff" around a circle or two to settle in. Maybe he'd take a nap.

"Okay, first," said Jerry, "Holbrook, will you switch the radio on – I know cows like music when they're being milked. After that, can you go up and pitch hay down the chute? Mary and I will put it in front of the cow's milking stalls? Pile it up under the chute. What we don't use tonight we can use in the morning."

"Okay," said Holbrook.

"Barber, can you and Mayor get the milking machines hooked up and ready? Farmer Parker has two of them. You guys know how to use them."

Barber and Mayor stepped toward the shelf where the milking machines were.

"I know cows are stripped by hand after the machine comes off," Jerry went on. "Will you need help stripping after you take the machines off?"

"We can strip them, no problem" said Mayor. "But with two of us, we'll need two milk pails. Somebody taking the full pails and hauling them over to pour through the strainer and fetching them back for the next cow can help make it all go faster."

Everyone nodded they would be watchful and grab the full milk pails, walk them to the cans for pouring through the strainers, and return them to Barber and Mayor empty.

"Randy, if you can find the filter cloths and set up the funnels we'll need to strain the milk into the milk cans – and then can you put a scoop of silage in the manger in front of every stall."

"Sure can," said Randy.

"Bases, you organize the milk cans, make sure they're clean and lined up for Randy. It's colder after sunset so if you can watch and wait for the cows to come down the driveway. Slide the back barn door open wide for them to come in. They'll know their stalls.

Close it behind them to try to keep the heat in. They'll warm it up, though.

Mary, come with me, we'll go call the cows – and then we'll put the hay in front of their stalls."

"I'm impressed," said Barber rigging a machine up to the teatcups. "Not bad for a city boy."

"Can everyone be here in the morning to do this all over again? Tomorrow we'll have to shovel the manure into the spreader right after the morning milking," said Jerry.

"Morning comes early on a farm, can we stay over at your place?" asked Barber.

"Already arranged - my mom said yes to your staying and called your parents. She called Principal. If Farmer Parker is still laid up on Monday, we don't have to go to school as long as we're here so we won't be marked absent or tardy.

Oh, and Big Mike is making spaghetti for later - for whenever we get our work done here."

"Meatballs?" asked Barber.

"He always makes meatballs and sausage and Italian garlic bread."

"Yahoo," shouted Holbrook from the hay chute wall ladder.

Jerry smiled. He and Mary stepped out of the barn and walked up the cinder drive towards the road.

"Did you ever think we'd all be running a farm, even if it's only for a day or so?" asked Mary.

"I'm worried about the hay," said Jerry.

"What's to worry? Isn't there a chute from the hayloft down to the milk barn Holbrook can drop it through?"

"I mean in the field on top of the hill, the hay that's been cut."

Jerry pointed up to the tallest hill on the back side of the place.

"That hill - it's the one overlooking the cemetery on the other side. I climb it to come home from our meetings. Thing is I don't know how to hitch anything up – like the horses, the hay lift, the hay wagon. We have to get the hay into the barn before it rains or it will spoil."

"Seems you knew what needed to be done for milking. Who'd-a-thunk that? How about the music to make happy cows? I didn't even know that one."

"I've seen Farmer Parker do his milking a million times."

"I'm sure we'll figure out the hay thing, someone will help us," said Mary.

Mary crossed the road and opened the barbed wire fencing at the base of the side pasture hill, pulling it back and out of the way.

Jerry briskly rubbed his hands together to warm them in the dusk air. He cupped them into a megaphone over his mouth and copied Farmer Parker's cow call best he could:

"Cahobosse! Cahobosse! Cahobosse!"

(Come Home Bossy!)

He paused and looked up the hill.

"Cahobosse! Cahobosse! Cahobosse!"

Wasn't long Jerry and Mary beamed with a pride. They could see, way up the hill, Holstein heads bobbing up and down, up and down - back and forth as the cows lined up single file and made their way down the steep dusty warn cow path, around the briar bushes. The cows pretty much knew Jerry by now. They seemed contented. Step by step they came through the gate, nostrils snorting steam, they crossed the road looking forward to being milked, and to a manger of oats. They welcomed Jerry's call for them to come in; headed right down the cinder drive and through the back barn door and into their stalls.

"Better count them, Jerry. Let's make sure they're all in and we didn't leave any up on the hill," said Mary.

Ole Charlie here was busting my buttons watching these young folks. Reminded me of the time, awhile back, young Jerry asked his brother, Gourmet Mike, when his mother would let him go out with girls, like to the picture show or to a school dance.

"Probably when you don't have to ask," was the answer Gourmet Mike gave him – and a good one.

Watching these young folk here - they ain't just milking cows, pitching hay, cleaning and filling milk pails. If someone was to ask a guardian angel to describe when a boy becomes a man and a girl becomes a woman I'd have to say this was about it. They were full-grown tonight. I'd have to say full-grown the minute they didn't bother to ask – to step up and help. Put a happy tear in my soul, it surely did. It reminded me of the millions of boys and girls who laid it on the line in the War because they were needed. I had seen it with my own eyes then and today. It was days like today the Pompey Hollow Book Club and all the American kids they represented just like 'em - grew up full.

The chores done, pails and milking machines cleaned proper, Jerry told everyone to go to the hen house and use that garden hose to freshen up. Then to head on over to the house across the way - he'd be along for supper after he gave a report and that they'd be back in the morning.

"You all go on, I'll get the lights," Jerry said.

With the barn empty Jerry stood there in the middle and took it all in, slowly turning full circle.

The cows were quiet for the most part. Contented they were milked and staying in the barn overnight out of the cold.

He thought back to the first time he came into the barn when he was nine. It was an autumn chill like tonight. He chuckled to himself about his first episode with Farmer Parker's manure spreader – and that tomorrow he'd be certain to stay in front of it. He walked over to get Buddy and turn off the lights.

"Let's go, Buddy."

Buddy didn't move when he called. He didn't stand and stretch like Jerry was used to seeing him wake up.

He felt the dog's heart, then sat down beside him and scratched under his collar one last time. He pursed his lips and looked up on the wall at the emptiness of the moment, thinking what to do. There was a wall calendar with a picture of a Ford tractor. Farmer Parker always said when the horses, Sarge and Sally, give out he was going to get him a Ford tractor. Jerry remembered that and the calendar in Homer and of Dick and Duba going on about sneaking in under a tent at the State Fair. Somehow tonight – in a moment like this - life didn't seem to be about sneaking in – life was about leaving, as well. Life had a more real nature to it – a higher purpose.

"Mrs. Parker, is Farmer Parker still up?"

"Come in Jerry, he'd love to see you, come on in, dear."

Farmer Parker was resting back on two pillows, a rolled up newspaper was in his hand watchful under the bedside lamp for a housefly that was bothersome.

"Son, we can't thank you enough. Your friends are good people. We'll have to do something special when I'm up on my feet again."

"Farmer Parker, there's something I've got to tell you."

"How'd the milking go? Alright? Find everything you needed?"

"We found everything. It's all clean and put away," said Jerry. "We hosed it down good."

"Maybe we'll have a cookout," said Farmer Parker.

"In the morning we're putting all the cans out for Mr. Vaas to pick up after that milking. Barber and Mayor are good with the milking machines, we're lucky."

"Maybe a hayride."

"Buddy died."

The man's shoulders slumped.

"Sure enough?"

He looked up at the ceiling, raised his fists gently tapping them to his mouth.

"He followed me down to the barn; I set him up on the ledge he always liked. I'm sorry if..."

"Now that was one good ole dog. A friend if there ever was one. He would wear himself thin running up that side pasture hill getting the cows down and into the barn. You've seen him do it. Gave them fits, he surely did. Kept them in tow. A good ole dog – Buddy."

"What do you want me to do with him?" asked Jerry.

"Where is he?"

"He's laying on the ledge in the barn. I left the lights on out of respect until I talked with you."

Farmer Parker pulled on his bushy eyebrows thinking, then he looked over at Mrs. Parker standing in the shadow of the bedroom door.

"Are the cows in pasture or in the barn?" the old man asked.

"We kept them in the barn tonight because of the cold. It'll make it easier than calling them down in the dark in the morning."

"Ole Buddy surely needed the rest. Why not we let him be tonight, let's let him get a good night's rest on his favorite spot, with his friends. Go ahead and turn the lights out – I'll have an idea where you might could put him in the morning. Come ask me then."

"I'm sorry, Farmer Parker, Buddy was a good dog."

"Thank you for everything, son, and thanks for taking Buddy with you down to the barn. He loved that old barn - couldn't have been a better place in the world for him to pass."

"I'm sorry," said Jerry.

"Night, son."
"Good night."
Jerry stepped away.
"Jerry?"
He turned.
"Yes, sir?"
"Why not let's leave the radio on for Buddy tonight. He likes to hear the music and Deacon Doubleday's early morning farm report. Calms him."

CHAPTER THREE

DYING IS A PART OF GROWING UP

Missus welcomed everyone to the table, told them all where to sit and started supper with a prayer:

"Bless us, oh Lord, and these thy gifts for which we are about to receive from thy bounty through Christ, our Lord, Amen."

"Buddy died," said Jerry.

Everyone paused and looked over.

"I already told Farmer Parker. He died in his sleep down in the barn."

"While we were there?" asked Mary.

"Yes," said Jerry.

"How'd he take it? His dying," said Mary.

"He was an old dog, I think Farmer Parker's been expecting it, but he was still sad. Like when Charlie Pitts died, we all knew he had cancer but we were still real sad when he died," said Jerry.

"At least Buddy wasn't alone when he died," said Mayor. "Shouldn't anyone ever die alone, like Charlie did."

"Charlie knows we love him though, every time we meet in the cemetery we sit around his stone," said Mary.

If they only knew, Ole Charlie here never was alone, they was there all the time, the very second I died, me being their Guardian Angel and all.

"Buddy was in heaven," said Barber.

"Was? You mean now he *is* in heaven, like he went to heaven," said Holbrook.

"No," said Barber. "He *was* in heaven. Some animals, dogs for sure, pick their heaven and go there before they die."

"Is that true?" queried Holbrook.

"I heard elephants do," said Randy.

"If you believe folklore," said Mayor. "My ancestors came over as pilgrims. I think they believed animals went to their heaven before they died, so they could know their surroundings and rest easier. Buddy's heaven was watching his cows being milked."

Jerry added, "He liked listening to the music in the barn."

"Folks, let's start passing the spaghetti bowl, the sauce, and the meat platter before it all gets cold," said Big Mike.

Big Mike didn't favor wasting breath talking about death. There was enough of it in the world without any help, he'd say. He was a believer in celebrating life.

"I think what all of you are doing is admirable," said Missus. I know some are inspired by your stepping up to help the Parkers the way you have. Isn't that right, dear?"

Missus looked down at Big Mike.

Ole Charlie here was sitting up on the side buffet as usual, taking it all in. I pretty much knew what Big Mike was thinking. It showed in his face. He was thinking 'bout the time they came in that car and picked him up and drove him off like a convict to the sanitarium that time they found out he tested positive for TB. For a whole year it was, his thinking he was going to pass-on from tuberculosis before ever getting to see his boys again.

He was remembering how his boys took over running the house and doing chores back then without ever once being asked, and never complaining or balkin' all while he was gone. Now his boy and their friends were about to come through for the Parkers. I could see it in Big Mike's face as sure as day.

"Does anybody know how Farmer Parker got hurt?" asked Randy.

"He was up on a ladder and slipped somehow - wrenched his back," said Missus.

Hearing about the ladder, Jerry started, and without thinking he offered...

"My grandfather fell off a ladder or a barn roof or something, didn't he Dad?"

The words almost choked the lad up as the second he had them out of his mouth he remembered Missus telling him what a sensitive subject that was for Big Mike. Big Mike was thirteen when his pap died from the fall off a barn roof.

She looked around the group.

"That was a difficult time," she said. "It happened when Jerry's father was about all of your ages. He was the youngest of seven and so hurt by losing his father, he could never bring himself to talk about it or think about it for the longest time. Isn't that right, Mike, and aren't you proud of these young ones for being there for the Parkers?"

Mike set his fork down, unclenched his lips.

"My father fell off the barn roof, but he didn't go right away," said Big Mike. "He was paralysed in a hospital bed for almost a year before he went. I quit school to earn money to help my mother out. I wanted to see him but we didn't have a car in those days and it was too far to walk to St. Paul in the Minnesota winter."

"Like you, Dad," Jerry said. "It's like the time you were in the TB sanitarium and I couldn't see you for the whole year."

The phone rang.

"I'll get it," said Jerry, interrupting his thought.

The distraction helped Big Mike hold back a tear – remembering that his dad died after the year so he never got to see him again.

Jerry stood up and went into his mom and dad's bedroom to answer it. In a few minutes he returned to the table and sitting down he looked over at Mary. She puffed a curl from over her eye.

"That was Marty - he knows how to hay it and is riding Sandy over in the morning to help us out."

The clatter of spoons on bowls and forks on platters filled the air. First taste of warm food and spaghetti sauce was when the book club realized what an enormous appetite they'd worked up. Missus gave reprieve and made no notice of table manners, set 'em aside for this supper. Figured she could soak the table linen tonight and wash it in the morning.

Big Mike was still thinking of his pap, I could tell. He was thinking how lonely it is when someone leaves and you think you may never see them again. He was thinking the sadist part is that you seem to have so many things you wished you would have said and didn't.

Then he thought this wasn't about his losing his pap. He sat up. Thought it best he break the ice.

"Jerry, do you remember the night I came home after that year of being away in the sanitarium? I sure do," said Big Mike.

The table got so quiet you could hear a thought. Every soul sittin' there wanted to hear the story and they knew Big Mike loved telling them.

"I remember," said Jerry quietly.

Big Mike sat back, gathered his thoughts; looked around the table.

"It was a Christmas Eve. I had been gone a year trying to get through a bout with tuberculosis, having a part of my lung removed. In the time I was gone, Jerry had grown eight, I think – maybe almost ten inches. He didn't know that Missus was keeping me up to date on my boys and the local news. Jerry wasn't even sure his mom had told me how he'd grown – and he was afraid I wouldn't recognize him, shooting up the way he had…the way you all had."

Mary and the club looked over at Jerry. They could understand a young boy's fear like that. They remembered members of their family or their friends being away at the War for so long - for years and coming home changed.

Big Mike went on:

"It was a bitter cold winter night; a windy snow storm was calming down to flurries. A medical aid was driving me home from the sanitarium and we stopped at Shea's Store so he could scrape ice off the windshield. Mike Shea came out to say hello and brought me a newspaper. Must have been Mike Shea called here and told Missus how close we were to getting me home for the first time in more than a year. You remember what you did when you heard I was close to home, Jerry?"

"Yes," said Jerry pursing his lips.

"The way his aunt told me, Jerry jumped off the front step barefoot, in his pajamas walking quickly through the snow toward the front gate, not taking his eyes off the top of the road up by Farmer Parker's hill."

Big Mike looked over at Jerry.

"Remember what you were looking at the hill for, Jerry?"

Jerry nodded yes and then looked down at his plate in a blank stare.

"He was looking for headlights from the car I'd be in. His Aunt Mary was driving in with our Christmas tree on her car roof. She rolled down the window and shouted, 'Jerry, you'll catch your death, go put something on.'

But Jerry kept walking as fast as he could, keeping his eye on the top of that hill watching for headlights.

Finally he saw some and our car came slowly over the snowy hill, inching down around the curve. The road wasn't plowed and slick so we were taking our time. We turned into the driveway and paused. I rolled the back window down as far as it would go which was halfway and stuck out my hand for a shake. Jerry's eyes widened. He grabbed my hand and squeezed it, walking alongside as we drove in.

Why I knew Jerry-me-boy right off, and my how he had grown. I was speechless, so happy to see him again.

'Jerry?' I said.

Shaking his head yes, his face grimaced a sad look. Growing all that much since I saw him last, Jerry wasn't sure I could recognize him anymore. It frightened him to think I might not remember my own son. He started rambling – trying to jog my memory – all while following the car holding on to my hand.

He said things like, 'Remember fishing at Little York Lake? Remember I rowed us out in the boat at Sandy Pond? Remember when you beat my airplane to Watertown? Remember teaching me how to make desserts? Can you remember me, Dad?"

By then we were close to the house and the family was on the porch waving and cheering. I shook Jerry me-boy's hand and said…

…you remember what I said, Jerry?"

"Yes."

"I said: You caught the croppies we cooked at the Imperial House, remember, son?"

'Room number six, Dad,' you said back.

Room number six," I answered.

That was the room we would stay in at the Imperial Hotel in Carthage; it showed Jerry I remembered him. I was sore and still healing from my lung operation. When I got out of the car and stood up straight I looked at Jerry and how tall he'd grown.

Son, I'll never forget what you said. You stood tall and looked me in the eye and said, 'I'm still the same, Dad—just like you're still the same.'

Big Mike looked around the table.

"You see - Jerry didn't know I was as afraid that he wouldn't know me after a year away and being operated on."

With that, Big Mike had said his piece. He choked up and looked down at his plate and fumbled for his fork.

"That was so beautiful, Jerry, did you really run out in the snow like that - barefoot?" asked Mary.

The lad nodded.

"That was a nice story," said Holbrook.

"There's a reason I wanted to tell it," said Big Mike. "All the time I was gone, my boys took on all the chores without once ever being asked. Like you're doing for Farmer Parker. I think you all should know how filled your lives are going to be down the road for helping Farmer Parker like this. The man will never forget it for as long as he lives. Each of you will be in his thoughts – no matter how long a time it is. He'll never forget any of you."

Missus knew Big Mike needed a moment.

"Mary, you'll be sleeping in Mike's room – he's at LeMoyne. Boys, you work out sleeping arrangements. There're plenty of blankets and pillows in the hall closet. I'll set an alarm and wake everybody."

"At five?" asked Barber.

"Five is fine," said Missus.

Mary leaned over to Missus.

"I got my records in the mail yesterday. On Wednesday I was going to have a square dance social at my house for friends. If we're still helping the Parkers on Wednesday, do you think maybe, should I cancel it?"

"If there are still things to do, chores at the Parker's should be over about the same time as tonight, dear. I don't see why there wouldn't be time for a nice square dance party," said Missus. "I know you'll all have the energy."

"Good, I have three new square dance records, will you guys come?"

Mouths full, all the lads around the table nodded they would be there.

"We'll see that you all have rides to your house and back here after the dance," said Missus. "Sounds like such fun."

"There'd better be some girls there to dance with," said Holbrook. "I'm not dancing with Barber like they did in Stalag-17."

"Oh, the movie," said Randy looking over at Missus. "Stalag-17 was about this real German prisoner of War camp holding captured Americans and British. To celebrate Christmas one time these guys played a scratchy phonograph record and danced with each other dreaming about their wives or girlfriends back home. It was funny how they did that but it's a great movie. It's playing up in Cazenovia. There's a Bugs Bunny cartoon with it."

"The bakery is giving everybody who helps at the Parkers these few days tickets to the State Fair," said Big Mike, "Dick, you can take them to the Fair on Friday with you. You'll get a ticket and gas money for driving them."

"I'm going with Duba, I can't fit them all," said Dick.

"Good," said Big Mike. "Then you and Duba can both drive them – there'll be plenty of room in two cars."

Dick moaned.

"Bring them home, too. You all plan on a time to meet up somewhere on the Fair Grounds when it's time to load up and come home."

"We'll meet on the Midway," Jerry snickered, knowing what Dick and Duba were up to. "Maybe we can meet at the shooting range."

Dick stabbed a meatball with his fork and snarled.

CHAPTER FOUR

SMALL TALK OF NAKED LADIES

There were boxes of cereal, some bananas and a pitcher of milk on the kitchen counter when Missus woke everyone at five. Barber walked in first, rubbing his eyes.

"We appreciate it," said Barber, pulling his sweater over his head, "but on a farm we always do the milking before breakfast. Cows have to get out to-pasture, especially being in the barn all night. After milking's done and we've loaded the spreader is when we can eat before we go back to work."

It was star clouded, a dark morning outside. The Pompey Hollow Book Club stepped from the house and walked the long gravel drive to the gate, each step joggin' their memories of what Big Mike had said last night about the significance of the adventure they were in. They crossed the road and took the short-cut on the north side of Parker's house filing up over the yard. Mrs. Parker was waiting for them on the back porch."

"Everybody come for breakfast after milking."

"Mrs. Parker, I think my Mom has cereal for us," said Jerry.

"Nonsense, I'll call her. You come here – don't bother to knock – I'll have a hot breakfast waiting for you."

Randy found the barn's light switch. Everyone stepped in and gathered about Buddy. The ole dog was layin' there peaceful like – looked like he was smiling - tuckered from an active happy life. His cataract grey eyes glazed over. Mary leaned and petted him on the head.

The morning farm report with Deacon Doubleday was on the radio filling the airwaves, bringing the barn to life:

"Good morning folks - this is the Deacon speakin' from the wired woodshed.

Only man in the great northeast wired for sight and sound.

Stay tuned for early crop reports, the weather and a look at the humi-diddy and all the news that'll get you through the day by starting off on the right foot."

"Maybe we should turn the radio down," said Mary. "I think we're supposed to say something nice for Buddy, aren't we?"

"Don't we do that when we bury him?" said Mayor.

"He likes the radio," said Jerry.

"Let's do it after we finish the chores," said Holbrook. "Getting the work done for his master is what Buddy would want more than anything."

"Holbrook's right," said Bases.

"Barber and Mayor, did you guys use strip cups last night when you milked?" asked Jerry.

"Why you askin'?" said Barber. "What do you know about strip cups?"

"I forgot that last night Marty told me to make sure we use strip cups when we milk is all - I don't know why."

Barber's been milking since not long after he could walk. This early in the morning, he took some offense to the questioning of his knowledge in a dairy barn.

"Well, where was Marty last night come milking time here?" said Mayor, "He wanting to run the show from Fabius now, is he?"

"He didn't mean anything by it; he's coming to help hay it – that'll take most of the day. Cut him some slack. What is a strip cup, anyway?"

Barber reached under his shirt tail and pulled one he'd tied to his belt.

"This is a strip cup. A cow's milk sack is divided into quarters. Four quarters, four teats. If a quarter gets bruised or hurt, a cow can get mastitis in the quarter that got hurt. If the strip cup says there's mastitis in the milk from that quarter it has to be thrown away."

"Good," said Jerry. "So you used one."

"Nah," he sneered. "I like to carry it for showing off to the girls."

"Yeah," said Mayor – "and I use Farmer Parker's strip cup here to hold my pencils".

"Everybody, simmer down - all of you," said Mary. "Barber and Mayor are as good as anybody can get in a dairy barn. Jerry doesn't know about farming, guys – it was good he asked."

"I was only asking," said Jerry.

"Give him a break," said Mary.

"Well make sure you remind Marty when he gets here the hay is that light green stuff that's laying up on top of the back hill," snapped Barber – and a pitch fork is…

"Enough!" said Mary. "Let's get to work."

"Well, we sure gave Buddy a show, acting like jerks – what a send-off," said Holbrook.

"Somebody, tell a joke," said Mary.

"I don't know any jokes," said Bases.

"Okay, so why don't cows have any money on them?" asked Randy.

"I give up - why?" said Holbrook.

"Because farmers always milk them dry."

It would take more than a ripple or two to rattle this club for long, even a bad joke.

Morning chores and work flowed smooth as butter. While the milking was being done, the milking machine suction cups clicking and ticking like a wind-up clock, Jerry, Holbrook, Bases and Randy pushed the end door aside and rolled the spreader into the barn by hand, turning on the spokes of its iron wheels. They'd shovel the manure from both gutters and move it forward to shovel more. All the while they were hoping the cows could hold off any further motions of the sort until after they were let out and back up on the pasture hill. Once the spreader was filled, and the gutters behind the cows emptied they rolled it back outside again.

"Mrs. Parker, any more bacon?"

"Why, Randy, a body'd swear you have a tapeworm," said Mrs. Parker. "Plenty of bacon, dear - help yourself."

"Mrs. Parker did you ever teach at the Delphi Falls one-room schoolhouse when it was going?" asked Barber.

"I did – and probably taught most of your parents a time or two."

"Know any secrets we can blackmail them with?" said Mayor.

Mrs. Parker smiled and looked out the back window. She saw Marty riding in the drive on Sandy, his palomino. She opened the back door and waved at him to bring the horse up on the lawn and hitch him to the porch railing.

"That pretty thing can't do the lawn any harm grazing and with any luck at all my roses will have some lasting benefit from his droppings, for sure."

Getting ready to walk back down to the barn after breakfast, Barber and Penoyer put their morning 'spiff' about Marty behind them figurin' he didn't mean anything by it last night – only trying to help. They were all best of friends. They gathered around Marty on the back porch, some with bacon in their hand.

"I see the cows are up on the hill, looks like you got through the morning milking," said Marty.

"Marty, we haven't done anything with Sarge or Sally, the work-horses," said Jerry. "They've been in the pasture all night; do we need to do anything for them?"

They stepped off the back porch and started towards the barn.

"Oh, a bucket of oats and let them share it will be about all you need. They'll use the drum trough for water. Is the top hill out back the only one with cut hay on it?" Marty asked.

"Yes," said Jerry.

"Do you know when he cut it?"

"We think three days ago. Before he hurt his back."

"Has it been raked?"

"I'm pretty sure," said Jerry. "Rows of hay that look like big long roles of carpet line the length of the field."

"Then it's been raked."

"Not sure when, though. If it's important, I'll run back up and ask Farmer Parker."

"Nah – we're good. We'll get it all in today if we can," said Marty.

"Let us know what we can do," said Holbrook.

"I'll need two helpers with me on the hay wagon. Well, three with one as a lookout."

"A lookout? For what? Indians?" snorted Holbrook.

"I'll be tending a team of horses I don't know; pulling a wagon I don't know that's pulling a hay-lift rig I've never seen or used before. I'll need another set of eyes, is all watching out for things."

"Name it," said Mayor.

"Two with hay forks tossin' the hay around even on the wagon. The hay-lifter will drop it – then it needs to be spread around. Later we'll need someone to hitch the team to pull the spreader around the hay field."

"You mean the spreader should go out right after the hay is on the hay wagon?" asked Randy.

"Not right away," said Marty. "We'll need the horses to haul the hay wagon down to the barn first. Then we'll need one of them, probably Sally, to pull the hay-fork lift rope with hay up into the haymow."

"Haymow?" said Jerry. "What's that - haymow?"

"Haymow, hayloft, kind of the same thing," said Barber.

"What's the top floor of Farmer Parkers barn have in it?" asked Marty.

"Just hay," said Jerry. "But he has a loft up on the right side beams with a shelf for straw.

"Then it's a haymow for the hay and a loft for the straw."

"Charlie Pitts hay was on a shelf, like a loft in the rafters," said Jerry.

"…and that would be a hayloft, then," said Marty.

"I never knew all this," said Mary. "Learn something new every day."

Marty scratched his head.

"After we get the hay in the barn," said Marty, "somebody can hitch the team up to the spreader, but if it were me, I'd let them rest and spread tomorrow after the morning milking."

"I'll take the honey-wagon up in the morning," said Barber.

"By the way," said Marty. "I saw a rope hanging from the cupola but I didn't see a hay-fork lift."

"Farmer Parker never got it put back up before he hurt himself," said Jerry.

"I'll get it hung," said Holbrook. "Randy can help me. I've seen him use it. I'm pretty sure I know how it works. If the ropes are all up there and ready, we'll be good."

"Try testing it with a bag of corn husks," said Marty. "Make sure it connects to the rail at the top. You will hear a click. Then it should roll on the rail into the barn over towards the center. Try pulling the rope to see if it will release and drop the bag."

Barber and Mayor appreciated Marty's knowledge of horses. It helped with horse farming. They both worked more sophisticated family farms where hay was baled by machines. They had tractors to work with. Handling hay with hay-lifts, hay-forks and a team of horses was foreign to them. It was time-consuming and back-breaking farming but that was farming in much of the Crown. Lads then kept a keen eye, listened and learned.

Everyone stepped out of the barn to help Marty hitch up the team to the hay wagon. Jerry ran back up to the house and climbed the stairs to say hello to Farmer Parker.

"We're going to get all the hay put in the barn today," said Jerry. "Marty knows how."

"Appreciate it, son," said Farmer Parker.

"Have you thought more about what you want us to do with Buddy?"

"I was thinking through most the night how much he loved running to the top of the pasture hill across the road when it was cow-calling time."

"I remember too," said Jerry.

"Most always it was around sunset. It'd give him enormous pleasure - stubby as his legs were - making it all the way to the top before some of the cows even had a chance to stand up. Son, you suppose your friends could see to it Buddy gets buried somewhere on top of the pasture hill?"

"We can do that, no problem," said Jerry.

"Not in the shade, mind you, see to it you put him in the sun directly. Buddy loved the sun."

"We'll do it this afternoon. The sun is hottest at three so we'll find a good sunny spot and do it around then or when we get off the hayfield. We'll say some words too, don't worry. Mary is good at that – saying words."

"Bring me his collar, son."

"Sure."

Farmer Parker handed the lad a grapefruit sized rock.

"And put this on his grave. This was the first stone I ever pulled from the hayfield when I was making it ready for haying. Buddy will remember it and appreciate the company."

Jerry carried the rock down to the barn and set it next to Buddy on the ledge.

Marty had Sarge and Sally hitched up to the hay wagon. He stood in between the horses, tightening some buckles. The wagon was settin' other side of the gate in the pasture in back of the barn ready for the long haul up the steep hill to the hayfield.

Holbrook and Randy were in the barn steadying the ladder. They were working on hooking the hay fork up in the hayloft cupola.

Mary and Mayor were already walking up the hill – carrying a bucket of drinking water and ladle. They figured to meet up with the wagon on top.

"Pull her up some, Marty, and I'll close the gate behind the wagon," said Jerry.

Stepping up on the hay wagon and sitting on the bench, Marty looked behind him and noticed his horse, Sandy, had dropped a fresh pile of fertilizer as a courtesy for Mrs. Parker's red roses.

"Yo, Holbrook? Randy?" he shouted.

No answer.

He finally got Holbrook's attention with a two finger-in-the-lip whistle.

"When you two get down off that ladder, d'ya mind putting Sandy in the back pasture for me?"

Randy waved okay.

"And put the saddle and bridle some place up off the ground where they won't get peed on."

Jerry clamped the wire gate closed and climbed on the wooden seat bench next to Marty.

Marty lifted and lowered the reins with a gentle slap on the rumps of Sarge and Sally.

"Ktch, Ktch," crackled Marty. "Let's go you hosses – giddyup now!"

Leather stretched and squeaked; chains tinkled and rattled; wood creaked as the iron trimmed wooden wagon wheels started rolling over the pebbles and dusty powder of the trail.

The team of horses pulled the wagon making its way down the slope. With a clunk, clunk, clunk, clunk sound of hooves it crossed over the back creek's wooden bridge before heading up the steepest hill in the area.

It was a slow, steady climb. Most of the heavy work was getting up to it. On top, the hill was as flat as a stove lid, perfect for growing hay.

"Farmer Parker usually talks to Sarge, Marty. He calls him by name - tells him what to do. Sarge always seems to understand him."

"Good to know," said Marty.

"Are you going to the State Fair?" asked Jerry.

"Yup. I've got Sandy in a horse show, Friday. Schools let out Friday – Fair Day," said Marty, "He may be too young to win anything, but we'll see."

"Dick and Duba told me they're going to the girlie show on the Midway. They're going to sneak in under the show tent."

"I wouldn't put it past them," said Marty. "Hope they're smart enough to leave their wallets in the car. Midway is full of pickpockets come fair time and naked lady shows have a particular way of emptying a wallet, or so my gramps told me."

"Do girls really get, ya know, naked?"

"C'mon Sarge, keep a-going…" grunted Marty.

"…well I'm guessing they have a way of making you think they do, but I don't reckon the law would let 'em get naked. They'd all be arrested and hauled off. I think it's an illusion. I'm guessing, mind you. I wouldn't know though."

Marty slapped the reins down again, gently but firm. The ride up the hill was a long slow ride but steady; an empty wagon is an even pull for a good team of horses.

"I think we're going up Friday."

"Look in the livestock show pavilion. Sandy and I'll be there for sure. Shaffer will be there with his rabbits.

"You ever been on the Midway, Marty?"

"Well of course, I've been on the Midway, who hasn't? But no I've never been in the girlie show tent, if that's what you're driving at. Oh, I stood around and listened to the barker a time or two, but I'd sure enough get my butt tanned three weeks to Sunday if my old man ever found out I went in – and he always has a way of finding out things."

Jerry watched two rabbits stop their chewing, sit up and wait as the wagon passed on by, up the hill.

"What's a pickpocket look like, anyway?" asked Jerry.

"If anyone knew that, there wouldn't be any, now would there," said Marty.

"So where should a fella carry his money?"

"They won't be looking at you guys – I wouldn't worry about it. What'll you have in your pocket, a buck - two, maybe? They'll be looking for bigger fish. They'll be looking for farmers at the fair looking to buy a bull or some livestock, maybe even a new tractor – with a big wad of cash on 'em."

At the top of the hill, the team pulled to a level spot on the dirt road just before the gate.

Jerry jumped off the wagon and pulled the wire gate back so Sarge and Sally could get through and into the hay field. He closed it behind.

As Barber had said, the cut hay in the field was a light green. Soft, rolls of it had been raked so it wound the length of the field. Five long rows of hay that needed to be lifted into the wagon and taken down to the barn.

"Do you want Mayor and me to pull the hay-lift up to the back of the wagon so we can connect it?" said Jerry.

"Naw, it's way too heavy. I think I can line her up straight enough and back into it. Sarge has done this plenty of times, let's see if they can do it."

Mayor and Mary came over to watch Marty back the wagon into the tall, forward leaning hay lifter that picks the hay rows off the ground as the wagon passes over them. It takes the rows of hay up and over its top dropping it on the wagon.

"The field is smaller than I thought it was," said Marty. "It might only take us two trips – two full loads down. We'll see."

CHAPTER FIVE

DUCK AND COVER!

Marty reined the horses until they pulled around in a near half circle. He was lining them up with the first hay row on the field. He knew the horses would know what to do – to keep the row of hay between them as they pulled. Barber climbed up and was now settin' alongside him as lookout.

"Ktch, Ktch, let's go, Sarge!" said Marty. "Giddy up, you hosses, follow the hay line - like you know - follow the hay, Sarge."

The wagon wheels rolled, metal hay lifter forks began to turn, screech and scratch, swoopin' and turnin', spiking the hay from off the ground and carrying it up the back lift a good ten feet before dropping it over the top and into the wagon. Mary and Jerry were standing in the back, waiting to spread the hay - keeping their balance on the moving wagon leaning on their pitch forks.

"Spread it out," yelled Marty. "It'll dry faster."

Sarge and Sally picked up their gate.

Now, barring any mechanical breakdowns, the team pretty much knew the routine, where to go, what to do. It was haying time again on this particular field the horses knew so well. It was a walk in the park for them. Gentle breezes and a pretty sun and a level pull.

"You showing Sandy at the State Fair this year?" asked Barber.

"Plan to, Friday," said Marty. "You showin' that ornery ring-nosed old bull of yours this year?"

"Art and Bobby are," said Barber, "He's got three blue ribbons. I'm thinking he's too old now, maybe. I'm going to have fun this year. Dick and Duba are driving us all in on Friday."

"Did they offer or were they trapped into it?"

"I think they were trapped, but Big Mike is giving us tickets to get in. He'll give you one too, for helping the Parkers."

"They'll try to lose you, once you get there, I reckon," said Marty. "I heard they'll be up to no good, on the Midway."

"Why does the Midway have a reputation? Is it all that bad?" said Barber.

"A State Fair is about agriculture and industry; new cars and cooking, maybe. The side shows on a Midway are mostly all about getting money from outta your jean pockets, and into some huckster's pockets."

"Sounds like you've been there."

"Well, I'm older than you guys; bound to have more experience - let's say I've been around some. Shucks, no harm walking the Midway, seeing the lights and sights. It's fun listening to it all."

"You ever see the girls?"

"Girls?"

"You know – the 'woo-woo' girls."

"Oh, them. Some guy out front in a straw hat, waving a cane, would parade some fancies in sequins and garter straps and make a lot of promises, but no, I never went in."

"I wonder what it's like inside," said Barber.

"Wondering is just what the Midway is all about. The more they can get you to wonder, the more they can get you to pony up all your pocket money to see if even half of what they say is true and to buy some overpriced popcorn with a valuable secret prize in it. Those Midway guys are slick."

Off in the distance Holbrook and Randy stepped through the gate and were walking the length of the field towards the wagon.

"Looks like the hay-fork lift is up and good to go," said Marty.

"T'ain't fair," said Barber. "Every time I'd ask my pap about it – the Midway and all - he'd tell me to tie my shoestring, or to run go fetch him a bucket of water - or why wasn't I inside doing my homework?"

"Oh, I reckon it's a father's job to stall on some subjects – it's the mother's job to pray they never come up in the first place. Deny them if they do."

By this time there were only one and a half rows of the hay left on the field waiting to be picked up. The hay pile on the wagon was about seven feet high, Mary and Jerry balancing on top.

"We might do it in one load at that," said Marty.

Holbrook was standing about fifty feet directly in front of the wagon looking north up into the sky.

"Hey, look! Look you guys! What's that?" Holbrook shouted, pointing off beyond the north side of the hill in front of them.

"Looks like an old biplane," shouted Marty. "Two wings, probably a relic '41, by the looks."

"I think they're giving rides up at the State Fair," shouted Mary.

"Why's it wobbling all over like that," yelled Holbrook, "I think it's in trouble."

By this time, off in the distance the plane broke through a high cloud bringing it into better view. Its single propeller engine could be heard sputtering and popping. The horses started acting up with the engine noises and whine.

"Whoa, Sarge, whoa Sally," said Marty, pulling on the reins – settling the team best he could. "Whoa there."

"It's coming right at us," shouted Holbrook.

"Oh, he's putting on a show for his passenger, is all," said Marty. "Just showing off."

The plane came closer and closer, sputtering, poppin', wobblin' all get out - up and down, side and back headed right for the hill.

That's when it started to dive.

"It's going to crash!" yelled Jerry. "Look! It's going down!"

"He's crashing!" shouted Mayor.

The plane dipped down – out of sight - disappearing below the horizon on the north end of Parker's hill.

"It's crashing, it sure enough is," blurted Marty. "Better get ready to go stomp the fire out. This whole field will go ablaze."

Marty no sooner got it out of his mouth when the plane scooped up and reappeared roaring bigger than life over the horizon barely clipping the edge of the hill with one wheel but snapping the top strand of barbed wire on the fence with the other, then bouncing back to ground and up off it again.

Blocking the sun, it was coming straight at 'em now, the propeller blade whining like a fighter pilot – climbing again in front of Holbrook just enough to clear him and then the wagon.

Sarge and Sally reared up this time kicking their front hooves, whinnying - twisting their heads about in fear.

"Everybody jump! Duck for cover!" screamed Marty, pulling back on the reins.

"He's crazy. He's going to kill somebody," shouted Holbrook.

"Easy, Hoss. Whoa there, boy. Easy now, Sarge," Marty gruffed.

Getting the horses settled, Marty laid down in the seat bench ducking his head, holding tight to the reins.

Everyone else dropped low, scrambling under the hay wagon.

"Not under the wagon," shouted Marty. "If she rolls the hay lift will crush you. Stay away from the wagon wheels too."

Everyone rolled out from under the wagon and laid on the ground next to it covering their heads.

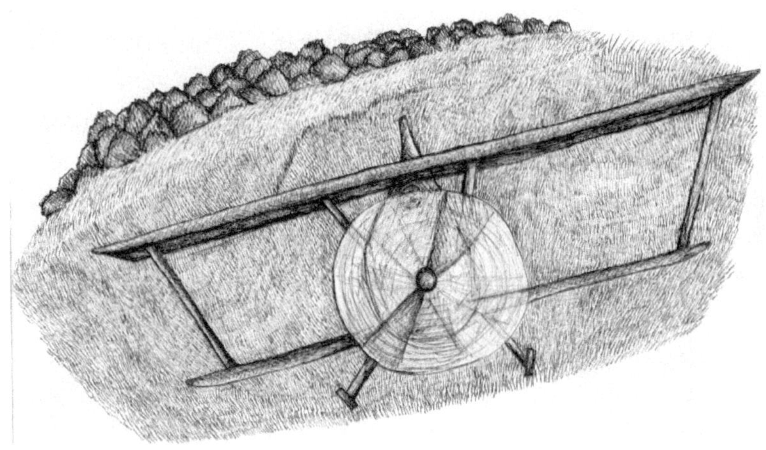

The biplane sputtered up again toward the sky skippin' then poppin' a backfire. Circling the hay field, it was turning up and down all over the place, wobbling almost like the pilot was trying to get someone's attention. Finally it came down, bounced on its left wheel, jumped up off the ground then down on its right wheel before settling both on the ground. It kept rolling along toward the end of the field like the plane was on its own and about to go through the fence and over the edge of the hill. The pilot was alone in the plane in the back cockpit– his arm lifted and a hand slapped at the steering stick swerving the plane around in full cir-cle. The slicing propeller kept idling – turning the plane, flashing the reflecting sun; the pilot's head slumped over. The plane rolled across the field every which way like a serpentine.

"He's hurt," barked Marty.

"Maybe he's had a heart attack," yelled Jerry.

Everyone started running toward the rolling plane.

"Somebody, try climbing on a wing, see if you can find a shut-off switch," shouted Marty. "Watch out for the propeller!"

"Be careful!" yelled Mary.

"Don't hit the stick," shouted Penoyer. "That could turn it the wrong way."

"We have to shut her off, it could set the hay field on fire," shouted Marty. "I've seen an Allis Chalmers backfire send a whole barn up in smoke."

"It could crash through the fence and fall over the hill," yelled Holbrook. "We have to stop it."

Holbrook grabbed a stabilizing wire holding the upper and lower wings together. As the plane turned he jumped on the back of the lower wing, pulling himself up using the wire. He climbed into the front cockpit and leaned over into the back cockpit where the pilot was. He bent his elbow over locking it to the rear cockpit. The pilot's head was now leaning back, his eyes closed under his goggles. Holbrook felt around with his hands, found knobs and switches and tried each hoping to turn the engine off. He'd reach and click. With one, the plane rattled to a full stop, the propeller shaking before going silent and slowly becoming still.

"Mayor," shouted Marty, "go grab the reins on Sarge and Sally and hold them steady! Don't let them spook. The rest of you help here. Let's get this guy out and onto the ground. The wing is canvas with lacquer on it, don't be stepping through it."

Holbrook and Jerry were on one side of the cockpit, Marty and Randy were on the other side.

"Take his earphones and helmet off," yelled Marty. He pulled the goggles from the pilot and dropped them on the floor of the plane.

Mary was running to the gate of the field where they left the bucket of drinking water and a ladle. Holbrook leaned in to unfasten the safety harness of the man. As he did, the pilot started - opened his eyes and sat up.

"Where am I?" he grumbled.

Holbrook and Jerry bolted - stood erect, eyes wide.

"Calm down, Mister. You're in the village called Delphi Falls," blurted Marty. "You dang near crash landed but you're okay."

"Doesn't look like a village," moaned the man. "Where's the village?"

"We're up on a hill next to it, the village is over there," said Jerry pointing to the north edge of the field.

The pilot opened his eyes, rolled them, turning his head about in a daze.

"I don't see any falls. Where's the falls? I don't see no village, no houses – I don't see no falls."

"I'm no doc, but my dad would say he's delusional. I think he's in shock," said Marty. "Quick, help me get him out of this contraption and onto the ground."

"Why young man, I take objective to your insinulation. I am not diluse…dilo…what you said. And this ish not a contraption; it is a fine piece of machinery."

"Well we'll discuss it all when we get you out and safe on the ground," said Marty. "Take his shoulder strap off."

Marty looked over at Holbrook and Jerry.

"In the state he's in what would he know about shock anyway? He's obviously in it – a state of shock. Just relax, fella, we'll get you out."

"That's shocking," the pilot squawked. "I heard that. What you said. I am def…defin…definitely not in shocked."

"Then what would you call it," said Marty amusing the pilot patiently, while putting the man's arm over his shoulder to help lift him up and out of the cockpit.

Jerry and Holbrook grabbed his feet and lifted.

"You were either running out of gas; having fainting spells or something that didn't look right, is all we know. We watched you near hit us. It could have been a heart attack. What would you call that, Mister?"

"I'd call it drunk," said the pilot.

Everyone paused, stood motionless, not moving a muscle and stared over at the pilot.

"I'm drunk," said the pilot.

"I can smell bourbon," said Holbrook. "I know what bourbon smells like."

"Here's two empty bottles back here behind the pilot seat," said Randy.

Marty turned his head toward the man's face, sniffed at the air.

"Why, he's gassed!" snorted Marty. "This man is as dead drunk as a hard cider skunk."

"Where're the falls," mumbled the pilot, as they rested him on the ground. "I don't see no falls."

The pilot plopped his head back, closed his eyes and passed out as Mary walked up with the bucket of water.

"Is he dead?" she asked.

"Dead drunk, is more like it," said Marty.

Mary knelt down and loosened his tie and unbuttoned his shirt collar.

CHAPTER SIX

FRENCH, MAIS OUI - - - FRENCH VICHY, MAIS NON!

"Bring him in. Set him on the couch," said Farmer Parker.

Holbrook and Mary helped the pilot to the couch resting him back on it. Farmer Parker felt the man's pockets for guns or knives. Mrs. Parker put a pillow under his head and covered him with a blanket.

"Only two reasons I know a body will drink that serious," said Farmer Parker. "The man's either a plum no-account or he's troublin' in some way. Let him sleep it off. We'll know soon enough which way the wind blows for him. I can't imagine owning an airplane he'd be a no-account, unless he stole it. We'll wait."

"Let's go back up the hill," said Marty.

"I'm feeling good now," said Farmer Parker. "I can help."

"You may think you're feeling good, Fay Parker," barked Mrs. Parker. "Dr. Brudny says one more day resting up and liniment – so you get back in that bed for one more day and you'll not be leaving me alone here with a drunken stranger in the house. What are you thinking?"

"We should have the hay in the loft by three and then we'll go bury Buddy," said Jerry.

"Who's tending the hay wagon?" asked Farmer Parker.

"Mayor and Barber are holding the reins until we get back up there, everything's fine." said Marty.

"How'd you get this man down the hill, anyway?"

"I whistled for Sandy and he galloped up to the top gate. We hefted him over his bare back. Being deadweight Sandy could walk him down the hill – easy as you please - like a pack mule."

Haying it on this particular sunny day would become an adventure of a lifetime for the Pompey Hollow Book Club. Not only were they doing good deeds for kindly neighbors, they about near got themselves killed by a drunken pilot diving straight at 'em in a 1941 canvas biplane.

Adding to their day though was the pride of knowing the spirited plane that put up such a fuss was as old as most of them. It wasn't long before everyone was back up on the hayfield ready to go to work again.

Not wanting to have missed out:

"What'd you do with him?" yelled Barber, as Marty and the rest walked toward the hay wagon.

"The Parkers took him in until we can see if he's okay," said Holbrook.

Mayor jumped off the wagon.

"They think there's a chance maybe he stole the plane," said Barber.

"While you guys were down there we were thinking of trying to take her around the last row and a half of hay," said Mayor. "But we figured sure enough if we did, something would break or bust."

"Well, let's get her loaded and down to the barn," said Marty. "Soon as Pilot wakes up, we'll see how he plans to get his plane off this hill."

All the hay loaded up, fork-lifted and dropped into the barn hay mow; Marty unhitched and walked the horses out back setting them loose in the pasture with a bucket of oats each. He whacked a gentle pat on their necks in thanks for getting through the day. He was letting' them know it was okay their bein' scared like they were with a plane comin' at 'em the way it did.

For Buddy's funeral, everybody lined up on the driveway for starters. Farmer Parker managed to climb the pasture hill following behind Mary while the lads carried the dog in a gunny sack. Holbrook was carrying the shovel. They searched around for good sunny spots. When they settled on one they rested the sack on the ground, Jerry untied the string, reached in and removed Buddy's collar, handing it up to Farmer Parker. Out of regard everyone stood there in silence while Farmer Parker ran his fingers back and forth against the collar. Holbrook dug a grave, cleaned it square and nice, respectful-like. Jerry laid Buddy down in it and each of them gently covered him with fresh dirt. Farmer Parker got down on one knee and patted the dirt down. He rested the stone on the middle of the pile of dirt. He whispered to Buddy that he put it and a few more to keep cows from stepping on the grave.

Then he stood.

"I've had some dogs in my lifetime," mumbled Farmer Parker. "Never said words like this before, ever I lost one. I'm not so good with words. I suppose wanting to say something says it well enough for me - about what Buddy meant to me. Good-bye, old friend. I'll never be able to replace you...and I'm too old to try."

Mary was in tears.

Jerry and Holbrook felt good about being a part of helping the old man get his friend to the top of the dog's favorite hill and in the sun. On the way down, Farmer Parker offered to help call the cows in come milking time that afternoon. The club wouldn't hear of it. They didn't want to risk the wrath of Mrs. Parker for obliging the old man and getting him out of his sick bed any longer than a burial.

"Let us get the chores and the night milking done and we'll come in and see you," said Jerry.

"Well, suppers here tonight," said Farmer Parker. "It's already settled - all of you will eat here. Missus and Big Mike are stopping by with some boiled corn and roasted acorn squash."

"Can you fit in everybody?" Barber asked.

"If you carry the picnic table from the back lawn and set her on the porch – that and bringing out the kitchen table should do it. Perfect day for eating out, not a black fly in the air," said Farmer Parker.

"Buddy can look down over us from the hill," said Mary.

In the barn, Holbrook turned the radio on for the milking and crawled up the wall ladder to throw down more hay. Jerry walked over to the ledge where Buddy used to sleep, where he laid when he passed. He set the water bucket and ladle on top of the ledge – making it a sort of shrine – not to worship an old dog – but to cause a body to maybe think a good thought about the dog whenever they took a sip of water on the day of his burial.

All finished and hands rinsed off with the hose, faces splashed, there was an hour before supper would be ready. They let the cows out of the barn and led them up the drive, across the road and up Buddy's hill and pasture.

Mrs. Parker and Missus were organizing vittles' in the kitchen. Most everybody else was gathered, settin' around the back porch recounting the day. Ole Charlie here was up on a side rail listening to every word and taking in the setting sun.

Farmer Parker and Big Mike were off in a corner with pride and smiles watching the youngins' growing up right in front of them and all - wondering where the time had flown…

About then is when the pilot leaned a shoulder to push open the screen door slowly, catching it behind him with his hand not letting it slam closed. He stepped out running fingers through his messy hair with his left hand, straightening his tie knot with his right. Pulling pieces of hay from his head he would hold them with his fingers and look at them wondering how hay got into his hair; how he got to where he was. Stepping out he wandered into the blinding setting sun - flinched a grimace, squinting his eyes closed, holding a hand over them. Barber stood and helped him take his leather flight jacket off and led him by the arm to a chair.

"You nearly killed yourself," said Marty.

Marty was a reporter for the school newspaper, he didn't like mincing words. The group wasn't quite ready for a scolding right out of the box as a friendly way to welcome a stranger to the supper table. Everyone quieted down and listened to see where this was going.

"What do you have to say for yourself, Mister?" asked Marty.

"That's enough, Marty," said Mary.

The pilot avoided looking into the lad's eyes – he looked instead over at Farmer Parker.

Marty was relentless.

"No, it isn't, he nearly killed us too!"

The pilot rubbed his eyes, still trying to wake up. He looked over at Farmer Parker again.

"You have a bottle? Anything would do."

"We don't use it, son," said Farmer Parker.

"Well? What were you thinking?" blurted Marty.

"There might be a bottle in the plane. Where's my plane?"

"The two bottles in the plane are both empty," said Holbrook.

"What were you thinking?" insisted Marty.

Pilot slumped in his chair, relenting.

"I wasn't trying to think," he mumbled - hoping to shut Marty up.

"The plane was doing the thinking."

"Why that'd be suicide talk," said Randy.

"...and *my* business now, isn't it?" said pilot.

"Not if you killed us and a team of good workhorses doing it, it wouldn't," barked Marty. "That there would be homicide."

"I 'spect your right," said pilot. "Sorry."

"Son," said Farmer Parker. "What could make a man in his prime, like you are, son – ever want to give it all up like that? It just doesn't make any sense to me."

Farmer Parker looked over at Big Mike.

"What am I missing, Big Mike?"

"You seem like a nice enough sort," said Missus through the screen door. "You must have someone who cares for you; your shirt has been creased with an iron."

"Son, whatever could be so bad it could make a young man want to kill himself?" asked Big Mike.

"It'd be no big deal. I'd already died, my friend, what's left to lose?" said pilot. "This would have finished the job."

"You'd died? Why you're making no sense at all," said Farmer Parker. "What do you mean you'd died already?"

Farmer Parker turned to Big Mike, again.

"What does he mean?"

Big Mike thought it best the pilot speak for himself.

Pilot looked around the porch, trying to see a familiar face in all the eyes staring back at him:

"It was predawn. That's what they called it anyway - an early morning dark. June 6, 1944 was the day I died. We were the 101st Airborne – stationed in southern England. Nine hundred planes revved up their engines and loaded me and thirteen thousand paratroopers. Some were my poker buddies. We climbed into bellies of unheated airplanes in the pitch of night. Anybody know how many boys thirteen thousand is?"

Pilot looked around at blank faces.

"It'd pretty much fill a football stadium – thirteen thousand is a lot of guys. Ike was flying us over the English Channel starting in the dark. We knew we were going to die; we didn't talk about it. We were headed over and behind the Nazi front lines deep into Hitler occupied France.

They dropped us from seven hundred feet up like New Year confetti behind the lines – on the Cherbourg peninsula – so we could decoy for the boys landing that morning on Omaha Beach."

Pilot paused.

He looked over at Farmer Parker.

"It was a top secret mission, and we were ready, but we weren't stupid. We knew we were going to be distractions – living decoys to give the Nazis front lines reason enough to have to turn around and shoot at something behind them. Pick us off in the dark and morning skies while the first of more than a million Allies and five thousand ships landed on Normandy beaches. We had to save France first and then Europe to win the War. It took us all willing to die to do it. Jump from a plane in the black of night. Fall into trees, onto roofs."

"Was it horrible?" asked Mary.

"Ever see a dozen eggs?"

"Yes, of course."

"Well crack a few of them. Adds up. Do that math on the five, six thousand dropped over Cherbourg alone."

Everyone remained motionless staring over at the pilot's eyes. Radio broadcasts of D Day played in their minds while they tried to imagine the fright in those brave young mens' hearts so the world could be saved from Hitler.

"Before daylight a farm went ablaze from cannon fire – lit up the whole sky making us easy targets. All the way down I could hear the 'yelp' or the 'ungh-grunts' of guys around me catching bullets, flak whacking into their guts or their kneecaps or heads - being wounded or killed...

Daylight was worse. The Germans flooded all the fields so if we hit ground we'd probably drown, with the weight we carried; at least stuck in mud until they could pick us off with machine guns."

Pilot looked up over the barn in the distance, at the setting sun.

"When you first jump out you can't hear the gun shots from down below, just the yelps and grunts a few yards away from you in the sky. Looking down, you could tell the dead ones. They'd plop when they hit ground, some would get dragged around by their parachutes in the wind until they'd hit a fence or a tree knocking their helmets off. The live ones rolled and tried to get loose from their chute before they got shot."

"How old were you?" said Mayor.

"Seventeen."

"My God," said Mrs. Parker from behind the screen door.

Big Mike and Farmer Parker pursed their lips, sensing the bravery of the sons of the world and the tragedy of that War – slowly shaking their heads thinking about it…

"Most were older. Lots of guys – some not even Catholics – squeezing rosaries, even blessing themselves, saying Hail Marys all the way down. Some kept repeating a one sentence prayer – but out we all jumped in the black of night.

We had to - for France.

All told, thirteen thousand guys.

We knew we'd get shot at like clay pigeons – that wasn't any surprise - but no one warned us they had flooded the fields where we were to land or that Nazis weren't the sorts to take wounded prisoners alive. Too much work carrying them.

They'd spend a bullet finishing a wounded guy with a headshot or through the heart if they thought they might live to fight again."

The pilot raised his eyes up from the table looking at the silence.

"I can't begin to imagine how frightening that must have been for you," said Holbrook.

"I think we've heard enough, for now," said Big Mike. "Why don't we…"

"…that wasn't even the worst part," added pilot. "How about the troops that flew into France – those guys in those wood and canvas gliders?"

"Gliders?" said Mayor. "You mean planes with no engines?"

Four-thousand guys in gliders – no engines - so they couldn't be heard flying overhead or landing – doing it in full daylight. Operation Deadstick. Their mission was to capture bridges by surprise and hold them for the Allied supply lines they would need after the invasion."

"Brave guys," said Randy.

"Brave but wounded or dead, mostly," said pilot. "Wooden gliders with dozens of men each, some loaded with heavy jeeps - who didn't have a lot of training on how to land with no brakes. Nazis drove eight-foot stakes in the ground everywhere to bust off their wings or kill them when they landed. Lots of them crashed or belly-landed, hitting trees, slamming into stone fences, barns - crushing them. Hiding in a tree once, I saw bodies from some gliders – the Nazis were lining them up side by side to take pictures. A bunch made it through though."

"How'd you finally get out?" asked Randy.

"A French farmer and his wife took me and two other jumpers in. They hid us up in their barn. They fed us when they came out to milk their goat so nobody would get suspicious. They drew a map showing us how to get to Cherbourg so we could make it through the back country and not get captured or killed."

"That was lucky," said Barber, "I bet the French were anxious to see you guys, the paratroopers, I bet."

"Some were," said pilot.

"What do you mean "some were?" said Mary. "France was our friend in the War, wasn't it?"

"What's your name?"

"Mary Crane."

"Well, Mary Crane, there were the occupied French, and, yes, they were friendly "allies" but then there was the Vichy supporters – they were French too. Vichy was all high and mighty French, friendly with Hitler. They stayed unoccupied, left alone to save their own skin.

The Vichy French arrested Jews and turned them over to Hitler to get killed – gassed, burned or shot in ditches. They even arrested gypsies and put them in concentration camps. French people are good, hardworking – nice, decent folks – the Vichy French were bastards - helping Hitler like they did – killing Jews. At least they were then."

Big Mike stood this time and interrupted.

"Okay, everybody," he started. "Let's take a break and give our guest some nourishment. What say we all eat? There's another morning or two of milking coming up before Farmer Parker is able to get back to work. Plenty of food here – friends brought it by. Let's chow down. Grab some salad and a plate while you're at it. Everybody get a good night's sleep."

Missus and Mrs. Parker came out with platters of food.

"By the way," said Big Mike, "What's your name, son? We never did get your name."

"Name is Ed, sir. Most call me Eddie."

"Well, Eddie," said Big Mike, "Welcome to Delphi Falls. You'd better eat hearty and rest up. You'll have all of tomorrow to figure how to get your plane down off the hill. You're going to need your strength."

"Any chance a man can work his keep a day or so to get gas enough and pocket money to make it to Binghamton?"

"If'n a body can stay sober, there is," said Farmer Parker.

"How do you plan to get your plane off the hill?" said Randy.

"I guess I'll fly it. Which hill is it on?"

"What's an old biplane like that need to take off, ya know, runway length?" asked Farmer Parker.

"Five hundred feet oughta do it."

"Well, hate to be the one to tell you, but it's a three hundred foot long hilltop – barbed wire at both ends. What's your next plan?"

Eddie's shoulders slumped.

"Pass Eddie the corn," said Big Mike. "A good night's sleep clears the head. Everyone will think better tomorrow and figure everything out. Kids, stay over, again. We'll call your parents and the school about why you'll be missing some more this week."

"Eddie, you can sleep on the couch again tonight. Tomorrow, bunk out on the straw in the barn," said Farmer Parker. "I'll come up with a chore or two."

Ole Charlie here could tell by their faces, Jerry and Randy were thinking it's going to take Minneapolis Moline Conway and his tractor with the front end lifter to bring the plane down off the hill. I could also tell from Big Mike's eyes that he was thinking there's more to this man's worries than a near ten year old War story, tragic as it was.

I was proud of my flock tonight. Tomorrow should tell the real story.

CHAPTER SEVEN

MARTY OPENS A CAN OF WORMS

Farmer Parker was settin' in the kitchen sipping coffee while his young book club friends mustered about, congregating on the back porch, all yawnin' and stretchin' in the dark before going down to the barn to milk. He stepped outside to join them.

"Don't know how to thank you for the hand, way you did," said Farmer Parker. "Helping with Buddy and all."

"Why you're a full-fledged member of the Pompey Hollow Book Club, Farmer Parker - you'd of done it for any one of our families," said Mary. "That's the way it is in the Crown."

"Dot Dot Dot – Dash Dash Dash - Dot Dot Dot," grinned Farmer Parker.

"That's right. It was your signals that helped us catch the Nazi crooks," said Randy. "You're an honored member of the club."

"How about we do a hayride this week as our thank you? Vittles and all. It should be fun. Sarge and Sally are up to a hayride. How about it?"

"We could do it at our place," said Barber. "Mary you could have your square dance party then too – like our harvest ride."

"Too cold for a hayride," said Holbrook.

"We can make it a regular hoedown," said Mary.

"Well, count us in," said Farmer Parker. "We'll watch the weather. Decide on the hayride when the time comes. I'll bring my jaw harp."

"And Eddie can meet Hal," said Barber.

"Let me call Mrs. Barber and see if Wednesday will work for her," said Mrs. Parker. "It's a church night, but it may work."

"Eleven bells today will be about the end of my three days cooped up here. Boss lady says I can take over my farm then. I get my reprieve."

"What about Eddie?" asked Holbrook.

"When he wakes, I'm going to let him whitewash the milking area in the barn. The stone walls are dusty. It needs a good going over."

"That was so sad," said Mary. "About the parachute guys and all of them dying like that, in another country."

"Parachute jumpers are volunteers," said Holbrook.

"Is that true, Farmer Parker?" asked Mayor.

"Think so," said Farmer Parker. "Jumpers and the navy kids being in a submarine were all volunteers, I think."

"Hal was in a submarine," said Holbrook. "He and Eddie will have a lot to talk about."

Holbrook, Jerry and Mayor looked through the back window into the darkened living room at Eddie sleeping on the couch. They tried to imagine what the man had been through.

Randy stepped in the house and picked the wall phone earpiece off the cradle and wound the crank. He didn't have to ask. That early in the morning, still dark, weren't nobody making telephone calls – not a lot to be said at that hour.

"Myrtie, can you get my mom?" he said.

"I don't recognize the voice."

"It's, Randy," he said, "Randy Vaas."

"Mom? Randy. Can Dad pick us up around eleven? Everybody needs a ride home."

Must have been some scratchin' on the phone wire.

"What?"

Randy stuck a finger in his other ear.

"Speak up, Mom – I can hardly make you out."

"We're still at Farmer Parkers."

"Oh – okay - but if we miss him will you tell him?"

"Thanks, Mom."

Click

Randy stepped back outdoors.

"What'd she say?" asked Barber.

"She said my daddy will be here anytime to pick up Parker's milk cans, we can tell him ourselves."

That caused some grinning and polkin' at Randy near all the way down to the barn. It was good starting the morning off on a good note.

Ole Charlie here felt blessed this particular morning, sure enough did. Not a family in the Crown ain't been helped a time or two by another. I can't think of anything that pilot needs right now – save his family – more than a good old fashion hoedown, piled up platters of food and friends; some dancing and a fire that'll near touch the moon. What a way to show him our thanks for his sacrifices in 1944. Hal's too.

Barber's farm is the place to do it. Like the Skeele's farm over Fabius way, Barber's is one of the biggest level pastures in the Crown. Best for hayrides if the weather's right. Big haymow barn for dancing.

Mary, Jerry and the gang were about to step into the barn and get to their chores when they looked up in the dark and noticed a small bright light up top of the hayfield hill.

"What is that?" said Jerry.

"It's moving," said Barber.

"Looks like somebody's coming down the hill," said Holbrook.

"I think it's a lantern. I think someone's carrying a lantern," said Jerry.

"You guys wait here," said Mary. "Let us know."

Holbrook and Jerry walked up towards the back gate – Barber, Penoyer, Randy and Mary went into the barn and started feeding, milking and stripping the cows.

It was kind of eerie watching the glowing lantern moving down the dark hill the way it was coming. About the time the glow made it to the wooden bridge, the clunk, clunk, clunk, clunk sound gave it away. It was horse hooves. Through the fog they could make out Marty on Sandy, coming up the knoll to the gate. Marty was holding the lantern out to the side.

"We thought you went home last night," said Jerry.

"I slept in the barn – on a straw pile. I left for home but started thinking about it and turned around at Doc Webb's place and came back. I wanted to see if I could find some clues. I needed to take a good look at the airplane, again."

"Did you find any clues?" asked Holbrook.

"I found this," said Marty.

He handed a leather valise down to Jerry.

"Give it to Eddie when he wakes up."

"Did you open it?" asked Holbrook.

"Naw," said Marty. "Didn't have to – pretty much got all the clues I needed looking in the plane."

"Like what for example?" asked Jerry. "What kind of clues?"

"I found a crumpled up sack he carried the whiskey in. There was a handwritten receipt in it. He got both bottles at the same time, yesterday."

"Anything else?" asked Jerry.

"Yeah. The gas tank was on empty," said Marty. "I tapped on it to see if the needle was broke."

"What does it all mean?" asked Holbrook.

Marty stepped down off Sandy, handed the lantern to Jerry and began removing the bridle and saddle.

"It means our friend Eddie has some explaining to do. He's not telling us everything. I want to ask him some questions. He may be in trouble he's not telling us about. He may need some help."

"What makes you think that?" asked Jerry. "Anybody can get drunk once in a while doesn't make him bad or suspicious."

"A man empties two pints of rye flying a plane eighteen miles on a near empty tank of fuel? He might as well been loading a gun, holding it to his head. Only two possible answers for that kind of behavior."

Marty was smart. Jerry and Holbrook were all ears.

"He was either so despondent he was thinking about suicide like he was talking last night."

"Or?" asked Holbrook.

"Or he had so much on his mind he wasn't thinking straight before his take-off," said Marty.

"Which do you think?" asked Jerry.

"Maybe a little of both," said Marty. "Let's wait and see what he has to say for himself."

Randy was pouring a pail of milk through the strainer when the barn door opened and Eddie came in. Looking sheepish, he tried to avoid eye contact as he checked for a whitewash bucket and brush. Marty reached up and turned the radio volume down. Holbrook walked over and handed Eddie his valise.

"I thought I lost this," said Eddie.

"It was in your plane," said Holbrook.

"Thanks."

Eddie unzipped the top of the valise looked inside, widening the mouth of it under a light for a better view.

"It's all there," said Marty. "We didn't open it."

"I wasn't worried about that," said Eddie. "Just forgot what I had in it, is all."

Eddie pulled out a handbill and ten printed tickets, fanned them out in his hand and offered them to his new friends.

"Like Sherlock Holmes, anybody? I got these ten tickets to the Sherlock Holmes Players – they'll be up in New Woodstock Sunday – matinee and evening show. Good for passage into either show, want 'em, anybody?"

"Eddie," said Marty, "you've been dancing all about, bobbing and weaving ever since you were able to stand on your own two feet without being carried. Now you may think it isn't any of our business – but it is. The truth of the matter is you about killed half of us and we all feel now you at least owe us what's eating at you so we can get it behind us. We might even be able to help."

"No offense, but how can a bunch of schoolkids help? What could you know about life, anyway?"

Oh, Eddie hadn'ta, oughtn'ta said that.

Even ole Charlie here knew that wouldn't set good. Mary, as the club president, pushed Holbrook aside and stepped around Randy to get up near enough to Eddie's nose to get his full attention. He was taller but she was about to bring him down to size.

"Listen, buster," she began. "Just who do you think you are, going about feeling sorry for yourself like you put on? So you were scared and had to jump outta an airplane – big deal. My daddy's ship was torpedoed. Half the kids we know lost somebody in the War. Little Bobby's mom was killed by a bomb and she was a nurse. We were all scared. Being scared doesn't give you any right to be rude."

"Well, I'm sorry..." he started.

"Well nothing," blurted Mary. "We dumb little schoolkids who don't know about life have caught burglars; we've chased off two escaped Nazi War POWs; and for three days us hick kids have run a farm for an old man who hurt himself on a ladder. You owe us more than sorries, buster. So spill it. You want our help – you'd better start fessin' up, got me?"

Mary stepped back, taking a deep breath.

Her friends stood around with their mouths open. They'd never seen their president quite so vocal. They was mighty proud.

"Yeh!" snorted Mayor, adding a knockout blow.

"…and we'll take those Shakespeare tickets," said Randy.

"Sherlock Holmes," said Marty.

"Whatever," snapped Randy. "We'll take those too."

Eddie turned a beet red, looked Mary in the eye, handed Randy the tickets. He stepped across the gutter and picked up the milking stool Barber was now finished with. He squatted down on it.

"I'm a house painter. Most of the year I make my living painting houses, rooms and stores for folks down in Binghamton. I'm married to the same woman since 1946; and we have two girls."

Mary, Holbrook, Mayor and Jerry sat down on the barn floor cross-legged. Randy and Barber were arranging the milk cans, but listening in. Marty raised an arm up and leaned on a cow.

"Painting isn't so good through the late winter. Every year about this time, I get a chance to earn some extra money. We need money to get us through the winter."

"Airplane rides at the State Fair?" asked Marty.

"Yep," said Eddie. "It always goes pretty good at the Fair. I've usually been able to bring home enough money to get us through the winter – and then some, if I'm lucky and the weather holds good for flying."

"Did your airplane break down?" asked Mary.

"Did it rain in Syracuse?" asked Barber.

"It was my best year ever. I had six hundred forty dollars yesterday morning – enough to get us through the winter and have some left over for a nice Christmas for the girls."

"So what happened?" asked Marty, suspecting the worst.

"Packing up to leave, I parked and chocked the plane right where I always do. I put three bucks in my shirt pocket. I decided I'd try to win a couple of kewpie dolls for my girls before I gassed up and headed down to Binghamton. I had enough money to get us through winter, and a painting job I could get waiting on me back in Binghamton and I was getting homesick…"

"…and?" asked Marty.

"And a guy came up to me offering me these here tickets free. Said they were sample tickets. Said they were trying to 'paper' the house he called it – held them out for the taking. Paper the house – that means they give away enough tickets so the play looks successful and seats are full."

"…and?" asked Marty.

"Well he had a French accent. I've been to France. So I asked him where he was from. I was thinking he might know the farmer in France who hid me out in '44. But in the back of my mind I was also thinking maybe he was down from Montreal or Quebec or somewhere in Canada. He said: "Moulins". I kept a straight face, mind you, I never flinched, didn't move a muscle. I told him I was leaving town, couldn't use his tickets and started to walk away."

"Why didn't you want the tickets?" asked Randy.

"Know where Moulins is?"

"No," said Mary. Tell us.

"Moulins is in Vichy," snarled Eddie.

"The bad French guys," said Holbrook.

"They were Nazis in French uniforms as far as I'm concerned. If we had jumped out over Vichy, the Free Zone, they would have been shooting at us."

Marty blurted:

"…and he insisted you keep the tickets, even slipped them in your valise all friendly Jand polite – only thing was he was a pickpocket – and lifted your money out of the valise at the same time he put the tickets in."

"I need a drink," said Eddie.

"No drinking," blurted Mary. "That does it! Jerry, we're calling an SOS. Barber, you figure out how you can get word to Dick and Duba."

"They're both in school today," said Barber.

"Figure it out!" blurted Mary.

"Let's get the cows back up on the pasture hill," said Jerry. "Mayor, you and Marty go hitch Sarge and Sally up and haul the spreader to the hayfield and spread it. Then put the horses to pasture."

"Everyone, let's meet in the cemetery," said Mary. "What time is it?"

"Seven thirty," said Eddie looking at his watch. "Easy you don't get too close with the spreader and hit my plane with that stuff."

"We'll all meet up at ten," said Mary.

She turned to Eddie.

Don't just sit there, Eddie," she snorted. "Start your whitewashing the milk room – it's not all that big a room. Do a good job, get it done and be ready to go with us."

"Where to?"

"To our meeting at the Delphi Falls cemetery," said Mary. "The Pompey Hollow Book Club is about to get your money back for you. Best you put a move on it and make that milk-room pretty for Farmer Parker to see before we go."

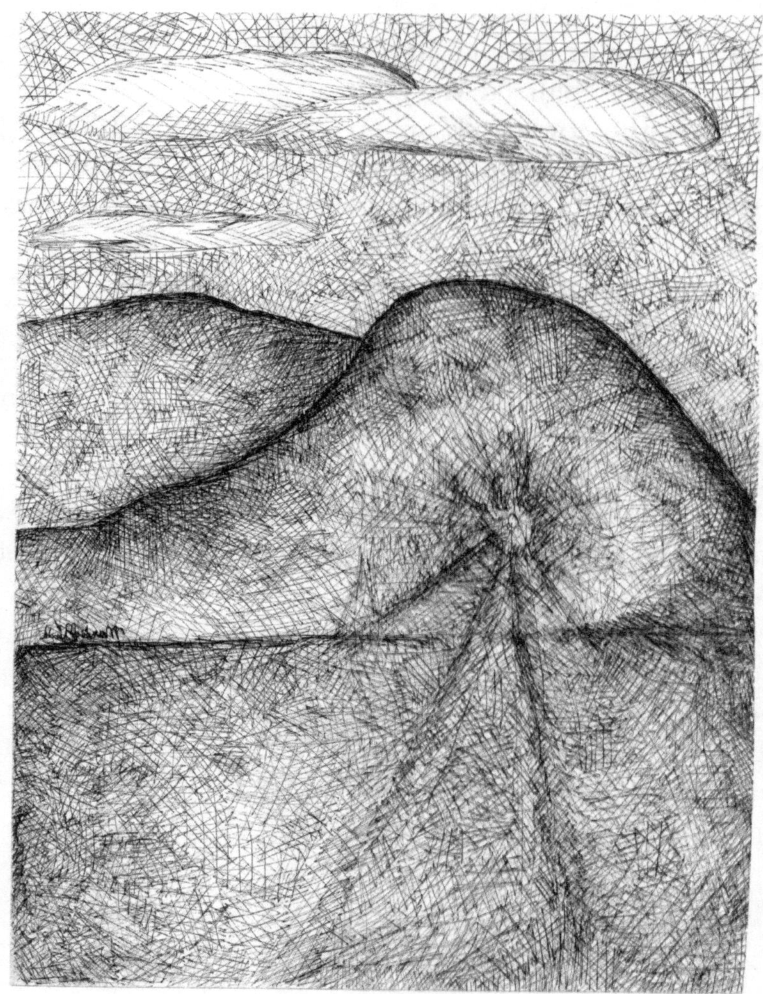

They Saw a Lantern Coming Down the Hill.

CHAPTER EIGHT

GETTING IT ALL OUT ON THE TABLE

After chores, while they were making plans to head on to the cemetery, Big Mike drove down around the hill. He was coming from the bakery for his early morning nap. A farmer's morning started around five or six – a baker starts loading bread trucks with warm bread around two in the morning. A quick nap and Big Mike would head back to the bakery. He caught their eye and pulled in Farmer Parker's and down the drive.

As usual the SOS business of the club was always held confidential until the older guys said they could talk about it.

"Mums the word, everybody. Cheese it," reported Mary out of the side of her jaw.

"Ribs and corn tonight," said Big Mike. "We'll see you get rides home after supper. Dick and Duba will drop you."

Big Mike saw Eddie coming out of the barn wiping his hands.

"Any thoughts on what you're doing about the plane, Eddie?"

With the new developments of State Fair pick pocket intrigue, everyone plumb forgot about helping Eddie get his biplane off top of Farmer Parker's hill. That was a first priority, so he could get home and the Parkers might go about their business – farming, even if he had to wait for them to try and get his money back.

"Just stepped out to get some air," said Eddie. "I've been white-washing the milk-can room and some of the wood racks. I haven't had a chance to think about my plane, yet. Later this morning, I will."

As he spoke, Eddie looked up and across down past the Cardner Road bridge on Big Mike's side of the road, next to the alfalfa field.

"Over there," he said pointing. "That field over there. Anybody know who owns it? I could take off in that field. It looks plenty long enough," said Eddie.

"I'm not certain who owns it," said Big Mike. "No one will mind the plane being there, using the field for take-off, I'm sure. Park it there while you earn up some traveling money. Have any idea how you'll get it down there, off the hill?"

"How about on the hay wagon," said Mary. She puffed a curl from her eye.

"It's way too heavy," said Big Mike. "I don't think the wagon wheels would hold all that much weight."

Big Mike turned and walked toward his car. He turned again.

"Tell you what. After my nap, and on my way back to the bak-ery, I'll stop off at the Conways and ask to see if Jimmy might bring their tractor over after school. That tractor might do the job."

"Jimmy is Minneapolis Moline Conway – to us," said Holbrook. "His tractor is enormous!"

"He'll get it down the hill alright," said Mayor. "The biggest tractor in the Crown - we've seen it lift a car."

"It has a front end lift thing-a-ma-jiggy," said Mary.

It was settled.

About then Farmer Parker came out listening to the tail end of the conversation. He had promised Eddie a full tank of gasoline and three dollars for his whitewashing the milk parlor.

"Farmer Parker, I'm hosing the barn floor off, touching up some beams along the way and the radio shelf with whitewash. I might as well hit it all so long as there's enough whitewash left. I got the time. I'll leave the doors open wide at both ends to air it out," said Eddie. "It'll make the barn and whitewash smell fresher come time for tonight's milking."

"That'll be fine, son," said Farmer Parker. "I'll kick in another few bucks for your trouble."

Mrs. Parker handed Mary a paper sack filled with tuna fish sandwiches and farm butter pickles wrapped in wax paper.

"The butter pickles are my own secret recipe," said Mrs. Parker. "Hope you enjoy them."

"Any chance I can sleep in the barn until I get my plane off the hill and am able to take off?"

"Help yourself, son," said Farmer Parker. "Use the straw loft. You can earn keep and food helping around the place until you leave. The chicken coop needs some repair. Hammer and nails in the shed. There's an old wood toolbox in there somewhere."

Marty nudged Jerry in the ribs.

"Ask him," he whispered.

"Huh?" grunted Jerry.

"Ask him to tell Dick about meeting us," whispered Marty. "Go on, ask him."

"Dad," said Jerry. "When Dick gets home can you maybe tell him we're meeting at the cemetery and we need him and Duba?"

There was nothing could put a grin on Big Mike's face more than an adventure. He'd been a fan of The Pompey Hollow Book Club since they started the club when they were nine years old back in '49 or '50. He's even collected reward money for them from time to time – giving them every penny. He winked at Jerry and smiled as he walked to his car.

Ole Charlie here looks forward to when they gather around in their meetings and set on my stone in the cemetery. It warms up the place.

Jerry turned the farm back over to Farmer Parker in good repair, cows milked, hay in, manure spread and chores done. Farmer Parker accepted it with a tip of his hat and a handshake. Big Mike got back in his car to go for his morning nap.

Mary rolled the paper lunch sack closed tight. Side by side they headed down over the wooden bridge and up the back hayfield hill. At the top they formed a quiet circle around the biplane, staring at it like it was an important exhibit in a city museum. They stood in the hilltop breezes imagining what the plane has done or where it's been since 1941. The stories it maybe could tell. They listened to Eddie talk about his learning to fly when he was only fourteen; his doing backward loops and barrel rolls in the sky; banking around farm silos and getting yelled at by farmers for scaring cows. He told of his flying above a railroad freight train and busting through the smoke from the coal engine stack just before going straight up in the sky missing the tunnel and mountain in Pennsylvania. He described how quiet it was and what it was like looking down at the snow-capped mountains in the Adirondacks under a full moon.

They imagined Eddie up high in clouds, in his leather jacket, his white silk scarf trailing out behind the cockpit in the wind. Drinking in his every word, dreams – every adventure, Mary passed around the homemade sandwiches and butter pickles made special for them.

"How high will she go?" asked Mayor.

"Couple of miles - maybe could push her up ten thousand feet. Top speed is right at 106 miles per hour – but she can hold that steady as long as she has fuel," said Eddie.

"Imagine that - one hundred and six miles per hour! Whew! Can you just imagine?" asked Mayor.

Holbrook grabbed the tail of the plane with two hands and gently lifted it off the ground.

"Look here, we can lift it on to the hay wagon," said Holbrook. "It's not that heavy. We could carry it down."

"That's the tail end," said Eddie. "The front weighs almost a ton or more – with the engine and all. We have to be careful we don't rip a wing hitting a tree branch or fence posts. Tipping it or dropping it wrong could hurt the propeller. I can't afford a new one. That would put me out of business."

"What are your girl's names?" asked Mary.

"Judy and Lucy," said Eddie. "Cute as buttons, they are."

"You should call them," Mary said. "Your wife too - they're probably worried about you."

Eddie tipped his head, shrugged his shoulders in a 'maybe' sign, and stepped up to the plane, avoiding the subject. Lifting a side engine panel, he pulled out a dipstick to check the oil.

Mary could see he was still looking edgy. The position he found himself in, losing all that money, nearly killing himself – having to explain a lot to his wife and family. She walked over to his side.

"So the way it is," she started. "We can get your plane down off the hill, but there's more but you'll have to listen and not walk away from me."

"I'm listening," said Eddie. "And don't think I'm not appreciative of you guys helping."

"We can get your money back too."

"Sure you can. A bunch of kids."

"You say that again, Eddie, and I swear I'll sock you in the nose."

"Sorry."

"…and stop apologizing, will ya?"

"Sorry."

"We have the Pompey Hollow Book Club – these are most of the regulars, but other kids join up all the time."

"A book club is going to get my money back? I don't think so."

"No, Barber came up with that name so we could get out of the house for meetings when we were nine and ten – even on school nights."

Eddie turned and grinned.

"So we've caught crooks before and on Halloween we even caught two Nazi POWs who escaped Pine Camp in 1944 and had been on the loose since, stealing everybody's old rubber tires and iron. The Army gave every town around here an ambulance because of us."

"I believe you," said Eddie.

"Good," said Mary. "So, here's the deal. It's not just about your plane anymore and you're not on your own anymore. You're not alone. It's about your family. It's about letting us figure out a way to get your money back for you. We could call an SOS. That's when the older guys come help us – like get your plane down and get your money back. Just wait. They're very good."

"What do you want me to do?"

"Come with us to the cemetery, watch and listen," said Mary.

Walkin' abreast, all of 'em - Marty on one end and Mary and Eddie on the other, the Pompey Hollow Book Club walked away from the biplane and crossed over the hilltop hayfield and started down the back hill into the piny Delphi Falls cemetery for a meeting. As they were gathering around ole Charlie's headstone, three cars pulled in, crunching up the cinder drive. Dick was in his Willys; Duba driving his pickup; and Minneapolis Moline Conway in his new Chevrolet with Jimmy Dwyer sitting alongside. They pulled to a stop, got out and strutted toward the gathering the way they usually do – looking like the James gang.

"What's up?" barked Dick.

"Spill," snorted Duba.

"How'd you guys get here so fast," asked Mary.

"Big Mike told Principal we were needed. He told him it was for an emergency," said Minneapolis Moline Conway.

"Principal called us to his office and told us to find you," said Duba. "Figured you'd be here."

"So what's up?" said Dick.

"Spill it," snorted Duba.

"Okay," said Mary.

She puffed a curl from her eye and looked at her watch. It was past 1PM.

"So everybody sit down. This might take a while."

"We've got all day," said Dick, lighting two cigarettes with his last match, handing one over to Duba.

"When I get through talking we can call an SOS if you guys say yes, Dick, and then we can meet some more before we all go have supper later."

"Ribs and corn," said Holbrook.

Mary looked down at Eddie sitting on the grass patiently.

"Eddie, the guys made me president. When we started we were pretty young. If we had any hope to catch crooks or help people out, we always needed guys who could drive to help, so we invented the SOS. The SOS is what we call it when we think we need the older guys."

"When did you start the club," asked Eddie.

"1949, most of us were nine or ten."

Eddie looked over at Dick and Duba.

"So you guys have had your licenses since 1949?"

"We knew how to drive. Nobody said anything about licenses."

"Didn't you say you learned to fly when you were fourteen?" asked Mayor.

"I did," said Eddie.

"Well, there you go," grunted Dick. "We learned to drive at twelve. We could rebuild a six cylinder engine at sixteen."

Mary wasted no time bringing Dick, Duba, Conway and Dwyer – the older guys - up to snuff. Then she let Marty tell the story of how Eddie had earned more than six hundred dollars – and how he was pickpocketed by a Vichy French crook handing out fliers for the Sherlock Holmes Players show for next Sunday. He explained the difference between our allies the French in occupied France and the French Vichy – our enemy in the War. Mary told how Eddie's family depended on his State Fair money to get through the winter. She told about the plane being stuck up on the hayfield hill and how the hill wasn't long enough for a take-off and our needing to get it down to the field next to the alfalfa field and bridge by the creek – so it could take off when Eddie earns enough money to fill the tank and go home. They didn't miss a detail.

There was a pause.

That's when Dick stood up and stepped in front of everyone.

"Listen up," blurted Duba, squatting down on one knee.

That was the signal; the older guys were taking on the SOS. Mary sat down.

"Okay," said Dick. "Everybody synchronize your watches. We'll all meet back here at five thirty – set your watches now at two. We'll go to supper together at five thirty, but we all leave from here.

Dick began organizing his thoughts and giving directive – as he had when they cornered the Nazi criminals on Halloween.

"Conway, you and Dwyer go get the Moline and haul the plane off the hill down to the field like she said - past our alfalfa field. Barber, you, Jerry, Randy, Mary, Bases and Holbrook all go with them and help. Conway's the boss. If you have to pull out a fence post or two so as to get the plane through, go ahead and do it, but be sure to put them back better than before. Fix all the wires."

"The tractor should be able to lift it up and over the fence," said Minneapolis Moline Conway.

"Perfect," said Dick. "Eddie, if there're keys to the plane, give them to Conway. Marty, you and Eddie come with Duba and me."

"Why me?" said Marty.

"You know the State Fairgrounds better than anyone here because of your horse shows. We'll need you at the library."

"Kids are still in school, for another three hours" said Mary. "How will you sneak Eddie into the library?"

"We've got some serious homework to do and not much time to do it and get ready. We'll head up to the Cazenovia Public Library," said Dick.

"This changes everything," said Mary. "Barber, find out for sure if we can have the square dance at your place on Wednesday night? It looks like we'll be here all week."

"Barn dance, hayride, everything," said Barber. "I'll get the word out to the Crown. This will give Eddie here a chance to meet Hal."

"I never thought of that," said Mary. "That's a nice idea. It'll give Farmer Parker the chance he wants of having a hayride."

"Eddie," said Randy, "Hal was on a submarine – he was a volunteer too, you'll like him."

"Where's the Sherlock Holmes Player thing – the theatre?" asked Duba.

"I don't know, it's printed on the flier that's in my valise," said Eddie. "I thought it was in New Woodstock."

"We'll stop and get your valise along the way," said Dick.

"If you get the plane down in the field, can you put a tarp over the cockpit to keep rain out?" asked Eddie.

The group assured him, and everyone dispersed.

The book club climbed the hill to try to rescue the biplane. Conway and Dwyer drove back to the Conway farm to get the Minneapolis Moline tractor. Dick, Duba, Eddie and Marty headed off to Cazenovia – by way of Farmer Parker's first to pick up Eddie's valise.

CHAPTER NINE

DARKNESS AFFECTS US ALL

For the first time as a guardian angel, a fright was comin' over ole Charlie here today.

Long before my passing and being laid to rest, I lived as simple as a body might. One horse, my Nellie. A cow, Bessie. A chicken coop in need of better chicken wire.

I didn't want for much – had my small barn, a two room house with a wood cook stove. I had kerosene oil for the barn lanterns and for my carryin' lantern; twarn't no electricity or necessary in the house. I had a privy chair in the bedroom for bad weather times and the outhouse out back for when times was good. I chose a simple life, I suppose, when I was in Germany in 1916 in WWI. I remember watching the Army boys and their horses choking and dying in the trenches from breathing in mustard gas. I knew if I ever got back home alive I would pretty much stay to my own self with my wife on the farm, thankful to be alive. I could still remember the boy's faces, taking their last gasps, eyes open lookin' up for a heaven.

After my wife died I would take the carriage to spinster Netty's place on Pompey Hollow Road on occasion. We'd set on her porch swing watching fireflies and listening to bullfrogs at sunset. We'd talk about my wife and how she could kick a jig on the front porch to a jaw harp and about our missing her but we'd never talk about that war I was in.

I was right comfortable with my barn, my carriage and the bullfrogs.

It's just that now this here French Vichy pickpocket thing and all the talk of State Fair girlie shows and those Sherlock Holmes stage performers from across the water are all new to me and not settin' right in my gut.

Problem being the rules guardian angels have to follow. We can't be manipulating. No interfering with people's lives more than nudging allowed. Other than being able to maybe stir up a draft to slam a door closed, most we could do was pray, hope and nudge – and yes, hoping is still a prayer of sorts.

I wasn't ever afraid of things I knew about. Guess the point is I would know what I would be praying for. I was afraid of the unknown. Most everybody is, ya know – afraid of the dark, as be said. I knew I needed educating on a world I wasn't accustomed to - and I needed it soon so I could deal with it all with proper prayer.

Might say I was in waters I never swam before – in up over my head.

Well, tonight's moon would be full and a full moon is opportunity for me, for any angel. I requested an Angel Congress on top of Big Mike's barn garage roof for later tonight. Angels can do that under a full moon – request an Angel Congress. I twinkled word out in the heavens I needed special help with my education about Paris show ladies-of-entertainment, with Sherlock Holmes stage actors and with a French Vichy pickpocket scoundrel.

Word came back to be on Big Mike's barn garage roof at ten o'clock. It would happen.

While I was organizing my Angel Congress here in Delphi Falls, up the hill in Cazenovia, Dick and Duba were running into obstacles of their own trying to get past the desk at the Cazenovia Public Library.

"Young man, I need to see a library card," said the bespectacled matron of the books. "No library card, no books."

"Ma'am, I don't have one, but we have very important research to do," said Dick.

"I'm sorry. You need a library card."

"It could be a matter of life and death - can't we just go into your reference section," pleaded Dick.

"We promise to be very quiet," said Duba.

"If it's life and death, then what you need is the Police station, you'll find Sheriff..."

"Ma'am, I exaggerated about the life and death, okay, but this is really important."

"You need a library card," said matron.

"Can he sign up now and get one?" asked Duba.

"Please keep your voices down. His parents would have to sign for him. Books are a responsibility – they are very expensive - a parent would need to sign for you."

"I'm twenty-five, could I get a library card on my own?" asked Eddie.

The matron looked him over, unshaven.

"Where do you live?" she asked

"I'm day-labor, staying at Farmer Parker's place down in Delphi Falls," said Eddie. "If you call, I'm sure they'll vouch for me."

"You boys go on in, but don't make noises, keep your voices down, and put all the books back where you got them from. If you don't remember – don't guess – bring them here for me to put up."

Dick's direction was plain and simple.

"Eddie, pull out anything you can find – magazines, reference books, anything on WWII that talks about French Vichy."

"Will do. Anything else?"

"Check and see if Hemingway wrote about the French Vichy, I think he did. Wasn't Humphrey Bogart in that movie?"

"I'll look in the index cards," said Eddie.

"Duba, you find whatever you can on English acting companies and the Sherlock Holmes Players," said Dick. "Check through local newspapers for articles about them."

"Okay," said Duba.

"Marty, you see if you can find a map of the New York State Fairgrounds in Syracuse."

In time Eddie carried a stack of Life magazines and Saturday Evening Post magazine from the early 1940s and set them on the table. He found two volumes on the Encyclopaedia Britannica with War pictures. He found the book – To Have and Have Not by Ernest Hemingway – set in North Africa under French Vichy rule. He and Dick started to go through them all page by page combing for clues.

"Look at this," said Dick. "I never knew this before. France was divided into two parts in the War. Here's a map.

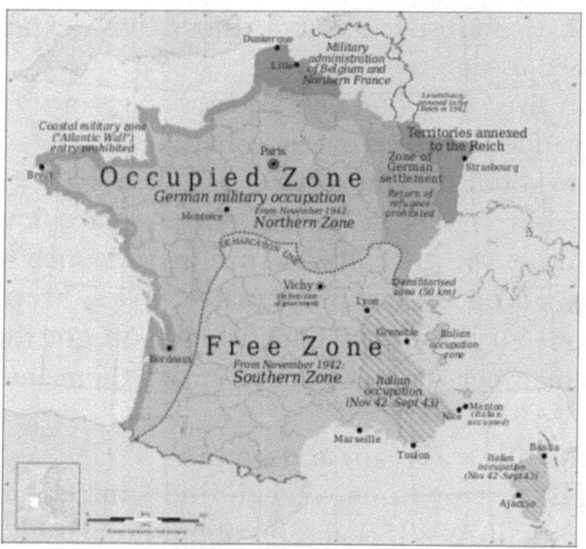

France in WWII – Occupied and Vichy (free)

It's like you said, Eddie, one part of France, under General de Gaulle was occupied by the German Nazi. De Gaulle escaped to England and hid out in London.

The other part had a bad French guy Marshal Philippe Petain who was like ninety and left over from WWI. He ran the second part of France, in the south – Vichy.

Marshal Philippe Petain shaking Hitler's hand.

He was friends with Hitler, so the Nazi left him alone. The Nazi let the French Vichy go through France and round up Jews to be slave labor or to be sent to the gas chambers for extermination."

"Here's an article about how the Vichy even caught Gypsies ever since WWI," said Eddie. "It was going on for years. They'd put them to work in the salt mines or iron mines. When WWII came along they'd put them in concentration camps."

"France controlled so much around the world and most of North Africa," said Dick, "Hitler used the Vichy to keep control of their countries with the French navy to keep the French navy out of the War."

"Any ideas?" asked Eddie.

"Not yet," said Dick.

"I'm not finding anything on the Sherlock Holmes Players," said Duba.

"We'll find the playhouse where they're putting on their show next Sunday and snoop around," said Dick. "Look in Eddie's valise for the theatre address."

"Seeing all this stuff is making me think," said Eddie. "Something's bothering me. You know what's bothering me about this whole thing?"

"What?" asked Dick.

"I was there a long time. The Nazi Germans kept bombing England all throughout the War. The blitz, they called it. They killed a lot of people in England, kids and families."

"Yes," said Dick. "They sent V-2 rockets they had, every day and night. They sent thousands of them. Sometimes they would bomb London using blimps – they called them dirigibles. So, what's your point?"

"The French Vichy helped Hitler all through the War – even all the time they were bombing England every day and night. Think about it, the Vichy were enemies, they arrested French citizens who were Jews and the Gypsies, even prostitutes - what they called "undesirables." They sent them to concentration camps to be killed or to work as slave labor."

Dick paused.

"I read where the Nazis would walk up to a Jew and if they were too old or too young to work they would shoot them on the spot and have other Jews drag them to a pit to be buried. Sometimes in wheelbarrows," said Dick.

"Take a look at these pictures," said Eddie. "Here are some of the wagons the Gypsies would live in.

This drawing shows how the Vichy made phony trucks out of canvas. They would hide under them to lure Gypsies so they could capture them. Sometimes they hid cannons under them, like this one."

"You're trying to make a point," said Dick.

"French Vichy were bad, really bad eggs."

"…and?" asked Dick.

"Any Englishmen who lived through all that Blitz, and the bombings isn't ever going to forget all what they did to the English," said Eddie. "Not in eight or ten years, anyway they won't. I saw London after the War. It'll take years to rebuild it. The Vichy was as bad as the Nazis."

"…and?" asked Dick.

"I can't see an English acting company hiring a Vichy member with the War still fresh in memories like it was. Maybe that guy, you know, the pickpocket was only pretending to be French Vichy; trying not to leave a trail."

"Are you saying?…"

Dick sat back and thought.

"I'm saying maybe he was pretending to be French Vichy. I can't see British actors being all that friendly with a real French Vichy – hiring them and all, this close to the end of the War."

"If we could only prove it somehow," said Dick.

"Too bad we don't speak French," said Duba.

"Wait!" said Dick. "Duba, say that again!"

"Huh?" asked Duba. "Say what?"

"What you said," said Dick.

"Too bad none of us speak French?"

"Hold tight," barked Dick.

He stood up and walked over to Marty who was looking through books at another table.

"Found anything on the State Fairgrounds?"

"Some old photographs of it is all. Nothing like what you're looking for - a map of the grounds."

"That's okay, you can draw one best you can from memory," said Dick. "I have a new job we need to get done."

"Name it," said Marty.

"I need you to memorize these pictures of the Gypsy wagons and the one made out of canvas – here, this one. You could even sketch that one on a piece of paper."

"…and?" asked Marty.

"Get with Mrs. Coco, the school art teacher – and Mr. Ossant in the school shop. We need a dummy gypsy wagon built that looks like it…maybe out of canvas."

"You mean you want a canvas tent that looks like a Gypsy wagon, with wheels and everything but it's not a wagon, just a tent that looks like a wagon?" asked Marty.

"A Gypsy wagon," said Dick. "Yes."

"Coco and Ossant helped us catch the Nazis, should help us again," said Marty.

"Yep," said Dick.

"I'll need a ride to school," said Marty.

"Hold on, we'll take you. Give us a second to try something."

Dick stepped around the library tables quietly leaning in and asking people sitting and reading if they spoke French. A lady paging through a book, looking for where she left off yesterday looked up and smiled.

"Why yes," she said. "I can speak and read French."

"Would you hold on for a minute, lady," asked Dick. "Don't go anywhere."

Dick waved Eddie over and sat him down next to the lady. He quietly whispered an introduction.

"Lady, this is Eddie – he was a paratrooper who landed in France behind enemy lines on D-Day."

"Well, I've never been to France," said the lady, but thank you for helping bring an end to that terrible War, young man."

"Eddie," whispered Dick, "this is important."

"What is?" asked Eddie.

"I need you to think. You have to try to remember everything that French pickpocket said to you."

"You're kidding, right?" asked Eddie. "That was days ago."

"You have to try to remember," said Dick.

Eddie looked around the library. He looked over at the lady smiling back at him.

"Did he speak French?" asked the lady.

"Ma'am, he spoke English but it was sure enough a heavy French accent, I do know that," said Eddie.

"What did he say?" asked Dick. "Try to remember."

"He said he was helping the actors paper the theatre seats next Sunday so there would be a crowd in the audience. He was French Vichy. He even called me "mon ami" and everything. He sounded like the French farmer who hid us out in their barn; but I knew the town he was from was Vichy. He made a big deal that the bigger the crowd the better the wankers would act and so the better his Sherlock Holmes show would be for everyone."

"The man isn't French," said the lady. "He's British."

"Huh?" bolted Dick. "Just from what he said you can tell?"

"He's a Brit. He's used a pejorative that is English – not French. A Frenchman would not have use the word. It is a local – probably London or Liverpool – a school boy word – and not a nice one."

"What word?" asked Dick.

"Wanker. That is a 'naughty' – well, let's say an undesirable word. It's an English slang used by the young from time to time. He's definitely English."

Duba and Marty gathered around. Dick went into detail how Eddie was robbed – pickpocketed – and the ruse was his trying to give away the Sherlock Holmes tickets. He went into great detail how Eddie nearly crashed his biplane and how they wanted to help him get his money back.

"Aren't you the same group who caught the POW escapees a few weeks ago?" she asked.

"Guilty," said Duba.

"Halloween, wasn't it?"

"That'd be us," said Duba.

"I want to help," she asked, "How can I help?"

"I can't believe I got duped like that," said Eddie.

"It could have happened to anyone," said the lady. "The man was with the Sherlock Holmes Players – I'd bet on it. Maybe only a stagehand though – but careful - he didn't want to draw any suspicion on the players so he pretended he was French."

"French Vichy," said Duba.

"He probably recognized your leather flight jacket," said Dick. "He wanted to throw your memory off-guard."

"Which he was able to do with the Vichy lie – at least for a while," said Marty.

"Exactly," said the lady. "For all you knew he was hired to pass out tickets. He would never suspect you looking for him – a French Vichy - at the theatre where Brits are playing. He's probably a back stagehand the audience would never see."

"Maybe he's the star," said Marty. "Maybe he's playing Sherlock Holmes."

"That could be, as well," said the lady. "His ego wanted a full house. So he was giving away tickets."

"This Saturday," said Dick. "We'll give him a taste of his own medicine."

"And get you your money back, Eddie," whispered Duba. "That's a promise."

"How can I help?" asked the lady.

"Lady, we might need to set up a camp somewhere in the woods. If we do we need to make it look like a Gypsy camp. Can you help?" asked Dick. "We're building the gypsy trailer and will have a big bonfire going."

"My husband and I have an antique trading shop," said the lady. "I believe we will have accessories you might need – including costumes and music."

"Where is your store?" asked Dick.

"In Hamilton. Come and we'll see what I have that can help."

The lady jotted down a number.

"You're probably in school tomorrow. If you can come after store hours, call this number, I'll make arrangements to meet you there."

"I'll call you if we need things. If we do something else, I probably won't but thanks for your help," said Dick.

"My pleasure," she said.

"Marty, did you copy the drawing of the canvas dummy, the Gypsy wagon?" asked Dick.

"I've got it sketched," said Marty. "I'll draw the Fairground map later."

"Okay, let's get back," said Dick. "Thank you Ma'am, we'll maybe see you tomorrow."

"Best of luck," she said.

She smiled and opened her book again – contentment in her eyes knowing how much she helped already.

As they walked out of the library towards Dick's Willys, Eddie asked, "What's next?"

"Back to the cemetery," said Dick. "Let's see how they're getting along with the plane. Then we'll get ready for supper. Later, when Duba and I pile everyone in our cars to take them home, we'll stop at the cemetery first and finish coming up with a plan of attack."

"...and we'll attack the French Vichy," Eddie laughed.

"You've got that right," said Dick.

"I get it!" blurted Duba. "The more we can make the pickpocket believe Eddie was convinced he is French Vichy, the better our chances of getting the money back."

"…and the more we can make him believe we're Gypsies, rolling in gold and silver and dripping with expensive jewellery," said Dick.

"Oh, wow!" said Duba.

"…and with a genuine Gypsy wagon," snorted Marty.

Eddie beamed a smile and climbed into the front seat of Dick's car.

"I think I'll telephone my wife tonight. See how the girls are –say hello," said Eddie.

CHAPTER TEN

DOWN TO EARTH PHYSICS

The engineering a body could learn in 1953 by living on a farm and having to think up solutions from time to time is amazing. Add to that what the kids born in the 1940s learned watching War newsreels at the Saturday morning picture show. They'd see young soldiers building entire bridges that could hold up under crossing tanks virtually overnight. They watched the building of tank and cannon camouflaged bunkers and no telling what else all throughout a world at War. War youngling's learned early that anything could be done if they put a mind to it, and worked together. A biplane stuck on top of the hill needed to come down. Minneapolis Moline Conway got his tractor up there to it, but after measuring off what parts he had on the tractor that might be of service to the situation and stepping-off measuring the plane; he concluded something would have to give.

"Oh, she'll lift it off the ground alright, that's certain," Conway said. "But I don't like the tilt we'd most likely have riding it down the steep hill. Because of its engine weight, it could tip us over, for sure."

"Pretty steep," said Holbrook.

It was a dilemma.

Holbrook, Randy and Mayor had already removed two gate fence posts from the ground in preparation. They could pull up more if they needed a wider space to get the airplane through. They had shovels, wire snips and all the tools they'd need to get the job done. Challenge was driving the enormous tractor down the steep grade of a hill carrying an awkward biplane on its forklifts without tipping over.

About this time Dick, Duba, Eddie and Marty had made their way up to the top of the hill and were walking towards the biplane. Dick gestured to keep quiet, letting the ones at it do their jobs.

"Let's sit down and watch," he whispered.

Sound advice.

He knew every person there. They were all smart as whips and would figure it out if they had the time and space to think. The four squatted on the ground thirty feet away from the plane and watched.

"I got an idea," said Mary.

Conway turned the tractor engine off.

"Let's hear it."

"The plane, with its crazy shape and different weight all around is hard to balance and could tip everything over, right?"

"That's it in a nutshell," said Conway.

"And it being canvas and all, it's pretty fragile in certain parts, making it harder to get hold of," she offered.

"I could tear a wing or shred the body with a wrong move," said Conway.

"Well what if we took it down the hill level and not tilted?" she asked. "Would that do it?"

"No offense, Mary," snapped Conway. "A hill is up, and a hill is down. T'aint nothing level about a hill, either way you're headed on it."

"Well, if it was level?..." asked Mary. "What I mean is what if we could make it level?"

"Then we'd be down there at the bottom and not up here on the hill," said Conway impatiently.

"It's not impossible," said Mary.

"Impossible!" barked Conway. "Even forgetting the hill, the plane doesn't have anything level enough on it to even lift it off the ground level. We can't take the propeller off and put it upside down, nose first on the forklift," said Conway.

"But the tractor could lift the hay wagon level, couldn't it?" asked Mary.

"You seem to forget, Mary, we're lifting an airplane," said Conway.

"No need to get snippy, Conway. Could the tractor lift the hay wagon level?" insisted Mary.

"Well, yes, but what's your point? We're not lifting a hay wagon."

"We could bring the hay wagon up here," said Mary.

"We've already gone over all that, Mary. We already settled that the hay wagon wouldn't hold the weight of the plane," blurted Conway.

"The wheels," said Mary.

"Huh?" snorted Conway.

"Didn't Big Mike say the hay wagon wheels wouldn't support the plane?"

"Yup!"

"What if we bring it up here with the horses and take the wheels off setting it flat on the ground. We then push and roll the plane onto the wagon on the ground and strap it down. The Minneapolis Moline could sure enough lift the flat hay wagon, plane and all – and it would be level."

Conway stepped off the tractor scratching his head. Holbrook and everyone else grinned. Dick elbowed Duba; who nudged Eddie; who winked at Marty.

Conway stepped around in a circle once or twice, thinking. He thought the world of Mary. Had complete respect for her presidency of The Pompey Hollow Book Club. But after all, she was a girl – and he had a tinkering notion he could be outdone by a girl – here with an audience and all.

His eyes twinkled – he could save face.

"It sure would lift her up level, and all. You're right there, Mary. But it still would be a front end heave and it could tilt us over going down," Conway said in a pensive tone as though he were putting Mary's king in check but being pleasant about it.

"Then, why don't you just turn the tractor around and back down the hill," she offered, with a checkmate tone in her voice.

Not one to hold a grudge, Conway put his cap back on.

"Well, somebody go hitch her up and bring the hay wagon up here," he barked, like he was running the show. "And bring a tool-box, set of wrenches and all."

By five o'clock everyone was in the cemetery again. The bi-plane was down in the field next to Big Mike's alfalfa field - with a tarp over it. The hay wagon was put back together and in the barn where it belonged.

By six o'clock they had pretty much laid out a first round plan of attack for the weekend at the State Fairgrounds and were pass-ing platters of ribs and bowls of canned corn around Big Mike's and Missus table. They would eat now and plan in better detail on full stomachs after supper.

Everyone was particularly proud of Mary's idea that got the plane down safe and sound. She had a right pleasant smile through supper, feeling good about herself, as she should. She knew it wouldn't be long before Eddie could go home to his wife and little girls.

"Missus, we're doing the barn dance and hayride tomorrow night at Barbers," said Mary.

"That'll be such fun, and a break for you all," said Missus.

"It'll be a chance for Eddie to meet Hal," said Barber.

"That'll be nice," said Big Mike. "We'll call Gertrude and see if we can bring anything."

Ole Charlie here had a few hours before the Angel Congress was to begin. I decided to sit up on the buffet side table and watch my flock enjoy their acorn squash with butter. I used to cut them in half and turn them upside down on a hot stove lid to toast. I admired the nice burnt crust Big Mike was able to get on the ribs, the way ribs ought to be done. I think he used honey.

CHAPTER ELEVEN

THE DICK TRACY CURSE

Leaning in to catch light beams from his dashboard, Dick scribbled notes. He stepped out of the Willys making his way over to the gravestone with a lantern light resting on it so he could read if need be. Everyone was sitting around on the ground waiting. Ole Charlie here was up on a pine branch above his head. I still had time before tonight's Angel Congress on Big Mike's barn garage roof was to begin.

"Listen up," barked Duba.

"We'll go through my notes on our strategy, first," said Dick. "We'll talk it out afterword. Then we'll set rules and make assignments. We have to figure out every detail any of our tactics will need attending to. We don't have much time between now and Saturday. Everybody okay with that so far?"

The silence was all the encouragement he needed to push on. Eddie rested back on my stone to listen.

"Strategically we're going to catch the bad guys basically by doing two things. We're planning to pull off both things this Saturday and Saturday night; Sunday only if we need to.

First, we're going to bait a trap that is sure to lure the pickpocket in so we can then - in phase two - set him up and catch him red-handed."

"What is red-handed anyway?" interrupted Mayor. "Everybody's always saying 'catch them red-handed'. What does it mean – red handed?"

"It means with blood on their hands," barked Duba. "In murder mysteries, they get caught in the act – or red-handed. Listen up. Don't interrupt."

"Oh," said Mayor.

"Red-handed to us would be to have Sheriff John or somebody important that actually hears the pickpocket confess. Mostly what we want though is for him to give us back the money he stole from Eddie," said Duba.

"Second," said Dick, "if there are any chances more people are in on the pickpocketing, we want big enough bait to catch all of them. If it's a gang, we want to bring them all out of hiding and catch them in the same net."

"Sounds perfect," said Mary.

Dick continued.

"So look at what we know? We know he's a crook. We know he's a crafty pickpocket…he's slick."

"Check," said Duba.

"…at first we thought he was French Vichy, but we're not so sure now what he is. Tell you later why but we think he may be an English guy playacting like he's a French Vichy to throw us off his trail."

"That's what I think," said Duba. "I think he's a Brit using a phony French accent."

"We're going to hedge our bets," said Dick.

"Huh?" asked Holbrook.

"This Saturday, Duba and I are going to put on a show. It'll be on the Midway, starting around noon. We want to draw the pickpocket out. Duba will darken his face, arms and hands; even wear earrings. He'll pretend he's like the gypsies you see in the movies."

"A Hollywood gypsy," said Holbrook.

"Yes," said Dick. "He'll be a gypsy who doesn't understand a word of English or of French either."

"Dumb as a stump," said Randy.

"He'll stay quiet and playact he's a man servant to a mean rich lady in the wheelchair," said Dick. "I'll be there pushing the chair."

"The French Vichy Nazis cut his tongue out for consorting with the enemy!" barked Barber.

Mary poked Barber to hush.

"...she's going to be a lady with polio, in her wheelchair out getting some sun at the New York State Fair," said Dick.

"Alice!" Mary grinned.

"Alice," said Dick. "She is smart; she probably knows French or can learn some of it quick enough to get the job done."

"And she sure loves an adventure," said Conway.

"We need to get her a wig so she looks old," said Mary.

Duba turned around to Eddie.

"You should have seen Alice and Marian ride the rope line on Halloween, zipping all the way down the seventy foot tree in their leg braces before we sent Conway up with the pumpkin."

"Leg braces?" asked Eddie.

"They both have polio," said Mary. "They wanted something to do to catch the Nazi escapees. We needed weights to tighten a rope...I'll tell you later."

"I'll push her wheelchair around the Midway until we get the pickpocket's attention," said Dick. "Duba will be carrying a handful of cash - running for her every whim, buying things — you know - kewpie dolls, ice-cream, cotton candy, spoiling her with State Fair junk. We'll be her servants, me pushing - Duba buying and carrying her packages. All the time we're setting up the lure.

Alice will do all the talking. If it works like we hope we'll lure him into the trap and catch them all red handed."

"You don't know what he looks like, the pickpocket," said Randy.

"Eddie does," said Dick. "The pickpocket won't recognize Eddie dressed in Farmer Parker's bib overalls, red bandanna and engineer hat. Eddie can find him for us and give us a signal."

"For it to work, the pickpocket or whoever his gang is will have to come to you," said Marty. "They'll have to smell money, right?"

"And if Alice sounds French Vichy enough, the pickpocket will believe her," said Mary.

"Believe what?" asked Marty. "I'm still not getting it. If Duba, the gypsy, is carrying all the money in his hand, what good is Alice going to be sitting in a wheelchair the whole time? How can anybody pickpocket her? I don't get it."

"If she'll even do it for us," said Dick, "Alice is going to catch the pickpocket's eye somehow, get him to come to her so she can let him in on her secret."

"Secret?" asked Marty.

"Her secret counterfeit money printing operation," said Dick.

"I am intrigued now," said Eddie sitting up alert. "Please go on."

"The Hardy Boys and the Secret of the Old Mill," blurted Jerry. "The crooks had a secret counterfeit printing press."

"And her counterfeit press operation will be in my gypsy wagon hidden up in the woods somewhere," said Duba.

"First she'll disarm the pickpocket. She'll tell him that she's on to him," said Dick. "She'll tell him she's been watching him pick pockets and as slick as he is, she could tell and what a waste of time that was for a talent like him. She'll tell him something like he was lifting nickels and dimes when he could be making money – real big money with her counterfeit cash."

"How's she going to prove anything about any counterfeit money to a pickpocket with nothing more to show than her flapping gums?" asked Marty. "He's going to want to see something."

"He's right," said Randy. "Talk is talk unless she can prove it."

"How is she going to put her counterfeit money where her mouth is, like they're saying?" said Mary.

"What happens if he asks her to prove it?" asked Holbrook.

"That could spook him," said Mayor.

"Well, that's when she takes bills out of Duba's hand," said Dick. "Her gypsy man-servant hands it all to her. She lifts the top her blanket to hide it when she fans the counterfeit money out and shows off a wad, just like this."

With that, Dick pulled an inch thick roll of crisp new one dollar bills from his shirt pocket. He removed a rubber band from around them and fanned them out flat like a hand of cards and held them up for all to see.

"She'll show him these brand new crispy green one dollar bills – and she'll show him the tens and twenties too. Here, check them out. Pass them around. Feel them. Examine them."

Dick passed the one dollar bills around to anyone with their hand out.

"This looks real," said Mayor.

"She'll convince the pickpocket he can make big money just by making change for the farmers at the Fair with the hundred dollar bills in their pockets. They only need a few ones for the Midway demonstration – to find someone who needs change for a fifty or a hundred dollar bill. Pickpocket takes their real cash folding money and hands the farmers counterfeit bills in exchange. Buy counterfeit money from her, real cheap - that'll be her story. Why should a pickpocket look all day for that one sucker big score when with her counterfeit money, he could get some folding cash from everybody walking by?"

"No one would ever know this stuff is counterfeit," said Barber. "It's really good."

"If we get caught with this, we're all in the pokey," said Randy. "I don't know if my dad…"

"Okay, I know there must be a trick to it," said Marty. "How'd you and Duba even get your hands on counterfeit one dollar bills in the first place?"

"We didn't," said Duba.

"Huh?" said Holbrook - holding one of the dollar bills up to the lantern light. "This sure looks real."

"That's because it is," said Duba.

"These are all real bills," said Dick. "Real U.S. currency one dollar bills – but the French Vichy faker will believe whatever Alice tells him they are and he'll believe it's all counterfeit," said Dick. "Counterfeit money he can buy real cheap and make a fortune making change."

"Exactly," said Duba, "whose not going to believe a lady in a wheelchair who has a gypsy man-servant?"

"Holy dang!" yelped Marty. "I have lots of questions to answer; lots of detail to work out! My minds a-spinning – but that sure will work. It had us all fooled and we're Americans."

"You believed these one dollar bills were counterfeit because we said they were," said Dick. "They will too, when Alice says it is."

"What next?" asked Barber.

"Marty, get your drawings to Ossant in the Ag shop as soon as you can. We'll need a canvas gypsy wagon like the pictures. A printing machine in the back is too much to ask for. Mary, you get with Mrs. Coco, see if she can come up with a costume and make-up for Duba. Maybe even an outfit for me smudged with printer's ink like I'm her counterfeit pressman. Ink on my hands, under my fingernails. No wait, Randy you go see Mrs. Coco, she made the ghost costumes for you on Halloween – you'll know what she'll want. Mary we need you to come with us to see Alice and help us talk her into this whole thing."

"If Alice says no," we'll need a new plan," said Marty.

"Everybody, let's meet up here again right after school tomorrow, before we go to Barbers for the hoedown," said Dick. "Marty have your map of the Fairgrounds drawn."

"One hitch," said Marty.

"What?" asked Dick.

"What if the pickpocket wants her to prove the money changing thing will work?"

"Hadn't thought about that, Marty," said Dick. "We'll come up with something by tomorrow's meeting."

With that they all climbed into one of the cars going their way and were driven home. The group was as exhilarated as they were on Halloween night while catching the Nazis. Ole Charlie here floated up the hill, easy like – enjoying the smile and look of satisfaction on Eddie's face as he climbed the hill to cross the hayfield and go down to sleep in the straw loft. It was a right nice feeling, seeing all my flock rising to such an occasion in such an admirable manner.

Big Mike's barn garage roof was aglow when I got there for the Angel Congress. Oh, it weren't a glow just anyone could see, only angels – but a pretty, rainbow sheen it surely was. Ole Charlie's first thing was to find angel Arnold – and hear more stories about his time with my Pap back in the Spanish American war. They fought together under Teddy. When I found him, Arnold didn't waste no time and told me about a time my Pap and when he and a bunch of others were ordered to stand at attention – early morning it was. They were somewhere in Cuba getting ready to head out on a charge. Seems Teddy Roosevelt was about to come in person and tell them all something important – some words of encouragement. Well, as Arnold remembered it, about every time the Sarge would start to tell the recruits – ya' know, the Rough Rider infantry – something he thought was important his horse would fart. Naturally, that early in the morning, someone would guffaw through pressed lips and ruin Sarge's concentration further. Every time he'd start up again to say something more, his horse would twitch an ear and let out another fart. This went on until he bellowed out:

"Who was the danged fool gave my horse his oats this morning?"

A voice came back.

"Oats, Sarge?"

"Oats, you heard me. Who was the danged fool gave my horse his oats this morning?"

"I thought surely the note said to give him cod liver oil and carrots. I even boiled the carrots. Boiled it all together, Sarge, cooked it up real tasty."

"That was my list for the Post Exchange, you idiot."

"No need to get personal," said a Lieutenant riding by.

The Sargent didn't say a word; he reined the horse and rode away sounding like a percussive band instrument to hitch his flatulent mount a bit more downwind.

After that story raised my spirits, as be said, Arnold asked me to follow him to the other side of the barn garage roof. Sitting there all alone, taking everything in, was a vested, moustached, masterly looking kind of man. Not quite a sneer on his jowls – but a keen eye, sure enough.

"Sir Arthur Conan Doyle," said Arnold. "Please meet the son of my very best friend – he's Charles Pitts on the scrolls – just ole Charlie here tonight. He was a simple man on earth, Sir Doyle. Runs a mighty good flock – but needs some of your help, I'm thinking. Something special he's up against now – could use some of your kind of advice. I thought you would be best to steer him over some potholes he'll have to explain himself to you."

The famous (I learned later) Sir Arthur Conan Doyle gave ole Charlie here the once over. He was pleasant enough about it but I knew I was getting a checking over.

I didn't know what to say, so I waited.

Angel Sir Arthur Conan Doyle meets Charlie - 1953

"My good man, it is a capital mistake to theorize before one has data," said Doyle. "You proceed first."

I later learned Mr. Doyle calling me his good man was a 'deduction' he made like that detective he knew, Sherlock Holmes. His deduction reckoned I was a good man just by being an angel and all.

"Mr. Doyle, sir, I'm not too all fired certain what Arnold had in mind – me and you meeting like this – but if I may take liberties with your kindness, it's been a frightful month. I'm up against women prancing all about barely draped – naked calendar girls and my flock coming to the age and all that goes with that."

"Naked bodies, drawings, pictures, calendars, not a totally unfamiliar test for the young. An ageless challenge, my good man, manageable though, quite manageable, I assure you," mumbled Doyle. "Is there more?"

"Then there are the pickpockets. Your eminence, sir, we're a simple country area – folks here are farmers and growers – they're not in a big city. The pickpockets have come here, right to our doors, they surely have."

"The lowest and vilest alleys of London do not present a more dreadful record of sin than does a smiling and beautiful country-side," said Doyle.

"London? London, you say," I said. "That reminds me, London - there are them Sherlock Holmes Player fellas from London, England. I think they're behind the whole mess. You think actors are crooks, Mr. Doyle?"

"Well you have me there," said Doyle.

He twisted his waxed moustache sprout, thinking.

"Very few professions where a person can be King Lear one mo-ment, a world at his feet and borrowing farthings from a barkeep for a crust of bread, the next. Actors are a whole science all their own."

"Are all actors' crooks?"

"Exaggerated perhaps, I say - keeping people's money after some of the performances I've seen does not make them crooked."

"You think you can help me, Mr. Doyle?"

"What exactly is heaven's destiny for you, Charles – have you been given your final assignment?"

"I'm pretty new at this. Right now it's tending my flock - they're young – twelve to sixteen maybe. I watch them for some years. I think later it will be tending their kin."

"Easy enough now then," said Doyle. "1953 is a wonderful time for a young person's values. They are impressionable at these ages now, and good examples have been set. My first flock came with the starting of a World Depression and moved through a world at war. Mine watched the years of depression. Yours watched an entire world at War whose story should be retold if only to teach the evil and virtue lengths of man's capability. It should be told as often as the Bible is read for its examples of our oneness of our souls and man's single purpose on earth. Studying both the War and the Bible could bring earth to forever calm. I'm sorry to tell you, Charles, your problem isn't today's flock; it will be this flock's grandchildren."

"One challenge here is maybe twenty-seven, he's a father, was a paratrooper in the War. The pickpockets I'm talking about took all his winter money and he almost took his own life as a result."

"He's a parent, is he?"

"Yes, your highness. He has two daughters. Can you help?"

"The young under your wing are smart, well-meaning and directed. They'll be fine. The paratrooper is both disciplined and loving. He will be fine too. He'll learn his lesson; let things take their course. Together they will prevail."

"Mr. Doyle, what'd you mean by saying their grandchildren would be the problems?"

"Today their kinds talk to each other. Their kind, all the world over talk together, watch, they're the young who witnessed the War. They are eager to learn. They are eager to learn because they have to leave the house to go explore – they have to reach on a bookshelf to look things up. They have to solve their own problems – and for many solving problems is what an eventful, fulfilled and fruitful life is all about."

"That's my flock, alright, but can you tell me about their grandchildren? Are you allowed? You said they will be my problem."

"Their grandchildren will not often look up from their hand. They won't know how to carry on a conversation if it isn't coded. They will seldom know the warmth of holding a hand, of looking into someone's eye. They'll lose the feeling of remorse, the quest to want to explore. They will age as they push a cold, worn button in their hand that will rule their lives."

"What's in their hand, again?"

"I know you are a simple man, my friend. May I call you Charlie?"

"Yes, sir."

"You're an honest, simple man, Charlie. In your lifetime had you ever, by chance, come across the character of comics – a Dick Tracy – in your travels?"

"Yes," I knew Dick Tracy. They had his comics in the Sunday paper at Hasting's store – about 1931 it was. I saw them in the '40s"

Dick Tracy – 1935

"Did you see on his wristwatch, it was a watch with a two-way radio-TV? He would speak into it - things like 'Calling all cars. Calling all cars.' As though he were calling his headquarter station from his wrist. Someone would answer."

"I couldn't read but I remember Dick Tracy cartoons and his two - way wrist radio."

"Such a wrist radio didn't exist, of course. It and TV was a story teller's imagination in 1935."

"I often wondered."

"But they'll be very real one day. Around the year 2020, I'm thinking, Charlie – the great grandchildren of your flock will be speaking to their hands in similar fashion as did Dick Tracy. Life as we know it now…life as I had dreamed it – with intellect and reflection, will shrink. Life for the children then will be spoon-fed, less literate. Life will be more about which flock they get in line behind and walk with while they look at their hands, pushing buttons for answers. They won't see what happens around them; they will not feel any of it, affect it, and even change it. By then anything they think they will ever need to know or see will be in their hand. They will turn into a physical apathy never imagined by a novelist. Man will have evolved both their neuro-mechanical and inner-electrical instincts from the insightful and sensitive humans to the robotic-like perfection of any of nature's insects and animals. They'll be called the children of the 'antenna generation' - *antennaegens*. The ant is born knowing to tunnel, hunt and forage. A bear is born knowing how to fish and hibernate. The grandchildren of 2020 will reduce themselves from having to think, to that of reacting to new instincts of nature – by reading the antennae in their hands – as animals and insects of today do with their antennae.

The thing that gives your flock the will to survive on their own this very moment is that they have to and want to talk to each other. They have to ask and feel and see in order to survive.

With anonymity of an enormous magnitude threatening the future – great grandchildren - *antennaegens* watching their hands as I predict, will become colonies of ants. The media will tell them what they can and cannot do – what they can and cannot get away with."

"What about now?" I asked. "What do I do about the ladies who tantalize the young lads, on calendars, in the sideshow Midway tents? They're here, very real and today, and in this world, now."

"…they are women, Charlie. Think of them as what they are – women. Respect that they're all mothers, daughters, sisters, or aunts. Don't paint them with common brushes. They are also God's children – equal in every way. Give your flock the proper values you know of about womanhood. That is all they will ever need to see in a woman's eyes, the mothers, daughters, sisters and the aunts they are as their first impression. They'll look beyond the circumstance of a moment, or the paint – like they looked beyond a horrific War throughout their childhood."

"So I pray for everything to work out?"

"You're a kind soul, Charlie, and you have a kind flock. Just pray. I'll be here whenever you need me."

"There seems to be many bad people around the world, aren't there, Mr. Doyle, sir?"

"My good man, there are those who might be enticed into acting against their nature, into being bad. These types have consciences and might typically be changed - saved in time. But there are those among us who are a devil-born villainous <u>bad</u>."

"Can those sorts ever be changed?"

"Can devil vermin like Moriarty or Hitler be changed, you ask?...

...only when they were in diapers, I fear."

CHAPTER TWELVE

LATE NIGHT SOS CALLED

Back in the cemetery, feeling better after my Angel Congress, I saw there were stragglers talking and waiting for rides. Something about their earlier cemetery meeting wasn't setting all that well with Marty it seemed. He's a detail kind of lad, a mathematical whiz kid. He sensed important small details were being overlooked and maybe he should step forward before they became big things. Pretty much everybody knew Marty was smart. Partly because of his inquisitive nature but mostly because he's alone riding his horse and then there's his getting up dark early since he was twelve to deliver his daddy's milk cans alone over to Apulia Station before driving himself to school. He's had his farm driving permit no telling how long. All this time ridin' and drivin' alone treats a smart young mind a proper edge in thinking time. Made him a tenacious school newspaper reporter too, it surely did.

Dick, Duba, Minneapolis Moline Conway and Dwyer had left the cemetery and drove off with most that needed rides. Holbrook, Mary and Marty were waiting for Mary's dad. Barber was passing time before he walked home.

Watching Marty think I remembered Sir Arthur Conan Doyle telling ole Charlie here that it took a scientist or mathematician to solve a mystery best. Mr. Doyle was one of these, can't remember which. Marty was both and had uneasiness in him walking with Mary toward her daddy's car.

"You're the president, Mary," said Marty. "Can I get your permission to take some steps that could help come Saturday?"

"What kind of steps?"

Marty didn't say a word.

Mary saw the concern in his eye. She trusted him. She puffed a curl from her own.

"Sure, go ahead," she said as she climbed into her daddy's Ford to go home for the first time after three days of working Farmer Parker's place and moving an airplane. She needed to rest up before the barn dance tomorrow. Holbrook climbed in behind her.

"Mr. Crane, can you give me a second to tell Barber something?" asked Marty.

"Go ahead," said Mr. Crane. "We'll wait on you."

Marty got to Barber, the meeting caller, before he stepped out of the cemetery for home on foot.

"We need to call a meeting, an emergency SOS meeting – tomorrow, noon at Shea's store," said Marty. "Can you do it?"

"For Dick and Duba?" asked Barber.

"For me. Mary says it's okay, I just asked. Can you get word out tonight?"

Marty sure enough gave Barber go ahead to call a special SOS meeting for tomorrow at noon – in front of Shea's store in Fabius.

"Pretty late, but I'll do it," said Barber.

But here's the twist – Marty also asked Barber to call Big Mike, Mike Shea and Doc Webb and see if they could be there too. This sort of parliament had no precedence. In the history of the Pompey Hollow Book Club, it's never been done before.

Well Mr. Ossant, the Ag teacher who built props for them was an exception. Randy's pap, too who'd pick 'em up and drive them to the Saturday morning picture shows. Mary Crane's daddy would sometimes bring Mary to meetings and wait. Big Mike pretty much helped out…and Myrtie. Other than that outsider adults had never been allowed in any top secret SOS meetings in the Delphi Falls cemetery or anyplace else. Not one time since they started the club when they were nine.

Well, ole Charlie here don't count neither; they most always meet in the cemetery and I rise to the occasions as necessary.

This being said, Marty knew he'd better make good or he'd risk consequences by Dick and Duba for gross insubordination. Depending on their disposition, this could mean a wuppin'. Marty earned his stripes on Halloween night alright, galloping a stampede and ropin' those skinned pineapple heads up Cardner Road the way he did. But SOS meetings were still their call. It's the way it's always been – the older guys - and only their call.

As was the routine in an SOS, Barber would get the ball rolling by calling a few kids and those few would call a few more, and so forth and so on in chain reaction. Some would call and some would even run down the road half mile to a house with no telephone.

By midnight nary a soul in the Crown from Cazenovia to Tully from LaFayette to Gooseville Corners didn't know about the SOS meeting noon tomorrow in front of Shea's store. Big Mike, Doc Webb and Mike Shea included.

As folks gathered about Shea's for the meeting, it might help you to know that in 1953 between grade and high school there was a full count of no more than three hundred fifty kids. High school alone was a hundred twenty. I'm here to tell you by noon the store's front and corner streets were filled with kids on lunch break waiting on the meeting to start.

Big Mike, Mike Shea and Doc Webb were in the background leaning on Big Mike's Oldsmobile.

Marty was inside the store looking out through the front window near scared to fright. He'd even put on a tie and his Sunday coat to make a point that what he had to say was given some serious thought and he didn't just ride in from nowhere. I do believe he even had a shine on his shoes. He was looking all about, waiting for Mr. Ossant and Mrs. Coco to show up. He could see Dick, Duba, Minneapolis Moline Conway and Dwyer leaning against a maple tree looking like they was wondering what was going on – but they were giving him the respect he earned helping them on a few adventures in the past where mercenaries, highwaymen and crooked varmints they caught or run off were involved.

About then is when he stepped out on the front steps of the store.

"Listen up," barked Dick, as a courtesy to Marty.

Marty smiled at him nervously, played with the knot in his tie, twitched his neck and began. To break the ice, Marty decided to make an announcement.

"Everybody know about the barn dance and maybe hayride tonight at Barbers, do ya?"

Smiles all around warmed the crowd, helped him relax.

"Oh, and members of the Pompey Hollow Book Club are still meeting today right after school before we go to the barn dance."

Marty thought it best to clear the air letting people know Dick's meeting was still on.

"In the past, we've always had a few weeks to solve something big or make right some wrong, right?"

Not quite certain what he said, the crowd gave his tie the benefit of the doubt and mumbled and grumbled agreement.

"We have an important mission we only have a few days to organize and act on – or we could fail," he said. "Show of hands if you're up to it."

Every hand in the crowd went up.

"That being settled I'd like to ask Big Mike, Mike Shea and Doc Webb to come up here and get sworn in."

Well I never…but sure enough the three of them all dressed in their suits and ties made their way through the crowd and just as serious as county judges they stepped in front of Marty waiting for him to speak.

"We have a secret mission we would like to keep secret. Can we ask you gentlemen for something we need and for your trust that we will do our best not to let you down?"

Well, I knew Big Mike had an inkling the mission was to help Eddie and I figure he filled in Mike Shea and the Doc while they were leaning on his Olds. All three nodded their heads agreeing with Marty to the terms. All three of them were fans of the Pompey Hollow Book Club.

"We need seven hundred dollars," said Marty. "We need two old hundred dollar bills and the others crisp new bills, the new kind like when they stick together. We'll need two new hundreds, four new fifties and the rest can be new twenties or five dollar bills. I can't tell you why we need them, but we promise it's for a good cause, and we'll try not to lose the money so we can give it all back to you on Sunday, every cent."

"Bully!" barked Doc Webb. "I'm in."

"We're all in," said Mike Shea.

"It'll be here at the store tomorrow," said Big Mike.

Every mouth in the crowd was now dropped-jaw open, eyes glassed over. Weren't a soul there ever seen seven hundred dollars before much less a seven hundred dollar decision made so fast it was like buying an ice cream cone.

"Our house didn't even cost seven hundred dollars," whispered Holbrook.

It were a moment to behold, it truly was. Even Dick and Duba and his cohorts admired Marty's spunk – and admitted amongst themselves they had completely forgotten the detail of where they were going to find the money they needed to use as their pretend counterfeit.

Marty now wanted to ask the three wise men gentlemen to let them plan in secret…but they were young once, they knew.

"If that's about it for us," said Big Mike, "we'll be heading back to work. Good luck, everyone."

Mike Shea stepped up and went in the store. Big Mike and Doc Webb made their way through the crowd, got in the Oldsmobile and drove off.

"I have a couple of announcements to make," said Marty. "I'll make them and then turn it over to Dick and Duba."

With what Marty had just accomplished they were all ears. He had them in the palm of his hand.

"There's a crook or two we're going to try to trap at the State Fair Saturday. Who plans to be at the State Fair this weekend?"

"Friday is Fair Day at school," we were going up then," said a voice.

Hands went up.

"Okay, please hear this and understand how important it is. Some of us will be in some get-up or costumes on the Midway. Maybe even Alice in her wheel chair. We're not sure of who it'll be or what we'll be doing but we'll all be undercover and sticking around the Midway."

"Do you need volunteers?" someone asked.

"Not sure what we need, yet," said Dick from the crowd. "Come to the barn dance tonight and if we need you we'll tell you then."

"Other than that we're pretty much set," said Marty. "What we need is for you to not recognize any of us if you see us. Just walk by them like you don't know who they are, can you do that?"

"It'd be easier not to recognize them if we knew who we weren't supposed to recognize, Marty," said Mr. Ossant.

"Fair enough," said Marty. "How about we tell you this tonight at the barn dance, so you'll know?"

"So what happened? Who are you trying to catch?" asked a voice in the crowd.

"Someone we met, a father with two kids got all his winter food money for the family pickpocketed on the Midway. Six hundred and forty dollars of his money that he'd earned giving plane rides. He was working the Fair like he does every year and his valise was pickpocketed as he was leaving for home."

"Anything else?" offered Dick.

"Who's in if we need you?" asked Marty.

Every hand went up.

"So that's it for now, go back to school. This is all top secret."

Marty caught Dicks eye and saddled over to the maple tree where they were standing.

"Dick, I hope that was alright. I worried about getting you the money you'll need to make this believable. A few dollars wouldn't do it."

"That was some real thinking, Marty," said Dick.

"I have some more thoughts," said Marty. "Let me tell them, you think about them, and we can meet again in the cemetery today before the barn dance, okay?"

"Shoot," said Dick.

"I have a problem with our barging into the Midway Saturday hoping he's there when we don't even know what he looks like. I think you, Duba and Eddie should go in on Friday to get a look at him and then we all go back Saturday to do our thing," said Marty.

"Good idea," said Dick. "Done. We'll scope it out Friday."

"The fact we don't know for sure if this pickpocket is a Brit or French Vichy, I think we have a problem using a gypsy as our lure. During the War the French Vichy locked up thirteen thousand gypsies, killed off hundreds more."

"What's your point?"

"If this guy is French Vichy, you'd be okay with the gypsy. I don't know if he'd believe he was mute, though."

"…and?"

"Well, if he's a Brit – think about it - won't he have sympathy for the gypsy and not want to be any part of ţaking advantage of him like he watched the French Vichy do all through the War?"

"Dang," said Dick.

"This is some powerful good strategizing," said Duba.

"You've been giving this a lot of thought. So what do you have in mind, Marty?" asked Dick.

"Why not let me play a traveling water-witchery, you know, bib overalls, sign hanging around my neck, the whole works. Something like WATER WITCHING $50 – Book today! Pay today! Guaranteed to find water or you get your money back in FULL!"

"I thought you were showing Sandy at the horseshow," said Jerry.

"The horse competition is on Friday," said Marty. We only have Saturday anyway because the Sherlock Holmes players are putting on their show in New Woodstock all day Sunday and then it will be too late."

"What if pickpocket wants to be careful and check you out first, you know, your water witchery? What do you even know about water witchery?" asked Duba.

"I'll have my water witching twig with me, and an apple in my pocket proving that my twig came from a tree that bears fruit with a seed."

"He knows," said Conway. "Only a water-witcher would know about the seed bearing fruit."

"That'll do it sure," said Duba.

"I get it," said Dick. "You'll have some cash on you that needs changing? You'll be a target for us, right?"

"Better than that," said Marty. "My sign will draw attention that I might have cash. Farmers will ask me for changing their big bills so they can play on the Midway. The water witching will be a front for me – for us. I have a wagon in the woods alright, but it's just something to sleep and eat and travel town to town in."

"Will there be a printing press in it?"

"Think about it. Nobody's going to believe we could print that quality of cash on the spur of a moment in a wagon in the woods. So no printing press, I'm suggesting."

"So if you don't print the counterfeit, where does the money come from?"

"It'll come from telephone calls to the telephone phone closet at the Lincklaen House hotel in Cazenovia."

"How'd you pick that telephone, at the Lincklaen House?"

"I saw it once – it has a door so no one can hear you talk. Besides, it'll be convenient to the New Woodstock playhouse where the Sherlock Holmes players will be performing Sunday, and most likely rehearsing Saturday night."

Telephone closet – Lincklaen House - 1953

Dick, Duba, Conway and Dwyer all sat down on the grass, totally confused.

"The money comes from the telephone closet in the lobby of the Lincklaen House hotel!" blurted Dick.

"Not exactly," said Marty. "I'll be playing a 'fence' for the counterfeit money. You know – the middle man. Water witching is my disguise. I don't sell the counterfeit money; I only deliver it to the customers. You and Alice are my shills. Customers show me the cash proving they have enough to buy some counterfeit and agree to pay me COD, and I give them a code to use to make the deal. They go wait by that telephone at the time I tell them to. When it rings, they say the code word, agree on the price for the amount of counterfeit they want to buy and the voice on the phone gives them another secret code that they are okay to come give me at my wagon. When they get there, they pay me first. Maybe I can get them to confess to what they pickpocketed. Then we nab him."

"So, who is the mystery voice calling the lobby phone?" asked Dick.

"Myrtie, the telephone operator will make the call for us, disguise her voice," said Marty with a big grin.

"Holy cow, amazing!" said Dick.

"But wait, there's more," said Marty. "Sheriff John Price will be sitting with her listening to this guy buying counterfeit money. He'll be witness enough to arrest the pickpocket."

"If he could admit to pickpocketing the money he's using to buy the counterfeit, and let Sheriff John hear that."

"Why not," said Marty. "One crook to another crook, Myrtie could ask where he stole his money and could he lay his hands on any more and he'd probably tell her. Probably brag about it."

"Okay," said Dick jumping to his feet. "We meet before the barn dance at the cemetery. Duba, see if you can get Alice there. Marty, have Barber get the club there, after school. Conway, you go see if you can get Mr. Ossant to come."

Marty felt better now about the small details.

CHAPTER THIRTEEN

THE PLOT THICKENS

Mary's dad drove in with Mary, Holbrook, and Randy. Eddie was already there, resting back on ole Charlie's stone marker.

"What are you doing here so early?" asked Mary.

"I got my chores done and heard about the meeting - decided to come over," said Eddie.

"Are you doing okay, Eddie?"

"I miss my family something fierce, Mary. I don't know if I can make it another week without seeing them."

"You'll have fun tonight at the barn dance. Try to relax. You'll be home soon."

"I'll try. I know the food will be good."

"Plan a jig or two tonight, Eddie. I have new square dance records we're trying out," said Mary. "Now don't you go embarrassing me making me ask you to dance."

"We'll see," said Eddie.

"Didn't you call them Sunday and have a nice talk?"

"Yes. That only makes it worse."

"Nice of Big Mike and Missus letting you make a long distance call to them, though," said Mary.

"They're nice folks. Everybody's been nice. I'm going to miss Mrs. Parker's cooking."

Mary sat down on the grass.

"Tell me about Judy and Lucy," said Mary.

"My little girls? How did you know their names?"

"You told me when we were up on the hill looking at your plane that day. Remember?"

"Seems like forever ago. Well, they're seven and five, Judy being seven. She looks most like her mother. Lucy is the tomboy, always climbing trees, playing catch."

"Like me," said Mary.

"She's a lot like you, Mary. She doesn't stand for much of my guff either, that's for sure."

"Eddie, you told us about the time you parachuted over France in the dark on D Day. We're you scared?"

"I think we were too young to be scared. None of us thought we'd come back alive though. We tried not to think about it. We didn't talk about it. Talking about it was bad luck, or so we thought – like three on a match."

"Three on a match - I've heard something about that," said Mary. "What does it mean?"

"It was a superstition that if you were in a foxhole and lit a match to light a cigarette a sniper could see it. If you lit your buddy's cigarette too it would give the sniper time to aim. If you lit a third cigarette – bang…you're dead by sniper fire."

"The War, every part of it was so awful. I hid under the bed and cried and cried when my daddy came home. I forgot what he looked like he was gone so long." said Mary.

"We had to do the D Day invasion, or we could have lost the War. The Germans were building war equipment faster than our boys could knock it out."

"My daddy doesn't like to talk about it. Can you tell me about it? Do you mind? About your parachute jump?"

"Mary, at the base I was stationed at in England, we jumpers lived in Quonset huts. There were always rumors going around, you know, whispers of things we guessed were going to happen. Everything was so top secret nobody knew for sure what was going on, but we all knew the allies were going to attack the Nazis in France, we just didn't know where or when."

"Were you scared not knowing?"

"It's hard to say. Nervous, maybe. Maybe numb. We'd been training and waiting for months. We were getting antsy just waiting. We kind of felt like if we were dropped in the dark we'd have a better chance of making it to the ground alive than if we jumped in daylight."

"It must have been awful."

"Well, then it happened - one afternoon, late. I remember it like yesterday, General Eisenhower and a bunch of photographers came driving up while we were standing around. It was overcast and windy, almost ready to storm. I could hear thunder in the clouds."

*Supreme Commander Eisenhower wishes
paratroopers luck.*

"Did you get to meet him?"

"Who? Ike?"

"Yes."

"Me? No. But I saw him in the distance. He talked to a group of us, they had some laughs. Word back was he worried about delaying the attack much longer because of the weather forecasts. He had five thousand ships ready to go – didn't want to risk them sinking in storms. He wanted to ask us guys, the paratroopers what we thought, could we make it in the rough skies."

"I wonder why he asked the paratroopers. They weren't even going to be in ships."

"We were going to be the first over France – in the dark."

"Amazing," said Mary.

"It's true. The Supreme Commander of the entire European Operation cared what some pup paratroopers had to say."

"What did you guys tell him?"

"Word was we told him to go for it. We were ready. All thirteen thousand of us were ready to jump. Just give us barf bags in case of rough weather in the dark but we were ready to go."

"Did they?"

"Nah, but they knew what we meant. They gave us seasick pills."

Mary sat there watching his eyes glaze into a stare at a caterpillar crawling on the ground by his foot almost as if he were in a plane over France looking down.

"Nine or ten thousand died that day, Mary," he said. "A bunch of the jumpers or glider guys died along with the rest of them."

"That is so sad," said Mary. "Imagine if their mothers and families back home knew what was going on."

"But you know what? They were there with us. That's what counted, Mary. The guys who died, they got to be a part of it. We all knew going in the world needed D Day to save France and then to save Europe from Hitler's domination. We knew the boys invading Normandy needed us paratroopers to divert fire so they could land on the beaches with fewer casualties. They needed the gliders to capture and hold the bridges."

"You guys were heroes," said Mary.

"The dead guys were the heroes, Mary, we were lucky. But all their families, wives and kids know they were heroes and helped save the world."

"That's a nice thought."

"We were young. We knew if we didn't help stop Hitler, the whole world could be doing his goosestep in every country on earth. We wouldn't stand for that is all. Seventy million people were killed in that War before it was over."

"Eddie, you did it for your Judy and Lucy, for your wife and me and all of us. The whole world will never forget your night-time paratrooper jump to help save the world."

"I wonder sometimes."

"Someday I'll get lucky and meet a guy like you, Eddie."

"That guy will be the lucky one, Mary."

"Eddie, I want you to listen to me, and listen good."

Eddie raised his head and looked in Mary's eyes, then looked back down at the caterpillar.

"I need the real Eddie to listen to what I have to say, not the pigheaded Eddie."

Eddie looked up and smiled.

"Want to hear pigheaded?" asked Eddie. "Something most people don't know?"

"Sure."

"Did you know every head of every allied country on earth, supported the D Day invasion..."

"Yes, I knew that."

"...except one."

"You're joking. I didn't know that – who?"

"France's own General de Gaulle said no to it, said he wouldn't support it – said he wouldn't go on radio and tell his people in France to be behind it."

"Can this be true?"

"He was living in London, sipping tea and eating crumpets all throughout the War. It is very true. He told Ike he wouldn't support it – that only he was the only boss of France – no one else."

"I think Hitler would have disagreed," mused Mary.

"If it was up to General de Gaulle we'd all be speaking German now."

"Eddie, in all your life you will never, ever do anything as scary as what you went through then. Especially the night you got in that cold noisy airplane with a bunch of guys with rosary beads and M1 rifles in their hands and you flew from England over to France to jump out in the dark and get shot at, right?"

"Pretty much."

"Well, we're on a mission right now. Only this time nobody will be shooting at us. It may not be as dangerous, but it's as important to us. It's important that some guy doesn't get away with this. It's an important one – to help get your money back so Judy and Lucy can have a Santa Claus Christmas like any kid deserves, and you can get your wife a necklace or something for putting up with you."

"I never thought of it that way."

"Of course you didn't, you're a man. It's only going to be a few more days when the very split second Judy and Lucy look up in the sky and see your plane coming in to land on an airfield in Binghamton that they will hardly remember you even being gone."

"If only that was true."

"It is true, Eddie. I'm a daughter, I know these things."

"You're pretty wise for a young lady, Mary Crane. You know that?"

"Yeah, I know – it's been my curse. And if that wasn't enough to run boys off, I can hit a home run, too."

Cars made their way up the cinder drive of the cemetery and emptied out. Dick, Duba, Minneapolis Moline Conway and Dwyer reshuffled and sat in one car with all the doors open, talking. They waited for everyone to show up. Eventually two lads lifted Alice out of a pickup and set her in her wheelchair and rolled her in front. It was then when Ole Charlie here rose up to the occasion, about three branches over the lot of them. This meeting seemed promising...

"Listen up," barked Duba.

"Marty, good job for what you did," said Dick. "We could have blown this whole thing the way we were going about it. We were making it so unbelievable it would only look like a trap to a crook."

"Couldn't sleep thinking about the money thing, all its details," said Marty.

"So, here's what we have now," said Dick. "We are going to do it as Marty suggested. Here's the official word - whatever we do has got to be believable. Everything we do has to pass scrutiny."

"The deeper we want to get into a crook's pocket the more scrutiny we'll have to muster," said Duba.

"That makes sense," said Mr. Ossant.

"I'll go through it all quickly," said Dick. "Listen up now. Friday is Fair Day at school. Everybody go and have a good time. Don't forget, Big Mike is giving us tickets. If you're showing an animal or plants or something like that, Friday will be the day they're judging. Duba, Eddie and I will go check on the Midway and see if we can spot the pickpocket. We'll all meet back here Friday night at nine. If we are able to spot him, Saturday will be our D Day at the State Fair, understood?"

They all nodded approval.

"And on Saturday nobody knows anybody at the Fair," said Duba.

"Mr. Ossant, we need a camper wagon, nothing too fancy, and a team of horses. It'll be the traveling wagon for Orville (Marty) here – and his traveling Water Witchery business. We'll need it by Saturday midday, so a campfire can be there long enough to get the smoke smell in the air and the char indicating it's been there awhile."

Marty beamed a smile, proud of the detail.

"Orville?"

"Make up any name you want, Marty, but let Mr. Ossant know what you come up with soon so he can get Mrs. Coco to put it on the sign on your wagon."

"Jedidiah," said Marty. "I have a card from the Cortland Carnival, says Jedidiah. He does séances, you know, he talks to spirits. I'll use that name: Jedidiah."

"Oh, we'll need a team of horses too," said Dick. Make sure they're unhitched from the wagon and have hay in front of them so it looks like they've been there some time."

"We'll leave cans of food, everything, pots and pans. I have to go to Albany for an FFA conference," said Mr. Ossant. "What do you want me to do with this wagon after it's finished, and I'll need Barber, Dwyer, Conway, and Mayor during every school break to help build it. I know where I can get my hands on an old buckboard we can rig up with a tarpaulin or something. That should do the trick."

"Farmer Parker will most likely lend you his team of horses," said Dick. "If he will take them and the rig deep into the woods somewhere, and draw a map of where it is so Marty can find it, and be camping after we come back from the State Fair. If he won't we'll figure something else out."

"Done," said Mr. Ossant.

"Alice," said Dick, "Duba and I have written a script for you to try to memorize. Do you think you can act like you're a tough gal from the big city – not afraid of snakes or pickpocket varmints?"

"Ha! You've never had to make a room filled with fourth graders behave. No, seriously, I was in a play in the seventh grade once and then in my school's senior play. I'll do just fine," said Alice.

"Me," said Dick. "I'll be the one pushing your wheelchair around the Midway, but you do all the talking. As a matter of fact, if you get to talk with the pickpocket turn your head and tell me to go get some cotton candy or something so you can talk in private."

"That's so important," said Mary. "Alice, then you wait for Dick to walk away before you start talking. That'll make it look real."

"Conway, you, Dwyer and Duba have to figure out where you'll be loitering around on the Midway – don't be together though. Two of you will have old one hundred dollar bills or new twenties on you. One of you won't have anything. Figure out between you who will have the money and where each of you will be standing at the Fair. Make sure you look like farmers working, in overall duds, like you're pondering going into a sideshow, or thinking about taking your chances for a kewpie doll before you go back to the stock show."

"Best if we have old wallets so nobody gets suspicious with us pulling a hundred dollar bill from our pocket," said Minneapolis Moline Conway.

"Conway, Dwyer and Duba - try to remember this signal. If you catch my eye and I have a cigarette tucked over my ear, whoever is closest to the pickpocket you ask him if he can change a bill for you. We're assuming here we make contact with him. If I don't have a cigarette over my ear and he gets close, he's going to be asking you if you can change his small bills into a big one. Now he will get close to each of you as Alice is telling him how easy it is to convert the counterfeit money into real money. She'll have him trying her scheme."

"What if I'm the one who doesn't have any money?" asked Dwyer.

"Then, if you don't have any money you say no and walk about your business."

"That will make it look real," said Marty. "It won't look rigged if it doesn't go too smooth…if someone says no, he's more likely to believe it."

"So, here's the deal," said Dick. "If pickpocket bites, and Alice does her job of acting like you have a stash of counterfeit money for sale, pickpocket will come up to you, Marty, and want to do business. You brush him off first time like – 'Who are you?' Or – "Go away, mister, you're bothering me. I don't know what you're talking about." That sort of thing, but when he comes at you again you ask if he knows the Lincklaen House in Cazenovia. Whisper to him you don't sell it, you only deliver it."

"That's perfect," said Marty.

"Ask him what time he can be there 'tonight' – tonight being Saturday. Give him a code word to use and tell him to be in the lobby phone closet at that time he said."

"Any code word?" asked Marty.

"Any code word. But be sure you pick up a phone somewhere and tell Myrtie the code word and the time she should call the Lincklaen House phone closet."

"Gotcha," said Marty.

"Marty, rehearse some chatter so you'll feel more comfortable prancing around the Midway selling your Water Witchery services. Don't forget your apple."

"Mr. Ossant, make sure you leave three copies of a map to the camp with the front desk clerk at the hotel Saturday," said Marty. Leave them in envelopes, one for me, one for 'Sherlock Holmes' and one for Sheriff John. That way Sheriff John will know where the camp is and go and arrest the pickpocket."

"Will do," said Mr. Ossant.

"I wouldn't mark one for Sheriff John. That could spook pickpocket if he sees it. How about 'Messenger'?" asked Dick.

"Marking it for Sheriff would scare him off for certain," said Mr. Ossant. "I'll mark it to Messenger."

"We'll see everyone here Friday night for a final go through," said Dick.

As people began leaving the cemetery, headed for the barn dance, Duba paused, turned his back from the wind, struck a match and lit a cigarette.

He leaned around with the same match and lit Dick's cigarette and then Dwyer's.

CHAPTER FOURTEEN

BARN DANCE

Lest you think Mary Crane did some magic to arrange a barn dance tonight, Wednesday, after mentioning square dancing at the supper table Sunday - she didn't have to.

It was about when Missus had said grace before meal and Jerry had told about Buddy passing on. While making pleasantries, it dawned on Mary her new square dance records had come in the post and maybe she shouldn't be thinking of the social she wanted to have when they arrived. She happened to be sitting next to Barber at the time.

"When's your social?" asked Barber.

"I was thinking Wednesday, but maybe another time now with us being here helping out."

After that supper Mrs. Barber learned about Mary's new records when Barber called home to say they were all staying over at Big Mike's and Missus place to help Farmer Parker - no notion how many days. It was Mrs. Barber telling Barber she was thinking she'd tell her church group about the square dance records and to tell Mary their barn would be cleared for tonight that got the ball rolling.

"And, son," said Mrs. Barber, "if the weather's looking decent, ask Farmer Parker - if he's up to it by then - would he bring his horses and hay wagon over for a hayride."

"Yes, Ma'am," said Barber.

You should know this is the way it was in the Crown, in 1953. There were three reasons country folk could for sure be counted on to drop what they were doing and come by the house without an invite.

Someone dying was one.

They'd come miles for the wake. Walk, if they had to. Ladies with hats on, men holding theirs over their heart - circling the yard waiting to take their sympathies inside, maybe a cheery word or two like 'don't he look nice' - or - 'ain't her dress purdy though'. They'd come to the house from the cemetery and set a cover dish on the dining room table to tide over through a spell of mourning. Ole Charlie here lost my Alice in 1931, I remember.

Second reason they'd come uninvited was if your barn burned down.

Barns could burn for reasons bigger than dropping a lantern or a crack of lightning. Greener hay can sometimes smoulder under a pile of dry hay and spontaneously combust - blaze up on its own accord. Sparks from a tractor muffler in the barn have also been known to burn barns to the ground.

Need you to understand barns of 1953 were thought through, time tested tools of trade passed down generation after generation over hundreds of years. Barns had souls. They held hay or mow needed to feed the cows through a winter. Pastures are snow in the winter. They had the straw to bed them. Without straw fresh calves would be born on concrete. They had the silage to nourish cows through every milking – and they had milking stalls. A cow needs to be milked at least two times a day; sometimes three or they can bloat and get powerful sick.

And as a wooden ocean vessel's keel needs inside moisture to hold the wood seal tight, a barn needs the dampness cows cause through evaporation of normal sweat and waste to keep barn beams and siding sealed and secure. Cows need a barn to survive and a barn needs cows to survive.

They had barn raisings in two days. They had to, to save the farm – and everyone would come. Day one was getting the first rafter up, fixing that with the pulley for hefting all the rafters. Day two was putting up the siding and roofing.

Third reason people would come uninvited was to dance. A barn dance was all it took for everyone to stop by unannounced bringing a smile and a pot of something with them, maybe even a fiddle or a jaw harp. Kids were a natural part of everything in the Crown and they came for the hayride, vittles and music.

Tonight was extra special to ole Charlie here as Sir Arthur Conan Doyle made honor by accepting my invite to witness something he'd never seen living in London or his travels. He'd never seen an American country square dance. Bustin' my buttons knowin' I could show off the Crown under a full moon, my brood a dancin' and prancing about – singing, kissing and squeezin' with opportunity. I'd show him something new for him – a good ole barn round and square dance, and maybe some old country folk-stepping.

We could talk angel shop, if'n he had a mind to, but tonight was more about watching down from the roof, enjoying the sights and sounds of my flock in the Crown and remembering the fun of our youth.

"Mr. Doyle, sir, the fire they're building over there in the rock pit. Wait till you see it reach the heavens, the sparks and all. Takes full time watching to keep her safe but she is a spectacle, that's for certain."

"Charlie, old salt, what an impressive farm this is. Several barns, this big house under us and endless fields of something cultivated. It looks like peas, if I'm not mistaken. Is the fire a sign of festivities?"

"This time of year it's mostly to get warm if'n you're chilled, I reckon. It'll draw a crowd later into the night."

"This is a large house we're sitting on, Charlie. Are houses in rural America always this large?"

"Most of the bigger houses like this one, Sir Doyle, were on bigger farms with rooms for helpers and workers. As farms get mechanized, people living in them now mostly board up some rooms – saving winter coal. This one we're setting on housed workers. A building up top of the hill at Gooseville Corners owned by the Conways was a hotel back in the day of coaches.

Carl Vaas's milk can hauling truck pulled in the drive and parked under a tree on the side. About the same time it came to a stop its doors busted open and out poured near half dozen young'uns, Randy leading the pack.

Seeing them come in, Mrs. Barber waved and stepped down off the porch with a dishtowel in her hand. She saw Judy Clancy standing by a tree picking up a chicken drumstick from her paper plate while catching up with Alice, Mary Margaret Cox, Judy Finch, Linda and some others waiting for the dance festivities to begin. When they sat chairs and benches around the dance floor, there were always two spaces reserved for Alice's and Marian's wheelchairs when the dance started.

"Judy," said Mrs. Barber, "dear, if you see your Jimmy, would you tell him Mr. Barber would like to see him and the boys for a visit up at the house."

"He's out helping set up Mary's record player, Mrs. Barber. What boys?"

"You know, the SOS boys – Dick, Duba, your Jimmy, of course, and Dwyer," said Mrs. Barber.

"Are they in any kind of trouble, Mrs. Barber?"

"No, dear, nothing like that. Mr. Barber just wants to chat with them a spell. Will you see they come to the house before the dancing starts?"

"Yes, ma'am," said Judy.

It didn't take long for word of the meet to spread to Dick and the boys. It had also spread through the Pompey Hollow Book Club. When the time came, Jerry, Holbrook, Randy, Mayor, Bases, Barber, Marty and Mary followed the older boys over to the house.

Mary was met at the door by Mrs. Barber.

"Honey, why don't you take this piece of apple pie and go see about getting the music started? Everybody's here who's coming by the looks at all the cars everywhere - I'm thinking - and they've all eaten mostly. There's more if they want it. It's time for some dancing. The boys will be down soon enough," said Mrs. Barber.

"Can't I go in with them?" asked Mary.

Mrs. Barber took Mary aside.

"I think this is a man-talk sort of thing, Mary. Best you go get people settled and the music started. They'll be along shortly."

Mary stepped backward off the porch scratching her head, turned and walked over to where Eddie and Hal were standing and talking. She handed little Bobby the paper plate and piece of pie.

"Mary, Hal here has been telling me how you guys protected his Bobby all through the summer so he could be with his dad. I think I'm going to owe you a big apology for not putting faith in your intentions straight off. I've sure enough been giving you a hard time."

Mary held her hand out and took Bobby by the one hand he wasn't holding the pie with.

"We did what you'd do – or most anybody, for that matter," said Mary. "We took a runaway kid out of harm's way. He was sleeping in an ally in Syracuse and we fed him and gave him a bed and a tub until his daddy could come get him and raise him proper. Isn't that right, Bobby?"

Bobby looked up with a bit of pie crust on his lip and smiled. Mary stroked the boy's hair with the tips of her fingers, looking for a part.

"Mary," said Hal, "The War seems so long ago, but meeting Eddie here tonight brings it all back into focus. Wished I could have done it all over different and not have gotten into that trouble, slugging the guy, but it's too late now to be thinking that way, I suppose."

"Hal," said Eddie, "I don't know a father alive who wouldn't have stirred up a hornet's nest after being told in the middle of duty or a chore that his kid's mother'd been killed by the Nazis."

"Paratroopers and submarine sailors are two sorts who couldn't get away with it, I guess," said Hal.

"You're right there," said Eddie. "Our jobs were dangerous enough as it was. They couldn't take a risk of someone in our jobs going haywire at the wrong moment."

"The whole War was dangerous," said Mary. "I don't understand how anyone could ever tell what was the most dangerous?"

"Easy," said Hal. "Wasn't a man or woman in the War couldn't get killed instantly, don't get us wrong. The jobs that were done only by the volunteers only seemed most dangerous – like it was guaranteed death. Find some job that required volunteers and best to get out of their way. They're the ones in danger at all times."

"Wow," said Mary. "I never thought of it that way."

Inside the house, ole Charlie here and Sir Doyle sank down through the roof and into the dining room where the young men had drifted in the dimly lit room and stood around the table. Already there were Mr. Barber, Big Mike, Doc Webb and Mike Shea. They were smiling and friendly-like, but the lads gathered about having a keen sense about them that they were either on trial or about to learn something.

"We only wanted to see the older boys," said Mr. Barber. "You younger boys don't need to stay."

"We're all in this together," said Dick.

"We can take it," said Mayor.

"Well, okay, fellas," said Mr. Barber. "I've been asked to be the talker here for what we have to say, so you'll have to bear with me. I'm a farmer's son, don't ya know – and not a preacher or public speaking politician – so be patient."

"You're doing fine," said Big Mike.

Dick and Duba and the boys looked at their adversaries, checking for a sign, something in the eyes. They could only see smiles.

Ole Charlie here was in the dark, as well. I couldn't give Sir Doyle even a clue of what was going on.

"What's the count, Big Mike?" asked Mr. Barber.

Mike Shea was ahead of them on face count.

"All told, there are eleven of them here," said Mike Shea.

With that Mr. Barber reached down into his pocket deep enough to pull a roll of dollar bills. He straightened and fanned them out, and handed the money over to Doc.

"Doc, what say you give two dollars each to the fellas here, and then we'll get started?" said Mr. Barber.

"Bully!" said Doc. He walked around the table to the front and handed each lad there two one dollar bills. He then stepped back and to the other side of the table with the gents.

First thought the lads must have had was they was being rewarded for being such upstanding citizens.

"What'd we do to deserve this?" asked Dick.

"I'm not looking a gift horse in the mouth," said Duba.

"Hold on fellas, I'm about fixin' to tell you," said Mr. Barber. "Everybody got your folding money?"

"Yup," said Holbrook.

About then is when the hammer came down.

"You are all a good lot," said Mr. Barber. "Everybody in the Crown would agree that's a pretty fair statement. Other than the drag racing from Hastings down the Oran Delphi from time to time when a body's sleeping – you're all pretty much the sorts we can be proud of. And when you're proud of something or someone you want to favor it in any way you can, to help them through life a bit more."

"It'd be selfish not to," said Doc.

"You don't have to pay us," said Minneapolis Moline Conway. "We do stuff because we want to."

"It's not pay," said Big Mike.

"It's more like a life learning experience," said Mike Shea. "We know how eager you chaps are and we know there's been some talk about what some of you are up to at the fair?"

"Consider us giving it a push," said Big Mike.

"Catching the pickpocket?" asked Dwyer. "You already gave us money to do that."

"This isn't about the pickpocket," said Doc.

"Huh?" asked Conway. "What, then?"

"Fellas, fellas," blurted Mr. Barber. "We gave you the two dollars here because we want you to have enough to go see the Hoochie-Coochie girls on the Midway at the State Fair, like you want to. The money will be enough to get you in. Might just as well go sew your oats - get it out of your systems."

"What!" snorted Conway. "I wasn't going to any girlie show. I wouldn't hurt my Judy for the life of me."

"My Ma would tan me sure," said Randy. "I'd never go."

"It only costs a dollar," said Holbrook. "You gave us two."

"A dollar is for the popcorn," said Big Mike.

"You're kidding, right?" asked Duba. "There's some catch to this."

Dick smirked. He was getting the message.

"I think I know what is going on. I'm guessing I know what this is all about," said Dick. "Somehow you heard we were thinking about going to the girlie show and you want to let us know you know."

"What do you mean, 'we', Dick?" barked Mayor. "I wasn't…"

"Taint it, son," said Mr. Barber. "But go on with what you were saying."

"Well, maybe we were thinking about it – gave it some notion - but that was then and now is now," said Dick.

"You want to put that in English, son?" asked Mike Shea.

"It's different now, is all," said Duba. "We've been so busy planning how we can help Flying Eddie, we haven't had time to even think about the girlie show. Matter of fact we already decided helping him was probably more fun anyway and we weren't going to go."

"So, what you're saying is maybe it's better you boys stay busy with life's important things and not be idle, thinking too much on other distractions," said Mr. Barber.

"I want it on the record, I was never going to go," said Conway.

"This ain't a court, son," said Mr. Barber.

"What did you mean, 'we', Dick?" barked Mayor.

The rest of the lads looked around, silent, some letting their imaginations keep options open, since the subject was brought up.

"It's only a dollar," said Holbrook. "Not that I was going to go."

"I wouldn't disrespect my sister or my mother by going to that sort of thing," said Randy.

"As for me," said Mayor. "I won't lie. I first figured I'd be afraid the whole world would see me going in or coming out of the 'hoochie-coochie' show, either way. That thought alone scared me from thinking about it. But then as I started to think that if I was scared I'd be seen, it must be no good for me to begin with, so I stopped thinking about it altogether."

"That's called a conscience," said Marty.

Mr. Barber smiled.

"That way of thinking is sure enough called 'character', son," said Mr. Barber.

In the background the music and square dance calling started up. The lads were getting edgy.

"Look," said Dick. "Sure we thought about going but we got busy helping Eddie and forgot about it. Here, keep your money. We're not going."

With that Dick and Duba laid their two dollars down on the table in front of the men standing there. The rest of the lads followed suit, stepping around and placing the money on the table.

"We're not worried about a growing lad thinking about things and their curiosity in worldly temptations – or about a world that is painted and perfumed to lure the unsuspecting," said Mr. Barber. "You've now about said you are, for the most part, with the character it takes to keep on the straight and narrow."

"We were never worried about your stepping too far off course," said Doc. "Why I never seen a better group of youngsters in my life. We never thought for a moment you were losing respect for motherhood and decent family values."

"You've all proved it to me," said Big Mike.

"I think guys like Eddie were youngsters once – jumping from planes. Don't forget guys like them," said Dick.

"So, why are we here?" asked Duba.

"It's stealing that ain't right," said Mr. Barber.

"Huh?" asked Conway.

"Word was some of you were planning to sneak in under a tent at the Midway without paying for a ticket," said Big Mike.

"We tried to teach you well," said Mr. Barber. "We may have missed some things, but it was for certain we taught you respect for someone's property – and that stealing was never a way of life."

"Mr. Barber," we've caught crooks and thieves," said Holbrook. "Since we were nine we've been catching them. They're the ones who steal things."

"Now we're going to catch a pickpocket. That's serious!" said Mayor.

"You slip in under a tent, get away with not paying for a ticket – you're no better than a pickpocket or some burglars sneaking into stores at night," said Mike Shea.

"We never thought of it that way, but you're right," said Dick.

"You keep saying 'we', Dick. What do you mean, 'we?'" snarled Mayor.

Everybody go dance, and have fun," said Mr. Barber. "Go on now, git!"

The dining room emptied, young men tripping over each other to get out - thankful to be alive. Holbrook and Jerry stepped off the porch, each with a piece of apple pie in their hand.

"Why did you keep saying the tickets to the girlie show were only a buck?" asked Jerry.

"You told me to find out how much it cost and I asked is all," said Holbrook. "What's the big deal?"

"Well now the whole world knows we were thinking of going," said Jerry.

"Look. We gave them the two dollars back, didn't we," insisted Holbrook. "They know we're not going."

"That's not the point," barked Jerry.

"You mean we're going?"

"No, that's not what I said. I mean we had considered going for purely scientific reasons, not for the other, well, you know…"

"I think that is the point. Neither one of us knows – and we thought going to a girlie show would answer some questions we had - you know - about girls."

"It was purely scientific," insisted Jerry.

"I'm not good with English, Jerry, but I don't think I'd use the word *purely* in a sentence about us going to a girlie show."

"Know what I wished?" asked Jerry.

"What?" asked Holbrook.

"I wished when everyone joked all summer about going skinny-dipping, somebody actually did – go skinny...ya know."

"Know what I wish?" snapped Holbrook.

"No, what?"

"I wished you had never seen that naked girl calendar. You haven't been the same since," said Holbrook.

"Well, they're not the same," said Jerry.

"Who's not the same?"

"Girls and boys."

"Well, yeh! Welcome to the real world," snarled Holbrook. "Girls have to wear brassieres for a reason, ya know."

"Yeh, I know that, but they don't have something else, that boys do," whimpered Jerry.

"What are you talking about?"

"They don't have a thingy."

Holbrook slugged Jerry on the arm.

"A what?!"

"I didn't see one on the calendar."

Holbrook slugged Jerry again.

"Shut up."

"How do they pee without a thingy?" asked Jerry.

"Oh, that," said Holbrook pondering.

"I don't think girls have to pee."

"Well, that could explain it," said Jerry.

"Explain what?"

"They always go to bathrooms to 'powder their nose'. That explains it."

Surprisingly enough, this seemed to settle the issue for a thirteen and fourteen-year-old for the moment in 1953.

Holbrook wasn't into starting a great debate here at a square dance social. There'd be plenty of time later to learn about girls and get his ears wrung out by his best friend, he thought.

"Let's go see if Judy Finch, Mary Margaret or Donna are dancing yet," said Holbrook. "Let's go dance with somebody."

"Head lady and foot gentleman forward and back…
…forward again with both hands round."

…and dance they did.

Mary's new record was the Virginia Reel square dance. She handed it to Judy Clancy to put on the Victrola record player and most had it memorized before the evening let out. Eddie danced; Hal danced. Even Dick and Duba took Alice's wheelchair with her in it and did a jig - spinning her all about the floor grinning from ear to ear to a lively tune. People clapped and cheered them on. It was a wonderful night for all.

Sir Doyle and I rose up proud and sat on the roof again taking it all in.

"Charlie," said Sir Doyle, "we have more in common than you may think."

"Other than our both bein' angels?"

"Why the Virginia Reel is an Irish and English folk dance, goes back many years. The early settlers here in the states must have brought it with them."

"Did you enjoy yourself tonight, Sir Doyle? Best an angel is allowed, that is?"

"My, yes. Why I've never seen such a clever plot to get growing pain issues out on the table and discuss them without a word of lecture or scolding," said Sir Doyle. "I'm truly impressed with what I've seen here in America."

With that, ole Charlie here sat and quandaried to my own self, a spell. I wanted to choose the right words to say what was on my mind without offending my esteemed guest.

"Well your lordship, Sir Doyle."

I carefully dusted off every word I was about to use.

"I think it's when a country has a king or queen telling you what they want you to do - you pretty much know the set of rules you're stuck with and where not to walk or tread. But when you're free, like the lads are here in America, they need to talk together from time to time just to stay on course and find the right path. That way they'll always be free."

"I certainly learned many things tonight, Charlie my friend," said Sir Doyle. "Thank you."

"I'm pleased you think so, and hope you'll come to all my Angel Congresses," I told him. "But something bigger tells me you're here for other reasons that ain't come up yet."

I used the 'ain't' word on purpose to let my guest know that being an angel now hasn't made ole Charlie here all uppity.

"I've had the same premonition. We'll see," said Sir Arthur Conan Doyle, angel.

CHAPTER FIFTEEN

SCHOOL FAIR DAY

Fair Day Friday means no school today. Rural pupils get the day off to show their livestock or greenery at state Fair competitions.

Dick, Duba, Minneapolis Moline Conway, Mr. Vaas and a small hoard of other parents loaded with young'uns wove their cars through the streets of Syracuse early enough to be at the ticket booth opening. In a caravan line they pulled into the Fairgrounds parking area like an Eisenhower tank division. Dick and Duba asked club members to wait while they decided their approach to the Midway to scope everything – get a lay of the land.

"Where's Marty? Marty has the Fairground map?" asked Dick. "Where's Marty?"

"Hang on to your shorts," gruffed Holbrook. "Marty is already here – he's showing Sandy today. Hold on, Mary gave it to me to give it to you. I have it somewhere."

"Where's Mary?" asked Dick.

"She went to Barbers' place to help clean up from after the barn dance last night," said Jerry.

"We're falling apart here," moaned Duba.

Holbrook pulled the drawing of the state fairgrounds from Marty's satchel and handed it to Dick.

Dick paused and stepped back towards his Willys and unfolded it.

"Eddie, you stick with us," said Dick. "Maybe leave your leather flight jacket here. Everybody else, go have fun, we'll meet you in the car show when we're done. If not there we'll look for you. For sure be at the cemetery tonight by nine."

"But we stay off the Midway, right?" asked Randy.

"Right," said Dick.

"Yeah, we might get lucky right off - maybe Eddie can point the pickpocket out," said Duba.

"Three of us won't be noticed. We'll be careful. You walk in the middle, Eddie," said Dick.

Studying the map, Dick, Duba and Eddie started away from the cars – people brushing by them milling towards the entrance.

"Eddie, I'm thinking you should head back after we spot the pickpocket so you don't risk being seen," said Dick.

Duba explained to the ticket lady that tomorrow, Saturday, they may have to come back out again to get a friend in a wheelchair and would she let them back in with the same ticket.

"You'll need new tickets for Saturday," she said. "This ticket is only good for today."

"I'll have new tickets."

"Come to me Saturday," she said. "I'll let you come out and take your friend in."

My-oh-my, what a wonder the New York State Fair is! For a coot like ole Charlie here, it's almost like being in Paris back in '16. Any age, any time, a fair makes a body pause and imagine things they never quite gave much thought to before…see other things they'd a sworn they wouldn't see all their lives – only in books. Why there were tall camels cantering along in long strides following a man wearing a turban around to the rear of a tent. A tiger was prancing back and forth in a wagon cage.

"They have some kind of circus show or acts in the main arena the night they close the fair down," said Dick.

The rabbit show was so filled with cages, they were stacked up taller than a body could see over, rabbits of every kind and color. There were Netherland Dwarf rabbits, Holland Lop rabbits, Dutch rabbits. The New Zealand rabbits were most like what ole Charlie here would take to spinster Nettie's place for rabbit stew. Cornered them mostly in the chicken wire stealing the chicken feed. Paul Shaffer was sitting on the stage in his Sunday best waiting for the judges to get to his cages. He usually wins blue. You'd know the name had you read a book called The Pompey Hollow Book Club by Jerome Mark Antil. The club started in 1949 saving Paul's brood of rabbits from being sold as livestock.

Marty was sitting prim and proper in the saddle while Sandy ran, stopped and turned with his snow white mane flying. A golden glow of the sun through the roof portals beamed down on the palomino. Win or lose, he was the prettiest horse. Ole Charlie here thought back to my Nellie, but not for long. Angels aren't allowed to think about themselves all that much, or our losses.

Scratchy deep voices on the sound systems echoed throughout the great halls. People walked about laughing and shaking each other's hands in pathways between stables, kennels and cages, wishing each other luck. Many of them only see each other this time of year, at the fair.

The food pavilion was the quiet building. Seems there's a religion to cooking, canning, preserves. It's hard to explain without getting sacrilegious. Pleasant ladies, mostly, in aprons fawning over the judges as they passed by. Mrs. Parker was standing watch over her three quarts of butter pickles, but going on so, catching up with her old friends - not a care in the world if she won a ribbon or not...

Seems this country went without for so many years through the dust bowl and famine, folks like to celebrate being able to preserve something to last through the cold or hard times. Was a spell there wasn't electricity in farm country, so no refrigeration. Right up through the War, there was farms still without wires, mine included. We didn't know any better and made do with our fruit cellars and canning. Crops through the 1800s in rural, New York was mostly tobacco. Leaves for rolling cigars. Cigar and cheese box factories sprinkled all over the countryside, and in towns like Cortland and Homer. Because of so much tobacco, people were dependent on their gardens and farm crops for food. After the tobacco, some started planting cabbage as it was a hearty survivor through cold winter months. Then when Big Mike and his best friend partnered up as bakers in 1931 many farmers went to growing the wheat the bakery bought to make bread and cakes.

Behind the food pavilion near the elephant tent, an elephant with a chain around his foot ripped a bale of hay apart snorting a bugle as Dick, Duba and Eddie walked by.

The bouncy flute, the snare drum and cymbal sounds of calliope music and the ratatatatic-tic-tic of spinning fortune wheels crackled through the air. Friendly noises and sounds letting them know they were getting closer to the Midway entrance and the beginning of an adventure.

"Slow down, guys. Eddie, keep your head down but your eyes peeled," said Dick.

It was when they turned the corner that a sideshow talker with a white and red-striped cane leaned down from the stage and gently poked it at Dick's shoulder. The talker pointing the cane was wearing red ribbon garter belts on both sleeves up above his elbows and a flat straw skimmer hat tipped to the side.

"Tell ya' what I'm going to do! Step right up close gentlemen, and I was certain you were gentlemen the very minute I laid my eyes on you rounding the corner. Why this is your lucky day. Step in close and look behind me. Now, it so happens that hidden by the curtain right behind me is something only a gentleman with some bonafidee' and worldly experience would appreciate."

Dick and Duba stood there gaping up at the stage, jaws dropped. With his head down, Eddie kept moving his eyes around the Midway.

"Step in closer here for I'm going to give you a free look at some pulchritude, magnificence certain that unnamed men in Paris have had to change their names for. Why behind that very curtain there is a lady – don't worry, gentlemen, I'm going to give you a free peek - a lady who is so bejewelled on stage with strands of finery so elegant – pearls so opulent they're under armed guard whenever she isn't letting gentlemen like you up close and personal to watch her take each and every one of them off in front of your very eyes revealing other certain qualities. Get my meaning, gentlemen? And she takes them all off, yessiree, every strand. Use your imagination. Be careful if you have a bad heart, though. We can't be responsible."

"Dick," said Eddie, nudging him.

"Dick turned his jaw to speak to Eddie while his eyes were locked on the talker's every word.

"Hold on," barked Dick.

"Step in closer, gentlemen; everybody come in closer, I'll share a secret with you. When the pearls come off, she starts up around the milk barn and she winds up down near the hen house. Why gentlemen, I'm going..."

"Hey, Dick!" blurted Eddie, poking him in the ribs. "That's the guy – he's over there by the third tent. I see the guy."

"Where?" asked Duba.

The three stepped out of the rest of the crowd closing in on the beauteous-bevy-of-Parisian-ladies talker.

"Count the tents," said Eddie. "Three tents over across the Midway. See that guy over there in the beret and the seersucker coat?"

"Flower in his lapel," said Dick.

"Carnation – red," said Eddie.

"Okay," said Dick. "Back out of here slowly before he sees us. Let's find everyone."

Dick and Eddie made it around to the side of the tent before they realized Duba was still back listening to the talker. Dick's arm reached around the corner of the tent and he grabbed Duba by the arm and yanked him around.

I might say Dick and Duba were exhilarated knowing they were about to go into another daring adventure with Mary and her Pompey Hollow Book Club. Of course they were still smiling, thinking about pearls and Paris...

Eddie had a sweat on his brow – angry he couldn't walk up to the red carnation and bust him in the nose for stealing his family's winter money.

They left the fair and drove to Fabius and Mr. Ossant's shop to see how the wagon was coming so they could report it at tonight's cemetery meeting.

CHAPTER SIXTEEN
FRIDAY THE 13TH

"Alice, are you ready for tomorrow?" asked Dick,"

"You being a wise guy or something, hot shot? Don't let this wheelchair fool you, slick – I can still kick your butt or have it done for me, ya' hear? So get lost...take a powder...

...how's that?" asked Alice.

"Perfect," said Dick. "Marty?"

Marty stood up tall and turned toward the crowd.

"Folks, farming's tough enough with water but impossible without it. Cows need water, chickens need water – follow Jedidiah to the water. Who needs rain? Nobody who knows Jedidiah needs rain. With Jedidiah you're drinking from your own well in a week, watering your crop or your money back. Who needs water? Need water, Ma'am? How about you, sir – Jedidiah knows where the water is."

"Perfect," said Dick.

"Pretend you're the pickpocket, Duba," said Marty, "ask me if we can do business. Go on, ask."

"Hey, buddy, I want to talk about buying some counterfeit. Can we do business?"

"I'm a Water Witcher trying to earn an honest living here, mister; don't know what you're talking about."

"You've got it, Marty," said Dick. "Good job."

"Duba, Conway and Dwyer, where will you guys be loitering?"

"I'll be in front of the girlie show tent," said Conway.

"Me, I'll be at the freak show tent, or maybe throwing base-balls," said Duba.

"I'll be shooting at the target range," said Dwyer.

"Don't forget. Watch for the signal – the cigarette over my ear," said Dick.

"How are we going to know who the pickpocket is?" asked Marty.

"You'll see us talking to him on the Midway."

"Then what do we do?"

"Slow down," barked Duba. "We'll get to it."

"Just act natural," said Dick. "But look for my signals. If you catch my eye, and I have a cigarette tucked over my ear, whoever is closest to the pickpocket you ask him if he can change a bill for you. We're assuming here we make contact with him. If I don't have a cigarette over my ear and he gets close, he's going to be asking you if you can change his small bills into a big one."

"Oh, we forgot to ask you something, Eddie," said Duba. "Does your plane have a two-way radio on it? You know - a shortwave?"

"Yes, it does."

"Turn it on come dark tomorrow night – Sheriff Price may need something, and he'll be on the shortwave at Myrties - the telephone operator's place."

"Does Myrtie even have a shortwave?" asked Randy.

"She has to; when phone wires go down she can report problems."

"Anything else?" asked Duba.

"One thing," said Mr. Ossant. "I can't get Farmer Parker's team of horses until mid-day tomorrow, but we can keep them all night if we need them. When I get them I'll take the wagon deep into the woods somewhere in Pompey Hollow. I'll draw maps to the camp and leave them at the Lincklean House for everybody. We'll tie the horses and they'll have plenty of hay, but I won't start a fire. Too dangerous. I'll be heading straight away to Albany and don't want to leave a fire burning in the woods unattended."

"Who's we?" asked Duba.

"Farmer Parker will be following me to the camp in my car, and taking me to Cazenovia where we'll drop off three maps."

"Why don't I go with them," asked Jerry. "I can get the fire going and make coffee and cook things while we're waiting. Two guys shouldn't spook him. Marty and I can be playing pitch or rolling dice or something when he comes."

"You don't drink coffee," said Dick.

"It'll make us look older if we're drinking from coffee cups.

"Okay," said Dick. "You go set up the camp, but let's not take any chances. When Marty gets there, maybe you hide out away from the camp. Don't make any noise - but be close enough to help Marty in case of any funny business."

"Maybe," said Jerry. "We'll see how it goes."

"Marty, soon as we handle our business on the Midway – after all the money is traded and we did our act," said Dick, "you go meet Conway at the Fair entrance and head down to the Lincklaen House. Get a copy of the map and go right to your camp in the woods. Help Jerry finish setting up camp like you've been there awhile."

"Will do," said Marty.

"The wagon has pots, pans and canned goods, for you, Marty," said Mr. Ossant.

"Conway, don't be stopping anywhere too long so Marty might get seen and recognized by the Sherlock Holmes actors. Drop him on the road somewhere like you're giving a ride to a hitchhiker and drive on. Marty you find your way to the camp using your map. Anything else?" asked Dick.

"Mike Shea thought maybe you might need this," said Mr. Ossant, stepping forward.

He handed Dick an envelope with all the money in it. Dick slapped his forehead.

"This whole thing is so nerve-racking," said Dick. "I'm forgetting everything important."

"…and this," said Mr. Ossant handing Dick the State Fair passes for all the crew.

"The devil's in the details," said Marty.

"Can Barber, Randy, and I catch a ride with somebody up and back?" asked Mary.

"Ride with us," said Eddie. "And anybody who wants to hear how it's going with Sheriff John through my shortwave, meet us at my plane."

"Eddie, after you drop us off, use my car, Mayor, you go with him. Remember, don't wear your leather flight jacket, Eddie; try to disguise yourself."

This is about the time ole Charlie here busted a button or two. I only wished Sir Arthur Conan Doyle was with me on this branch to see what happened next. I only wished, is all – about near brought a tear to this ole Guardian Angel's eye, it surely did."

"Everybody circle around," said Dick. "Everybody get in a circle and grab hands."

They did.

"Mary, you're the best at it," said Dick. "Will you give a prayer that we do alright tomorrow, and we get Eddie's money back?"

There were a few snorts and giggles, but everyone began to have the sense of how important the next twenty-four hours could be in the lives of a humble happy family in Binghamton. They knew tough times. They all realized that it could have happened to their family.

"Dear God, please help us do right tomorrow so Lucy and Judy can have a nice Christmas and they can break bread every day as a family, and Eddie can stay at home and be a painter. I don't know what to say, God, but you know what I'm trying to ask for. Please help us, amen."

Mary looked over at Eddie.

"Eddie, are you crying? Don't cry, Eddie, be happy. We're going to get your money back. I promise."

"My platoon of paratroopers grabbed hands and prayed in a circle before we boarded the plane. Just wishing they could all be with us here now, is all."

"...and they are, young man," said Mr. Ossant. "If it weren't' for all you brave lads that dark stormy night in southern England offering up your lives to help save the world, we wouldn't be here today free to make something right...to right a wrong. Every member of your platoon and all the others will always be alive in our hearts."

Mary reached out and grabbed Eddie's hand and squeezed it.

"Don't worry. Everything is going to work out," she said.

The meeting broke up, one by one they climbed into cars and the tires crunched down the cinder drive of the cemetery.

Ole Charlie here was about to be prayerful when I heard the voice clear as anything.

"You did well, my friend. You did very well."

It was Mr. Doyle, for sure.

"Don't I have a nice flock?" I said.

"You have a fine flock, Charlie, you certainly do. The big details come tomorrow. Keep a prayer."

CHAPTER SEVENTEEN

THE DAY OF RECKONING

"Mrs. Parker, nice of you to feed us," said Mayor.

"Farmer Parker and I wouldn't have it any other way. We know you all have a big day planned in Syracuse at the State Fair. Tomorrow we may be saying good-bye to our Eddie. My momma used to tell me nothing says better at pretty words than a morning farm kitchen filled with hungry mouths passing the syrup and enjoying a moment with one another's friendships."

"I'm going to miss your home cooking, Mrs. Parker," said Eddie. "How did your butter pickles do yesterday?"

"I got a ribbon, only placed, but seeing all my old friends was worth going."

"I'd love to take a jar home to my wife," said Eddie.

"Well, you had better be bringing that wife of yours and those sweet young ladies around for a visit sometime before it snows. Of course, you can take a jar, but we're counting on seeing them."

"I will bring them up, I promise."

"You'd better bring your wife by, Eddie," said Duba. "We don't want to be starting any talk around Delphi Falls – you know, a strange man living in the barn, coming in for breakfast and all. People do talk."

"Oh, you stop," said Mrs. Parker. "Those summers left the barn when I got my college degree and met my Fay at a barn dance up in New Woodstock."

"Can you dance, Mrs. Parker?" asked Barber. "I saw you clapping and tapping your feet at the barn dance, but I didn't see you dance."

"We could cut a rug in our day," she said.

"Everyone, Myrtie would like for you all to come to supper tonight – in New Woodstock," said Mrs. Parker. "Sheriff John will be there with her waiting for a signal to go arrest your pickpocket. Pass the word about her supper. She's counting on you all coming."

"Mrs. Parker," asked Jerry, "did you live through the Depression?"

"It was more like nobody 'lived' through the Depression – but somehow we made it through," said Mrs. Parker.

"Did you ever go hungry then," asked Mayor.

"We learned to go without. I could make a chocolate layer cake in 1940 with everything but chocolate," laughed Mrs. Parker. "Why, young man, sugar was so scarce Duane Skeele, up in Fabius, would draw a hundred gallons of maple syrup come springtime in the '40s and sleep in the horse stall all night keeping the fire going."

"Eddie," said Holbrook, "Things will be tight for you all winter if we don't come through for you."

Marty changed the subject.

"Eddie, if you fly back here, don't you be landing on top of the hayfield hill," chuckled Marty.

"Hey, Marty," said Mary, "I like your old straw hat and suspenders. You ought to have a piece of straw hanging from your mouth. Are you going to wear shoes or going barefoot?"

"I want to look like a hayseed, but not too huckleberry. I have some old boots my dad had and worn out. They'll do the trick. I have a leather and burlap shoulder-strap bag for my witching twig and the apple."

"A regular Johnny Appleseed," said Randy.

"Well, I did get the idea out of a library book. I saw a sketch of one on Johnny Appleseed, sure enough," said Marty. "Mom sewed it together for me."

"Alice," asked Dick, "you ready to do your thing?"

"Let's see the color of your money, wise guy. I don't waste no time on any two bit flim-flam artists – show me the green or get lost, buddy...

...How's that?" asked Alice.

"Perfect," said Dick.

"Good heavens," said Mrs. Parker.

"Neither good nor heavens' got anything to do with her act today, Mrs. Parker," laughed Mary. More like bad and down below."

"You like it, for real, everybody?" asked Alice.

"Sounds real enough to me, like the streets of a big city – like in the movies," said Conway.

"Whew! Well, that's such a relief," said Alice. "I've never been so scared in all my life."

"I remember a time in the woods you looked pretty scared," said Mary.

"But she was dead, then," said Jerry with a snort. "Remember? She was murdered and carried into the woods on the back of her killer."

Holbrook sneered, remembering the panic he caused thinking she was dead, lying in the field this past summer.

Dawn was breaking so the passel of them decided to walk on down to the barn to say hey to Farmer Parker finishing up his milking. The barn was lighted with the friendly bulbs hanging and warmed with the smells of the new lofted hay and warm fresh milk in cans. The radio was tinkling out a player piano-roll tune introducing the morning's wake-up farm report.

"Eddie?" asked Farmer Parker looking up from stripping a cow.

"Yes, sir," said Eddie.

"Heard you might need to go to the Fair to help 'em out. That'd be fine. You go do what you have to do."

"Thanks," said Eddie. "I want to be there in case they need help."

"I decided I'm staying here with Mrs. Parker?" said Mary. "I'm going to help make some salads and things for Myrtie's supper to-night. I saw the fair yesterday and I'd be a bundle of nerves worry-wart there today."

"Does the biplane take a regular octane or is there an oil mix to it?" asked Farmer Parker.

"Regular gas. Any octane is good. I usually buy the cheapest," said Eddie.

"Well, you'll find four five-gallon cans of gasoline setting next to your plane. Regular octane – we'll get more if need be to fill the tank."

"That's mighty nice of you," said Eddie.

"You earned it, son," said Farmer Parker. "That was our deal. The Mrs. and I were beginning to favor having you around."

"You're good people," said Eddie.

"The gas cans have to go to Hasting's store in Delphi Falls when they're empty."

"I'll take them," said Barber. "When I go home later tonight, I'll take them. Someone's picking me up."

"My dad could haul them in his Dodge, if you want," said Randy. "He goes right by the store."

Ole Charlie here was making notice how chatty and jittery ev-ery young soul standing around in this familiar old dairy barn was being this particular morning. Why the last time I saw these sorts of nerves with nobody shooting at me, like they were in '16, I was waiting in line to get my angel wings that time I learned I was go-ing to be Guardian Angel to this flock.

Oh, it wasn't caring for the flock what scared me near to fright, made me nervous; or the responsibility of it neither. I was a simple man in those times before I passed. Come from simple means. No electricity or necessary in my house, a wood cook stove. I couldn't read more than a measuring yardstick. Not being able to spell Guardian Angel is what was making me a nervous jittery wreck first day up. How would I ever know what line to get in if there were signs naming the lines? It's fun now, knowing I can be as smart as - if or when - I want and need to be at any given time. This handy 'optional extra' for an angel, came with the wings.

But today ole Charlie here can only watch and pray is all.

Conway pulled in the drive, loaded Alice's wheelchair in his truck and lifted her into the cab.

Everybody packed up and headed for Syracuse and the State Fair. As they reached the fairgrounds each car or pickup waited in the parking lot for the next. Conway stood in the back of Duba's pickup and counted heads.

"Everybody," said Dick, "have fun, but today you don't know Marty, me, Conway, Duba, Dwyer or Alice, get it?"

"We get it," said Holbrook. "Jerry and I are going to see the wild animals."

"If any of you see us, just walk on by," said Duba. "And if you see any other kids from school, tell them too."

Dick turned to Eddie.

"Eddie, we've been thinking. We need you to take Mayor and head back," said Dick. Can't take the chance they see you. They may be on the lookout."

"Probably a good idea," said Eddie. "A crook is always on the lookout for trouble. Give me some directions."

"I'll go with you," said Mayor. I'll show you how to get back."

"Take my car then," said Dick. He threw Eddie the keys. We'll double up. I'll ride with Duba.

"I understand," mumbled Eddie.

"You okay, Eddie?" asked Duba. "You look a little pale."

"I'm okay. I'm okay. I get this way when I'm nervous, is all. I'm okay. That bum…"

"There's nothing to be nervous about, Eddie," said Dick. "We have it all under control. We are going to get your winter money back. We've done stuff like this before. What can we do to set you at ease – and give you confidence that we'll come through for you?"

"What did you paratroopers do for nerves?" asked Duba.

"A lot of us drank or smoked," blurted Eddie. "I didn't smoke."

Dick stopped, turned, and reached deep into his pocket. He pulled out a five-dollar bill.

"Go ahead, get yourself one," said Dick.

"One?" Eddie asked, looking confused.

"You said you could use a drink to calm your nerves," said Dick. "So, get one."

"Thanks," said Eddie.

"No driving my car after you had a drink though."

"I'll get a pint and wait until we get back to the plane," said Eddie.

"One drink," said Dick. "But be at the cemetery tonight at nine for the meeting."

CHAPTER EIGHTEEN

THE SET UP

Dick pushed Alice's wheelchair through mysteriously wondrous alleys of the State Fair, each of them taking it all in. They turned onto the Midway making their way slowly so they wouldn't draw attention. The wheelchair stopped one tent away from pickpocket. Dick turned about watching the fun. The 'Ring the Bell' game where farmers and city folk alike stood in line to slam the wooden sledge mallet, ring the bell and win a kewpie doll or a pocket comb - impressing their sweethearts. Allowing Dick and Alice the time to get ahead of them Minneapolis Moline Conway, Duba and Dwyer made their own way through the front gate and then split up. They spaced themselves about thirty feet apart. They were careful to stay a fair distance from Alice's wheel chair. Conway took post listening to the talker for the girlie show; Dwyer was at the shooting gallery; and Duba was in the line for the baseball throw at the wooden milk bottles. Ole Charlie here got best watchful advantage of the whole Midway, sitting on top of the Italian hand carved merry-go-round.

"Slam! Ding..."

"Slam! Ding..."

"Hurry, Hurry, Hurry! He's part man. He's part alligator — come see the illusion..."

Alice turned her head about taking in the Midway sights and sounds before locking her eyes on pickpocket hoping he would know she was watching him; that she had an eye on him. It was about fifteen minutes when the water witchery man, Marty strutted up the Midway in his straw hat and sign hanging from his neck.

"Water! Water!" He sang out. "Who needs water?"

He'd zig and then he'd zag through the crowd pretending he was searching out farmers who needed wells.

"Why wait for a rain barrel to fill when you don't have to, folks," he preached. "Don't waste another planting – water is what you need and with Jedidiah and my magic stick here, water is what you'll get. It never fails. Now who needs water on their farm? Water anyone? I find water in a day or you get your money back – every cent of it. What's fifty bucks compared to a field of corn, mister?"

With a watchful eye Alice waited for pickpocket to notice Marty, maybe size him up as a mark. In time Alice was satisfied that pickpocket had caught her eye. He had moved about the crowd lifting a wallet or two. Alice reached over her shoulder and tapped Dick's hand, signalling him.

"He's such a crumb, that guy," said Alice. "Let's get him."

"You ready?" asked Dick.

"I'm ready as I'll ever be. Push me closer but keep towards the middle of the Midway. Keep away from prying ears, somebody might recognize me."

As Dick pushed the wheelchair Alice lifted a large purse from under her lap blanket. She figured it might be a lure. It was almost as large as Eddie's valise. Pickpocket was a spiff. He had a shine on his shoes, he had a starched collar.

"That's' an expensive tie he's wearing," Alice whispered to Dick. "Get me closer."

"I wonder if he's French Vichy today or a Brit?" said Dick.

"By the looks of his beret, could be either," said Alice.

When pickpocket first looked over, he locked his eyes on Alice's purse. Alice was patient, waiting to catch his eye. That done, she jerked her head twice, motioning him to come over. Pickpocket winced and looked around behind as though he wasn't certain if she was signalling him or someone nearby. Again she jerked her head twice. She rolled her eyes and boldly raised a hand and wiggled her finger a 'C'mere'. She wanted to talk. It finally worked. He started toward the wheelchair.

Seeing him Dick pretended to make no notice and turned to look around the Midway like a tourist at the same time getting a fix on where the chess players in this game of battle were - Conway, Duba and Dwyer...and Marty, of course.

"I'm sorry, but were you motioning to me, milady?" asked pickpocket.

Alice leaned her head back, looked up at Dick.

"Get lost," she said to Dick. "I have business."

Dick stepped away from the chair and walked over by the Bell Ring.

"Lady, I'm a guest in your country spreading the word of the Sherlock Holmes Players. We're bringing London to the American stage, tomorrow in the town, New Woodstock. May I interest you in free tickets for you and your mates? Free – it's such a demeaning term of value, isn't it, Mum? We're papering the house; ticket sales for the first performance have been a tad dozy. What papering the house means is..."

"Save it," barked Alice.

"There'll be two perfor....huh?" quirked pickpocket.

"I have a proposition to make."

"Why, ma'am I'm a simple thespian. Actually I play Sherlock..."

"Put a sock in it, pal," gruffed Alice.

"Excuse me?"

"Oh, I didn't catch them all, you're pretty quick – but I did see a few. What'd you make picking those pockets? A few bucks? How many wallets?"

"I must be going, nice to have met you."

"You haven't met me, and you don't know me. But I know you, boy do I know you."

"I beg your pardon."

"Beg all you want. If I didn't think you were good enough, I wouldn't waste my breath on you. How'd you like to make some real money? I mean real money, not this ten and twenty dollar variety."

"Lady, are ye a copper?"

"Last chance, sailor - you want to make thousands or just twenties? It's time to stop flapping your gums and make a decision or I'm going, going, gone."

"Pickpocket knelt down next to the wheelchair.

"Talk to me, milady. How do you Yanks say it? It's your quid?"

"It's your nickel," said Alice.

"I'm listening."

Alice caught Dick's eye and signalled him to come back and stand guard behind the chair. She didn't open her purse until he was there. She unsnapped it, reached in and took out five crisp brand new twenty dollar bills.

"See this?" she said.

"I do indeed, milady," said pickpocket.

"Pick a mark," said Alice.

"Excuse me?" said pickpocket.

"Over by that tent, over there, the shooting gallery – pick a mark."

"I'll play your daffy game. Okay, the young couple. He's shooting the rifle, she's holding three kewpie dolls," said pickpocket.

Pickpocket didn't point to Dwyer.

"Nah, they're too much in love, way too young, he's probably still in college waiting tables – and they're broke," said Alice.

"How can you tell, Mum?"

"She already has three kewpie dolls and cotton candy. He's spending the last of his money," said Alice.

"You're absolutely right. My but you are smashing, Mum. How about the fellow in overalls next to them – with the reddish hair?" said pickpocket.

"Perfect choice," said Alice.

It was Dwyer.

"He probably still has the down payment money his daddy gave him this morning to put on the new tractor in the farm equipment pavilion."

"…and this means what, exactly?" asked pickpocket.

Dick knew it was time. He watched over until Dwyer looked around at him catching his eye. Dick turned his head to the right and then to the left indicating he had no cigarette over his ear. The signal was in. Dwyer turned his head away.

"Take these twenties over there and see if the red head has a bigger bill," said Alice.

"Let me understand this. You're telling me to take five twenty dollar bills and go get it changed into two fifties or a single one hundred dollar bill? Am I missing something?"

"Let's just say it'll show me I can trust you, sailor. Then let's say it'll be your ticket to making a couple of thousand today – if you're smart - and that's in Yankee dollars."

"Well, this I clearly understand," said pickpocket.

"I do talk pretty clear, don't I, sailor?"

"You certainly do, mum, and after we sort through this we'll have a proper introduction."

"You don't like sailor, sailor?"

"I detest the sea, Mum."

Alice handed him the twenties. He stood up, brushed off the knees of his trousers, straightened the knot in his tie and worked his way through the crowd to the rifle range. At first he feigned walking by Dwyer, then turned as though on a spur of the moment and began speaking to him. He pointed to the girlie-girlie tent and reached in his pocket and pulled out the twenties, holding them in front of Dwyer. Dwyer shook his head yes, reached in his pocket and handed pickpocket a tattered hundred dollar bill taking the twenties. Not knowing if he was feeling a sense of accomplishment or a sense of confusion, pickpocket walked back to the wheelchair. He knelt down and handed Alice the hundred dollar bill.

About that time, Alice did something causing Dick to near spit up. She handed the hundred dollar bill back to the pickpocket.

"Here, keep this, you earned it," said Alice.

Dick's eyes got as big as cucumber slices. He bit his lower lip and hoped he was dreaming. Giving Big Mike's, Mike Shea's or Doc Webb's money away was not a part of the plan.

"This is a hundred American dollars, Milady. Why are you giving it to me?"

"You earned it, sailor, and it didn't cost me a nickel."

"I'm sorry, but not having my morning tea, I thought I heard you say that giving away one hundred dollars didn't cost you anything. Did I get that right?"

"Mine wasn't real. That farmer made you one hundred dollars and it didn't cost a nickel."

"What are you saying?"

"Mine was counterfeit."

Pickpocket believed her every word. He believed the real money was counterfeit, just as Dick and Duba felt he would – because she said it was.

"Lady," said pickpocket. "Are you sure you're not a copper?"

"Go ahead, try it again, sailor. Pick a mark."

"Let me see. Farmers have the money you say? Tractors and such. Only makes sense, now doesn't it, this being an agricultural exhibition. I say…"

"How about that tall gentleman over there by that cage?"

"The cricket cage?" asked pickpocket.

"It's a baseball cage where they toss baseballs to hit bottles," said Alice.

"Precisely, that's it."

"Go over and see if he'll change these twenties."

Alice handed pickpocket five more brand new twenties.

Pickpocket took the money and stood up. He gave a thought to disappearing. After all, the wheelchair lady picked this mark. It was probably a set-up, he thought. He paused at first, and then he decided to at least try and walked toward the baseball cage.

Dick caught Duba's eye - turned his head both ways signalling there was no cigarette. The mark was set. Pickpocket worked his way over, walked by him and turned back inquiring if he could make change. Duba said no, he couldn't. Pickpocket shrugged his shoulders over to Alice and walked back to the wheelchair.

"He didn't have more than a twenty on him," said pickpocket.

Now he was a believer, but Alice didn't leave anything to chance. She'd try again.

"Okay, last time, or I'm out of here, sailor," said Alice. "Make it good. Now what sorts of gents want to hide their folding money, hide it the best?"

"Those who are afraid of temptation and the pocket lifters," said pickpocket.

"Exactly," said Alice. "See the two farmers over there by the girlie show?"

"I do," said pickpocket.

"The one on the left, doesn't he have a crease on his back pocket, probably a wallet with a lot of money in it? Take this and see if he wants to change small bills for it."

Alice handed pickpocket two crisp new one hundred dollar bills. Pickpocket looked at the two crisp new hundred dollar bills - almost as though he could take it and run and be ahead three hundred Yankee dollars. But his greed kicked in.

"Wish me good speed," he said.

Dick placed a cigarette over his ear, turned and watched for Conway to notice it while pickpocket was straightening his beret and tie. Conway did. The signal was in.

Pickpocket stood up and walked over to the crowd gathering in front of the girlie show. As the crowd shuffled he made his way over sidling up to Conway. Casually he opened his wallet and lifted out the hundred dollar bills. He began folding them small as though he wanted to go see the girlie show but didn't want to risk losing them. He pretended he wanted to hide the two hundred dollar bills. Conway took notice.

"Want to trade those?" asked Conway.

"Pardon me?" asked Pickpocket.

"I want to get rid of some tens and twenties. Want to trade my small bills for your hundreds?"

"Perfect solution," said pickpocket. "Why is it we men always worry about losing our big bills but not smaller ones?"

"Beats me, friend," said Conway.

They made the trade and Pickpocket worked his way back to the wheelchair.

"This is amazing," said pickpocket. "I never dreamed it would be so easy. The bills you have are brilliantly done."

"Nothing but the best," said Alice. "They come in by boat from Canada. You want some of them, sailor? Beats, how'd you call it - lifting pockets?"

"I certainly do, if the price is right, I certainly do."

Pickpocket handed the two hundred dollars to Alice.

"Keep it," she said.

Dick was about to have a heart attack. He took the cigarette from his ear and lit it, choking on his first drag.

"Can you come up with a thousand U.S." said Alice.

Pickpocket looked at the three hundred he just made, knew about seven hundred he had stolen and looked over at Alice.

"I can, absolutely," he said.

Alice leaned her head back, caught Dick's eye.

"Get lost."

"Just as well, Dick had to go find a toilet where he could puke, cry or whatever was going to be his reaction to this fourth grade school teacher giving a known criminal, thief, crook three hundred real U.S. dollars that didn't belong to any of them.

"A thousand greenbacks will get you five thousand in assorted bills."

"My, my," said pickpocket, adjusting the knot in his tie.

"There's a catch," said Alice.

"I'm certain there would be," said pickpocket.

"You can only use five hundred of it here in Syracuse. Take the rest with you, out of town, back to England, but not here. We don't want locals to get wise and close in."

"Makes good sense," said pickpocket. "Perfect sense, indeed."

By this time Dick had reappeared. Alice caught his eye and flagged him over to the wheelchair.

"Sailor, it's time you meet Jedidiah," said Alice.

"Jedidiah?" asked pickpocket.

"He's the link to the funny money. I'll arrange it. Go get me a hot dog and lemonade will you?" Alice handed him ten dollars.

"Oh, no," said pickpocket. "My treat."

Pickpocket walked to a hot dog tent and stood in line, smiling, thinking of his soon to be riches.

Without moving his lips risking drawing notice, Dick pleaded.

"Are you crazy, Alice? Are you nuts? You just gave a crook three hundred real bucks that, I might remind you, doesn't belong to us."

"We'll get it back tonight," said Alice. "Don't worry about it."

"Want to clue me in as to how?" asked Dick, his heart palpitating.

"He's going to give Marty a thousand bucks tonight, right?"

"Well, yes, it looks like it," said Dick.

"So there. That'll be Big Mike's, Mike Shea's and Doc Webb's three hundred dollars plus we get Eddie's seven hundred back."

"Oh," said Dick, somewhat relieved. "But Eddie only lost six hundred forty."

"Well, we'll let Sheriff John worry about the change."

By this time pickpocket returned with three hot dogs and three lemonades.

"I love American hot dogs. They're such a tasty delight with all the garnishments."

"Let's eat first, and then I'll get you to Jedidiah so you both can talk business."

"And you get?" asked pickpocket.

"I get a finder's fee. Jedidiah takes care of me, don't worry."

"Such a nice arrangement," said pickpocket.

The three of them, a fourth grade school teacher in disguise, a sixteen-year-old upstart who dreamed up this SOS and a pickpocketing actor from Liverpool – standing together in the early afternoon sun, enjoying their hot dogs and lemonade. The smells of cotton candy and salt water taffy rifted through the air; the milling crowds growing with the day. The bait was set, the lure had worked. Now it was time for the big show - to spring the trap. While waiting for Marty to come up through the Midway again they listened to the carny noises and sounds only around once a year like honking geese in the spring. Bells ringing, clickers clicking, talkers promising their crowd the moon – anything they would believe. The three enjoyed it all. After all it was the New York State Fair.

Pickpocket was a pleasant enough sort. An interesting bloke as he would say. He happened to be a no-account crook is all and had to be stopped. Dick looked at his watch. Marty was only going to walk through putting on his show every hour on the hour. They had time. Pickpocket bought them another round of hot dogs and lemonade.

CHAPTER NINETEEN

WATER WITCHERY

"That's Delphi Falls Road up ahead," said Mayor. "You'll want to hang a left."

Eddie pointed towards the right.

"Is that a store over there?"

"That's Hastings, yup," said Mayor.

"I ought to get my girls something before I take off to Binghamton tomorrow."

"Why don't we go to the plane and put the gas in it. We'll bring the cans back and you can get a look around the store?" said Mayor.

"Good idea," said Eddie.

"If you don't see anything you like, we can always try Shea's up in Fabius. They'll have more stuff. Dick won't mind your using the car for that," said Mayor.

He parked the Willys on the side of the road, and the two walked through the field to the plane. With Mayor on one side and Eddie on the other, they lifted the tarpaulin and folded it like a bed sheet and put it on the ground by the fence. Eddie pulled the unopened pint of whiskey from his pocket and set it in the back cockpit of the plane. One gasoline can at a time; Mayor would hold the funnel while Eddie poured the gasoline, emptying every can.

"This'll be plenty to get me to Binghamton," said Eddie.

"Let's take the cans to Hastings and you can look for things for your kids," said Mayor.

"Hold on a second," said Eddie. "Let me check something out."

Eddie climbed up into the back cockpit. He picked up the two-way microphone knob.

"What is that telephone operator's name, again?"

"Myrtie?" said Mayor.

Eddie pushed his thumb down on the button. With his other hand he turned the dial on the two way radio receiver.

"Calling Myrtie. This is Flying Eddie calling Myrtie. Come in, Myrtie," he spoke every word clearly into the microphone.

There was hissing and buzz as he turned the tuning dial.

"Myrtie, come in. Calling Myrtie. Come in Myrtie."

He fiddled and spoke, turned the knob and tried again and again.

"Myrtie, come in. This is Flying Eddie calling Myrtie. Come in Myrtie."

Finally it happened.

"Myrtie here…come in please."

"Roger, Myrtie, this is Eddie and Mayor calling from my plane down here at the Parker's farm, come in…"

"You're breaking up, breaking up bad – where are you flying?" squawked Myrtie.

"I'm on the ground," said Eddie. "Can you hear me?"

"I hear scratching – can make out some, Eddie. Sheriff John said you might test. He will be here at seven…come in…"

"Roger, Myrtie…just checking the system…we'll be here waiting to hear from you from seven on…"

"Roger," said Myrtie.

"If its breaking up then, we'll take her up for better reception," shouted Eddie.

"I'll tell Sheriff John," said Myrtie.

"Over and out," said Eddie.

Mayor's eyes were as big as quarters.

"That hill is going to be a problem – blocking the plane's antenna reception," said Eddie.

"When you're flying with the open cockpit and all, how can you hear the radio?" asked Mayor.

"With these," said Eddie. He lifted earphones with a microphone attached from the floor. "You put these on and plug this knob in to the two-way."

"Holy cow," was about all Mayor had to offer.

"Let's take the gas cans back," said Eddie. "Help me pack them in the trunk."

"What then?" asked Mayor. "We have all afternoon to kill. After we get back, we'll charge the battery of the plane so the two-way will be strong."

"How do we do that?"

"We'll find something to chock the wheels of the plane so she won't roll anywhere and we'll start her up. You can sit in the cockpit fifteen minutes while the battery charges. While we're waiting on that I'll walk to Farmer Parker's and see if he needs me for a chore. I'll come back and turn it off when it's time. Just don't touch any knobs or switches while it's running."

Mayor beamed at the thought of his sitting behind the stick of a real, honest-to-goodness 1941 single engine biplane with its motor revving and propeller spinning. Life could never get better than this for a lad, he was thinking. They gathered the cans and headed to the car.

"While I sit in it idling, can I put on the helmet and earphones?" asked Mayor.

"Sure. Put on the goggles, too. Just don't touch any buttons."

Meanwhile back on the Midway at the New York State Fair, the water witchery master was about to go into his act again. Marty had timed it so he would make one quick round every hour on the hour until the trap was set. The last thing he wanted to do was to get a customer who needed water.

Alice caught Marty's eye from about four tents away. He was hanging the sign around his neck looking around the crowd for Alice or Dick. She reached behind and tapped Dick's hand to signal Marty. He was to clue him in that they've identified the pickpocket mark and they were ready to begin the charade. Dick put a cigarette over each ear and turned about. Marty saw them, tipped his straw hat and nodded. The signal was in. With that, Dick took one of the cigarettes from an ear and lit it.

"Sailor," said Alice. "You ready to make the connection?"

"I am, milady," said pickpocket, wiping mustard from his chin.

"You'd better be able to come up with the money or there'll be a big mess."

"I have it, I assure you – I'll have more than a thousand dollars American in my bag at the playhouse. I will not let you down, mum. You're commission is safe."

Marty pranced his way past the rifle range.

"Water! Water!" Marty bellowed. "Water on your farm!"

He slowed his walk, waiting for the fish to bite.

"There he is," said Alice. "Over there with the sign."

"The chap and his water-witchery, mum? Why he's been strolling through here all day. Are you certain?"

"Why wait for rain, you don't have to, folks," Marty preached. "Don't waste another planting – if water is what you need – with Jedidiah and my magic stick here – a water well is what you'll get. My stick never fails to find water..."

"That's his front here at the Fair, but he really can find water for farmers," said Alice. "He's the source for what you want. Go do your business, sailor. Make it good."

Pickpocket straightened his tie and walked over to Marty.

"Who needs water on the farm?" barked Marty. "Water anyone?"

"Sir, I need to ask you a question," whispered pickpocket.

"The answer is yes, I can find water anywhere," said Marty. "I find water in a day or you get your money back — every cent. What's fifty bucks compared to the cost of planting a field of corn, mister?"

"As a matter of curiosity, how are you able to find water using a stick, if I may ask?"

"It's a branch from a tree that bears a fruit with seeds in it. Nature points it to water the same as a sunflower turns to the sun. It will find water as far as twenty feet down."

"Simply amazing," said pickpocket.

Marty began to turn away.

"Young man, I have a thousand — how do you say — greenbacks — to spend if you have any of the other goods I've been told of," said pickpocket.

"Beat it, friend, I'm just trying to earn an honest living here, nothing more. Water! Who needs water on the farm?"

Pickpocket pulled the three one hundred dollar bills from his pocket. He fanned them out, counting it.

"That's a little short fella, take a hike!" Marty barked in a loud raspy whisper. "Water, who needs water, folks?"

"I've got another seven hundred at the playhouse in town New Woodstock. I promise I have it all. A thousand, I believe I was told. Milady over there will vouch for me. We can make an exchange to-morrow. I have to be in a rehearsal all afternoon. I'm in the play."

"Over in that wheelchair?"

"That's her."

"You have all the money?"

"Can you show me some identity? How do I know you're not a copper?" asked pickpocket.

Marty started, reached deep in his pocket and pulled out the card for Jedidiah and his Séance gatherings.

"Why that card's not about water, it says séances — say, what gives, Gov?"

Marty gulped.

"See that name? It's Jedidiah – that's me. I do water when ground isn't frozen. I do séances when it is. Have to make a living somehow."

Beads of sweat were sparkling Marty's freckles. He took charge again.

"You have the money or not, fella?"

"Every greenback, my good man."

"Do you know the Lincklaen House hotel?

"Well, yes, in fact, I do. We're staying there. In town Cazenovia. It's a short jaunt from our playhouse in a New Woodstock school."

"There's a telephone closet in the lobby of the hotel. Get in it before eight o'clock tonight, and wait for a ring."

"I was going to work the Midway until nine, be at the hotel about ten. Might we do this tomorrow?"

"See ya'," snorted Marty turning away.

"No wait, I'll be there. I'll be there. Precisely at eight o'clock. Tonight it is then, in the phone closet."

"Now you're getting smart. When it rings, answer it. Somebody'll ask for a code. The code you give 'em is - Mary had a little lamb…"

"Mary had a little lamb?" groaned pickpocket, in total disbelief.

"Get it right or the deals off."

"I will, I will. 'Mary had a little lamb.' I've got it."

"Not so loud, fella. And you'd better have the cash on you when you get there."

"Might'n I get some of it from you now?"

"Do you see any bags on me or trunks dragging around behind me? Do you?"

"So sorry, I didn't mean…"

"Answer the telephone, give the code. You'll get a code word back and directions where to pick it up. How simple is that?"

"Will it be far from the hotel?" I don't have an auto, you see."

"Figure it out. Just answer the telephone and give your code. By the way, what's your name, fella?"

"Call me Sherlock Holmes," said pickpocket. "We'll do business tonight – you come see us perform tomorrow. Sherlock Holmes at your service, sir."

"Be there with the money."

"I suppose I might hail a cab."

"Not my problem. You'd better have all the money or you'll walk away empty handed – and that means without the three hundred in your pocket. I'll call it a three hundred buck fine for wasting my time. Lincklaen House lobby telephone closet at eight. Now get lost before we get spotted."

Pickpocket watched as Marty walked away, up the Midway.

He folded the bills, put them in his pocket and turned to go talk with wheelchair milady. He looked at the spot where he left her and her helper. They were gone. He stepped back into the middle of the Midway and looked for them carefully in front of every tent, each attraction. Wheelchair lady had completely disappeared. Pickpocket was okay with that. He figured he was up three hundred American, if nothing came down. He had nothing to lose. He turned about again to see the water witchery gentlemen. Marty had disappeared as well – completely out of sight. Pickpocket had some time before his fellow actor ride to the Lincklaen House in Cazenovia came. He wedged himself into a crowd at the girlie show tent (lifting some unsuspecting farmer's and young men's pockets along the way).

As Marty stepped through the columns of the State Fair's main entrance, Duba jumped from behind one.

"Boo!" he barked.

"Where is everybody?" asked Marty.

"Mayor and Eddie went to the biplane. Conway took Alice home for a nap."

"He was supposed to get me to Cazenovia," said Marty.

"Alice was worn out from being keyed up all night. She said she wanted a soak in the tub and a nap after setting in the sun in her wheelchair all day."

"She was perfect, though," said Marty. "That pickpocket guy bought her story all hook, line and sinker of it."

"He'll never know what hit him," said Duba. "I'm driving you."

"Okay."

"Dick and Dwyer are taking the lot of them - Randy, Barber and Holbrook - over to Myrtie's to wait for Sheriff John. Myrtie is making them all supper. Jerry is already setting up your camp, with the fire and all. He went there with Farmer Parker and Mr. Ossant when they took the team of horses and wagon in. He stayed there."

"I need to use a telephone."

"I'm taking you to the Lincklaen House to get your map first," said Duba. "Then I'll drop you on the road near your camp – wherever that is."

"First I've gotta' tell Myrtie what time to call the hotel; you have a nickel for the telephone?"

Duba walked Marty over to a telephone booth handing him some pocket change. Marty dropped in a coin and dialled 'O'.

"Operator, I need the exchange operator in New Woodstock, please," said Marty. "Can you connect me?"

"One moment, puleeeze…"

"How much do I put in ma'am?"

"It's an operatoorrr' call, sir. No charge."

"It's free?"

"There is no charge for an operatoorrr' call, sir."

"Oh, I see. Thank you."

Marty put his hand over the mouth piece and explained it all to Duba.

"There's no charge to call an exchange, only to call people."

"Operator, how may I help you?"

"Hello. Hello. Myrtie, this is Marty."

"Marty, are you coming for supper?"

"I can't, I'll be at the camp. I'm supposed to give you the time you're to call the telephone closet at the Lincklaen House."

"Oh, that's right."

"Call it right at eight o'clock, Myrtie. Let it ring until he answers it."

"I most certainly will," said Myrtie. "What do I tell him?"

"You ask for his code. He'll say the code, it's – 'Mary had a little lamb.'"

Myrtie howled through the phone.

"I know, I know – it sounds stupid as all get out. It's all my brain could come up with. I was nervous thinking the guy might get wise and pull a knife or gun or something."

"It's perfect, sweetie. Just perfect," said Myrtie.

"Okay," said Marty. "When he answers with the code, tell him to ask the front desk for an envelope for Sherlock Holmes written on it. That will have a map to the hideout where he pays for and picks up the goods. Tell him when he gets to the hideout his code word is going to be 'Séance'. Tell him he'll need to say 'I'm here for the Séance' before he'll be let in."

"My, what fun," said Myrtie. "I have all of this written down, so don't you worry about a thing, honey. Be careful tonight."

"Thanks, Myrtie."

"Anything else?" asked Myrtie.

"Tell Sheriff John his envelope is at the hotel lobby desk for him marked 'Messenger'. He'll need it to find the camp and make the arrest. Tell him not to lose it; no one will know where the camp is without that map. I don't even know where it is until I get my copy."

"I'll tell him," said Myrtie. "My, but you've thought of every detail."

As Marty hung up, Duba pulled around in his pickup and wait-ed for him to climb in. They headed off to Cazenovia to get Marty's copy of the map and get him to his camp hideout.

"Duba, something's come up, we may need your help," said Marty, as they pulled into Cazenovia.

"You just think about it now?" asked Duba.

"He said he didn't have a ride. I have an idea."

"Shoot," barked Duba.

"In case we need it, can you make a sign that says TAXI and put it on the door of your truck?"

"Huh?" said Duba.

"I just remembered, pickpocket mentioned he didn't have wheels. If you're parked in front of the Lincklaen House pretend-ing to be a taxi, you could watch for him and be the one to give him a ride to wherever my camp is."

"Why me?"

"After Sheriff John gets the map everyone at Myrties will head into the woods and surround my camp. That way pickpocket can't run away. Jerry is already there. You're the only one not doing anything."

"I see a problem," said Duba.

"What's that?"

"What if a state trooper or deputy stops and asks what I'm do-ing with a taxi sign sitting in front of the hotel?"

"Well then don't be sitting in front of the hotel until eight o'clock. This ain't New York City, for crying out loud – nobody in Cazenovia is going to pay any attention to a sign on the door of an old truck. Park somewhere else and kill time listening to the radio."

"Can't."

"Can't what?"

"Can't listen to my radio."

"Huh?"

"No antenna. Can't tune in my radio with no antenna," said Duba.

The pickup pulled up to the hotel. Marty ran in and got his copy of the map. Two maps were left there, one for Sheriff John – (his envelope marked with 'Messenger'.) The other for pickpocket marked with 'Sherlock Holmes'. After they studied Marty's copy, Duba drove down Albany Street then over to the Cherry Valley and down to Pompey Hollow Road where he dropped Marty off to find his camp on foot.

"There's a dirt path up to it somewhere near about. From the map it looks like it may be a hundred yards in. Look for the path near spinster Nettie's place and turn in there, I'm thinking," said Duba. "There's a car path goes in quite a ways. Mostly apple trees all about, some maple."

"How do you know all this," asked Marty. "Car path and apple trees?"

"Us guys would take girls in there to neck."

"I swear, is that all you and Dick ever think about, necking and girls?"

"Pretty much," said Duba.

"Well, if you know the place, drop me off there then."

"They said I'm not to take you in, just in case we're being followed and watched. I think you have about a mile hike. Good luck."

Duba headed to Fabius to paint a taxi sign and get food provisions for his vigil later. It could be a long night. As he painted the sign, he devoured two peanut butter and jelly sandwiches, a dill pickle, and half a quart of milk. He paper-sacked some vittles' for later. Returning to Cazenovia he edged just up the street from the Lincklaen House entrance and parked in front of the movie house. He sat there a full forty-five minutes looking at the movie posters, waiting in silence before he lit his last cigarette. Smoking that one, he leaned over and checked his glove box for another pack. Then he sat some more. Before eight he would turn the truck around and park it in front of the hotel and attach his taxi sign so it would be clearly visible for pickpocket. Until then being quiet and incognito, was his plan.

It was during one of those quiet incognito moments it happened. A thought came to Duba, a vision, like a mirage that can happen after a body walks through a desert or sits too long in a pickup watching movie posters with a missing radio antenna and two house flies. He was inspired. He bolted into the Lincklaen House and right up to the lobby desk clerk.

"Do you have an envelope for 'Messenger,'" he asked.

The desk clerk in her starched white blouse and collar picked the envelope marked 'Messenger' from a basket labelled 'Important Papers'.

"This note says Messenger will be picking this up at seven o'clock, sir. It's only six o'clock. Are you Messenger, young man?" the lady asked.

"I'm the courier to get it to 'Messenger', Ma'am."

Duba likened Courier was to 'Messenger' as General might be to Sergeant.

She handed him the envelope.

"Thank you, sir," she said.

"Thank you, lady," said Duba.

He was going to wait in his pickup and personally hand the envelope to Sheriff John the very second he drove up? After all, Sheriff John was a busy man.

He climbed back into his pickup and adjusted his rear view mirror and side mirror so he would see the reflection of Sheriff John's vehicle when it turned from Albany Street and pulled in front of the hotel.

A sigh come over him for his stealth and cunning. As reward he reached in the sack beating the two houseflies to half the chicken salad on white. Then half the egg salad sandwich with black olive slices. The bag of Wise potato chips kept his hands busy. The lad believed the noise of their crunch would keep him alert. He washed everything down with one of his two bottles of Nehi orange soda pop, conserving one to go with the other two sandwich halves.

He tried several positions before he settled on resting his head against the back window of his pickup (just as a sharpshooter might rest the muzzle of his rifle on a firm object.) It steadies the hand, or in this case the head. He fixed his eyes on the side mirror pinpointing the exact spot where Sheriff John's car would be driving to behind him.

The efficiency made his leg cramp and him hungry. He ate the rest of the sandwiches, finishing his last Nehi orange soda pop, allowing he could stretch the cramped leg out and up onto the dashboard.

All in all, the Pompey Hollow Book Club had quite a day.

Alice and Marty outdid themselves with performances on the Midway. Alice would have some stories to tell. Mayor and Eddie got the battery charged on the biplane and found Raggedy Ann dolls for Eddie's two little girls up at Sheas. Mr. Ossant, Farmer Parker and Jerry got the horses and wagon up to a hidden campsite and dropped off the maps at the Lincklaen House. The wagon even had an empty trunk in the bed with a padlock on it. They felt pickpocket might think it was filled with counterfeit money. Leaving Jerry at the camp they then drove on to a Future Farmers of America confab in Albany for the afternoon and would return late. Mrs. Parker thought Fay could use a night off so Mayor and Eddie offered to do the milking for him.

Marty found the campsite with time to spare. He and Jerry had wood stacked up, a campfire ablaze and were stirring some eggs and Spam in a skillet, looking for some pepper, an onion and if there was a sack of coffee grounds anywhere.

Holbrook, Randy, Bases and Barber were being dropped off at Myrtie's in New Woodstock by Randy's pap, hair all combed, fingernails clean, waiting as proper houseguests for supper. They had stopped at Shea's store along the way and picked out a nice box of candy for their hostess. Mike Shea marked it down forty cents knowing it was for her.

Myrtie was dashing about her second story flat in New Woodstock tending operator duties in her bedroom, keeping an eye out the window for Sheriff John all while cooking supper in the kitchen.

Duba kept his vigil in the pickup mirror, bound and determined to impress the one man he and Dick had differences of opinions with from time to time, if he'd catch them speeding or drag racing: Sheriff John.

As the evening wore on, Myrtie and the lads enjoyed a bottle of Pepsi, talking about their satisfaction in the team Dick sent to the State Fair. Holbrook and Randy were settin' on Myrtie's side-porch swing wondering whether to split the Almond Joy first or the Mounds bar after supper. Alice was at home soaking in the tub making notes in her diary for a book she may write. She would be along for supper whenever Conway picked her up. Dick and Dwyer were husking corn for Myrtie, feeling confident about the detail they used in luring pickpocket. Good boys as they were deep down, they were giving Marty credit for the detail.

Duba was still sitting in his pickup, beaming.

Superior thinking, along with a glaring setting sun reflected in his eyes rendering him mesmerized. (Looking into that blinding sun his eyes started wriggling and rolling, closing and crossing, then turning - his lids trying to keep up with it all.)

Sheriff John was on his way to pick up his copy of the map. In fact, he was about a block from the hotel. He slowed his car to enjoy the setting sun. It was about the time he was passing the library on Albany Street getting ready to turn that Duba dozed off.

CHAPTER TWENTY

WHO'S ON FIRST?

"Mrs Parker, Mayor and I got the milking done. They're back up in the pasture, and the spreader is loaded for tomorrow. We'll be going down to the plane now to listen for radio signals from Sheriff John in case he needs us."

"It's dusk, Eddie," said Mrs. Parker. "Why don't you boys come in? Let me feed you before you go down there. You'll need your energy tonight. Myrtie's not serving until late."

The two agreed, stepped over to the garden hose by the hen house and freshened up for an early supper.

Ole Charlie here set above the stove watching the pork chops in the skillet. A perfect burnt edge to the fat.

"Eddie, I know you're leaving tomorrow, said Mrs. Parker. "We have something we want you to take to your wife and little girls."

"You and Farmer Parker are way too kind, Mrs. Parker."

"Oh, they're not from us, they're from everyone. We all chipped in. The packages will be here for you to take with you tomorrow, but you have to promise to put them under your Christmas tree and no peeking."

"You have my word," said Eddie.

"And we all know your word is good, Eddie. I wanted you to hear that from me. You've been through a lot in your lifetime, son."

Mrs. Parker handed Eddie a plate of vittles.

"So many boys your age have been places and seen things God didn't mean for anyone to ever see. Try not to think about the bad people who did that to the world. Why, don't even give them the benefit of dwelling on them for minute. Think of all the good people, like you, who put a stop to it. Those boys and girls, men and women risking -and many times giving up - their lives to put an end to it."

"I know. I still have the dreams of our jumping and being shot at - not as many as I used to though."

"Young man, you have a family who cares for you and needs you. I think you know that, but I'm not sure you realize how much you need them."

"What do you mean?"

"When that man took your money, the first thing that came to your mind was how disappointed your family would be with your coming home empty-handed."

"Yes, Ma'am – it surely was."

"But you'd be wrong, Eddie. You'd be so wrong. All they ever want is *you*. You're all that's important to them. I'll even make another wager (and I'm not a betting woman...")

"What's that, Mrs. Parker?"

"I'll wager that a big hug from your wife and your two little girls in your arms would have gone a long way to clearing your head while you were figuring something out for the winter – like helping on a farm or something. There's always work on a farm."

"You're right."

"So turn to them first. They will never let you down."

"Thank you. That's sound advice."

"Get some more potatoes and gravy, hon. Use that spoon."

"Mrs. Parker, I get the feeling you're trying to tell me something you haven't told me yet."

"Look here, Mayor," said Mrs. Parker. "Did you see Eddie suspect something more? I want you to see how inquisitive those boys in WWII were. Just as our Eddie here did. Learn from it, lad. Off at War they watched and listened to everything, never knowing what was in store for them. But never a doubt that their *will* would be done."

"You can tell me, Mrs. Parker. What are you thinking? I can take it."

"Eddie, everyone is going to try their best to get your money back for you tonight."

"I know. Mighty kind of them taking chances like this."

"But what if they don't?"

"Don't get the money back?"

"Yes."

"I never thought of that."

"What if they aren't able to get your money back?"

"Well then, Mrs. Parker, I'll get a night's sleep in the straw loft, get up early and have a nice breakfast, if I'm still invited, that is. I'll thank all my new friends for trying, and then I'll crank up the plane and fly home."

Mrs. Parker had a gentle smile in her eye.

"Why don't you boys take the coffee percolator and our canteen cups to drink from? Bring them back when you come back tonight," said Mrs. Parker.

Eddie and Mayor stepped out and onto the back deck. The moon was full; the stars were sparkling down a shower of budding lifetime friendships.

"Take this kerosene lantern. It'll outlast flashlight batteries," said Mrs. Parker.

She handed Eddie a handful of kitchen matches. She held the glass tub up while Eddie lit it. He and Mayor stepped off, walking across the lawn and down towards the field where the plane was.

"That's a nice lady," said Eddie.

"Do you ever see any of the guys you served with in the War?"

"A few, but we make a point of not talking about it much."

"Us kids used to listen to War news on the radio or watch it on the Newsreels at the picture show. We'd be so jealous we couldn't fight Hitler and the Japs with you guys. But hearing what it was really like the way you tell it is different than listening to it on the radio. You guys are all heroes."

"You know, after a few years of watching the enemy throwing dead naked bodies onto wagons, stacking them up like hay bales, you kind of try to get it all out of your mind."

"At seventeen, too," said Mayor.

"Oh, the Nazis had twelve and thirteen year old kids on the front lines towards the end. They were getting their heads blown off too."

"Eddie, can you teach me how to fly sometime?"

"I'd be happy to, my friend. There's nothing to it. How about I give you a ride up tomorrow, and, if you like it, I'll give you some lessons next year when I come up to the State Fair?"

Mayor beamed. He held the lantern up to look into Eddie's eyes to see if they looked sincere. They did.

It was about then when they both heard electric crackling and popping sounds snapping through the quiet full moonlit night.

"Wait! Listen!" said Eddie.

The two halted past the alfalfa field.

"What is that?" asked Mayor.

The crackling broke through the night again, then a hissing.

"Did we leave the two-way radio on?" asked Eddie.

"I think I did. Charging the battery with the plane running - we turned the plane off but forgot to turn the two-way radio off."

"Run," said Eddie. "I think someone's trying to call in."

Mayor set the percolator and tin cups down by the side of the road. They took the lantern and ran through the field to the plane.

"Keep the lantern back, away from gas fumes," said Eddie.

HISS-POP-SCRATCH

"Sheriff John call…"

HISS… POP…

"Come in Eddie…"

CRACKLE - HISS.

Eddie jumped onto the wing of the plane and stepped into the rear cockpit, grabbing the microphone.

"This is Eddie, come in, Sheriff John…"

No answer.

"This is Eddie, come in, Sheriff John…"

HISS-POP-SCRATCH

No answer.

"We don't have a good connection," barked Eddie. "We won't have a good connection until we're up in the air. It's this hill blocking the signal."

"Are we going up?" yelled Mayor.

"Run up to Farmer Parker's. Use their telephone, and get Myrtie on the wire. See if she knows what Sheriff John wants – ask why he's calling. He should be up there with her. If he is, you can ask him."

"Roger Wilko," shouted Mayor.

Mayor leaped from the plane's wing and ran like all get out grabbing up the lantern along his way.

"And see if Farmer Parker has a leather jacket or heavy coat you can wear. We might have to take her up; it gets mighty cold, especially at night."

Eddie kept clicking the switch on the microphone in case it worked but didn't want to risk wearing out the battery. It wasn't fifteen minutes gone by when Mayor ran back through the field again. He was toting a sheepskin corduroy jacket and a pair of work gloves Mrs. Parker loaned him.

It was then Mary's dad drove up Cardner Road and stopped and dropped her off in front of the field and drove on. Seeing the two standing around the airplane with the lantern, she walks over.

"I delivered my newspapers early and was coming to see who was going to Myrtie's," said Mary. "How can I help you guys?"

"You're a paper-girl?" asked Eddie. "What other surprises are there about Mary Crane?"

"That's about it, when I'm not selling popsicles and drumsticks from my cart summers in Delphi Falls, I'm delivering papers on Berry Road. My dad delivered them for me while we were here helping Farmer Parker. What's up?"

"The sheriff didn't get a map to the camp," yelled Mayor. "He doesn't know where it is."

"I thought it was supposed to be at the hotel waiting for him?" said Mary.

"There's been a foul up, there was no map there for him," said Mayor. "He doesn't know where the camp is. If he can't find the camp he can't make an arrest. Problem is we don't know where it is either."

"I was making salads and deviled eggs with Mrs. Parker when they left," said Mary. "Mr. Ossant was driving his car, and following Farmer Parker and Jerry driving the horses and wagon. It was a great looking wagon. It looked real. They never mentioned where they were taking it."

Eddie jumped off the wing.

"Mayor, did Sheriff say anything else? Did he give you any ideas, any clues?"

"Yes!" said Mayor. "He said to see if you could try to find the camp with the biplane and maybe radio its location into him."

Eddie took off his leather flight jacket and handed it to Mary.

"Here, put this on. You'll need it. When I tell you, jump into the front cockpit, both of you. We're going to go up and find us a campsite," shouted Eddie.

Grinning from both sides of the cockpit, Mayor and Mary started to climb on the wings.

"Have to move the chocks away from the wheels," yelled Eddie. "I'll do it."

"Do you have to crank the propeller?" asked Mayor.

"Yep, then I pull the chocks."

By this time Mary was standing on the wing leaning in over the side of the front cockpit.

"Grab the flashlight, Mayor," said Eddie. "Neither of you touch anything unless I tell you, understood?"

"I understand," said Mayor. "This is so great."

"I'm not touching anything," said Mary.

"Find my leather helmet and earphones. Take them into the front cockpit with you both. Look around; they'll be in the back cockpit somewhere, probably on the seat. Take the goggles off them and give those to Mary. She'll need goggles. Mayor you wear the helmet and earphones. Then crawl into the front cockpit - both of you."

Mayor grabbed the apparatus, did what he was told. Mary pulled the goggles on over her eyes. She took them off and tightened the straps and put them on again tucking her hair back.

This was when Eddie stepped up on the wing to check some gauges. He paused to gather his thoughts. Mayor flicked the flashlight on and was inspecting the front cockpit where he and Mary were to sit, places they might be able to grab on to and all. The radio kept hissing.

"Are you both ready?"

"We're ready!" said Mary.

CHAPTER TWENTY ONE

FINDING THE CAMP

"Stop! Wait a minute. Hold everything," shouted Eddie stepping off the wing and backing away from the airplane.

"You two jump down here for a second - both of you. Come on!"

"What did we do wrong?" asked Mayor.

"Oh, it's not you, it's me!" said Eddie. "Get out. We need a plan. I've got to give you guys a heads up."

Mayor and Mary crawled out of the front cockpit and jumped to the ground. Mary lifted the goggles from her eyes and strapped them on top of her head. Mayor was still in his helmet holding the wire attachment to the earphones.

"Here's the deal," said Eddie. "I'm used to my co-pilots and guys I fly or jump with having been trained. I either need to train you two quick or go alone. We'll get nowhere fast and waste everybody's time if I don't give you some training. Ready?"

Mayor stood at full attention and saluted Eddie.

"I'm ready, sir."

"I'm ready," said Mary.

"Alright. When we get up there it'll be dark and we won't be able to hear each other well. If there's no radio systems between us, flyers use hand signals. Let me show you. Put your hands together and point them up like this."

Eddie held both hands together high above his head straight up.

"This is called twelve o'clock. Just like a clock – twelve o'clock high – up here - means to look up or fly straight up or straight forward. Twelve o'clock low – or down here - is when you point in the opposite direction – to descend or go down. Can you do that?"

Both made the twelve o'clock low signal.

"You're doing it right," now this is what three o'clock looks like; and here's nine o'clock..."

Carefully and patiently Eddie demonstrated to Mayor and Mary how to signal him from the front cockpit to indicate which direction he should fly the plane.

"Won't we do everything backwards if we're looking ahead and you're behind us?" asked Mayor.

"Good thinking but you won't be doing it, Mayor. Mary will be in front of you directing me where I fly. You're going to be behind her on the radio talking with Sheriff John telling him whatever she tells you. I want you to know how to do it."

Mayor beamed.

"Okay, you both have that down. Mary, have you ever heard about coordinates?"

"Coordinates? If it's not about skirts and blouses, I don't think so," said Mary.

"Okay. I know it's dark, but take a look over there. See the coffee percolator setting on the side of the road?"

"Yes."

"Now take a look at that pine tree up there about thirty feet."

"I can see it.

"Now draw a line in your mind from the percolator to the pine tree. Let me know when you can imagine it."

"Okay."

"So, using that line, where is the plane?"

"The line from the pine tree to the percolator goes right through the airplane."

"That's right, so that would be our east-west coordinate for where the plane is."

"I get it," barked Mary. "So, if we find the north and south co-ordinates for the same plane, we can pinpoint on a map exactly where it is sitting. Am I right?"

"You've got it exactly right, Mary."

"Now what?" asked Mayor.

We'll get her in the air. I'll fly low, maybe fifteen hundred, two thousand feet. You two know the area – this part of the Crown. There are a lot of woods around here. Mary you're gonna' steer the plane."

"Huh? No way! I don't know how to use that stick," said Mary.

"Not the joystick. Put all the seat cushions on the floor in the front cockpit and kneel on them so you're up a ways taller than the front windscreen. You give me the clock signals. You will be telling me where to fly – which way to turn. I'll fly the plane. You take me any which way you want me to go until we find a campfire with a wagon."

"I got it. I can do that."

"Okay, turn around and show me a bank right signal," said Eddie.

Mary gave the signal for three o'clock.

"Now, a bank left."

Mary showed the signal for nine o'clock.

"Whenever you tell me to bank, Mary, make sure to grab and hold on to the windscreen so you don't fall out."

Over and over they practised the arm signals.

"I know you can do it. Remember we won't be able to hear each other up there most likely. Once we find it – their campfire - give me the twelve o'clock high or wave signal or something - then we'll circle to confirm it. If we confirm it's the camp, we'll bank right and go find some coordinates to it, east and west, north and south. You shout them to Mayor and Mayor will radio those to Sheriff John. The sheriff can plot them on a map and know exactly where the camp is."

"Mayor, you know this area better than I do," said Mary. "At first I'm thinking we can start in big circles and then close in until we see the campfire. What do you think?"

"I rode horses with Jerry in these woods. I think we should start heading down Pompey Hollow Road," said Mayor.

"Why so far?" asked Mary.

"I'm guessing the camp will be in the woods east of that somewhere," said Mayor. "I don't think they'll have taken the wagon past Cherry Valley."

"Not around here?" asked Mary.

"The hills here are too steep around the falls. The horses couldn't get the wagon up these hills or cliffs into the woods."

"Oh, right," said Mary.

"You two figure it out. We can cover a lot of ground. You'll just have to show me where you want me to fly," said Eddie.

"After we find them we find the crosshairs – the coordinates," said Mary.

"Exactly," said Eddie. "You ready to take her up, Mayor?"

"I'm ready sir," Mayor snapped a salute.

"Me too," said Mary.

"Where do I sit again?" asked Mayor.

"Sit on the seat in the front cockpit, on the seat – crosslegged so Mary has room in front of you. Gather all the seat cushions and give them to Mary to kneel on the floor in front of you. We need her to be able to see over the front windscreen."

Eddie wet his finger with his mouth and held it in the air to see which direction the wind was blowing. Planes took off better flying into the wind.

"It looks like we'll be taking off from the other end of this field. The ride down there will give us a feel of it – how smooth or bumpy it is. Blow it out and bring the lantern with us, Mayor, and we'll leave her lit down there."

"Why?" asked Mayor.

"We'll be flying blind in the dark. We'll need the light from the lantern to help us come back and land. It'll help us find where the end of the runway is."

Mayor blew out the lantern.

"Climb into the front cockpit, get settled, Mayor. Mary, you get your cushions set. Lean forward into the front windshield. Hang on to it when you have to. The goggles will let you see in the wind without having to squint."

"How come you fly it from the rear cockpit, Eddie?" asked Mayor.

"A Bi-Plane is a tail-dragger. It sets on the ground, nose high. The pilot always sits in the back for a reason. This plane is flown by the seat of the pants. Back there I can feel the slightest change in the plane in flight. Best view of the wings and horizon too. Helps keep it level."

While the wheels were chocked, Eddie reached up and turned the propeller slowly through all cylinders to prime each with fresh fuel. He would turn it and pause. Turn it again and pause. He stepped up on the wing, reached in and turned the magnetos to the right and left and then climbed down again.

"You sure we can take off in this hay field?" asked Mayor.

"Big wheels, she's at ease in a hayfield, if there're no woodchuck holes. No worries."

Mayor beamed, got comfortable in the front cockpit. Mary adjusted her goggles and took a look down the field under the full moon.

"Fasten your helmet and earphones," shouted Eddie.

Mayor obliged and strapped the helmet to his chin – earphones on.

This time Eddie grabbed the prop with force, flat- handed, giving her a hard downward pull. The second time he tried - she fired up, coughed and spit smoke. He pulled the chocks from in front of the tires and climbed up into the back cockpit turning the magnetos to the right.

"Hand me the cord attached to the microphone on your helmet," shouted Eddie.

"What for?" barked Mayor.

"You're going to be calling and telling Sheriff John the coordinates when Mary finds them. You'd need your hands with the mic. When I plug this in to the RCA you won't need your hands to run the hand microphone."

"This is so good!" shivered Mayor with a grin.

Mary got secure kneeling on the cushions – her head above the windscreen and touching the bottom of the upper wing.

Eddie plugged the jack from Mayor's earphones and microphone into the two-way.

"Yikes," shouted Mayor. "That popped sharp in my ears."

"Well, that means your live now, buddy, better watch your language. You got ears all over the county listening in. Well crew, what's say we go flying and try to find us a campfire?"

"Roger Wilko," barked Mayor.

Mary gave a thumbs- up.

Eddie eased the throttle forward to get her moving. The propeller sliced through the air with a roar, the big tires rocking the plane gently forward. Mary's hair was flying straight back with the prop wind.

"When we get to the end of the field, you jump out, Mayor, and light the lantern. Leave it about twenty feet from the end of the field. We'll use that as a landing spot when we come back," Eddie shouted.

Mayor indicated a thumbs-up.

The plane rolled down the length of the field. The full moon lighted some of the way not darkened by tree shade. When it reached the end, Eddie touched the stick and the plane turned near full circle now facing back the other way, awaiting take-off. Mayor started to climb out of his cockpit with the unlit lantern.

"Stay put, Mayor. Second thoughts! I don't want you walking into the prop. It's easy to do if you don't know the plane - too dangerous. You both sit still; I'll put the lantern out there."

Eddie climbed out and stepped down on the field. The plane was rolling slowly. He quickly pulled shorn hay stalks from the ground down to dirt so the lantern could be stable and wouldn't get blown over by wind causing a fire. He lit the lantern setting it firmly in the space he cleared and crawled back on the wing and into his cockpit. He circled back around to just over the lantern.

"Here we go!" he yelled. "We're flying on your signals from here on out, Mary."

FULL POWER! Pointed straight down the hay lot runway, Eddie eased forward on the stick. Mayor was pushed back in his seat with the pressure. Mary was hugging the windscreen. The tail lifted off the ground levelling the plane on two wheels...gaining speed. Eddie eased back on the stick lowering the wing flaps, thirty miles per hour, forty miles per hour, fifty, sixty, and off they lifted. It floated up weightless.

Mayor's heart bounced like a somersault.

Mary grabbed the windshield and grinned. It was almost like she could reach out and touch treetops. Up, up, over the tip of the trees next to the bridge – over the creek. The plane climbed up higher over Farmer Parker's side pasture hill. Above trees, in the moonlight they saw the reflections of the white and black cows scattered around the top of the pasture. Mary could see Buddy's gravestone. As the plane rose into the sky lights below as far as Delphi Falls and Gooseville corners sparkled like stars. The full moon seemed to have rested on the wing of the plane almost within reach.

Mayor gripped the side of the cockpit with his elbow, taking it all in as if he was on a magic carpet. He leaned over and watched sights he had only dreamed about. The engine whined and roared.

Still climbing, Eddie leaned forward, reached up and tapped Mayor on the shoulder.

"Call Sheriff John now and let him know we're up and looking. Tell him we'll report in when we find something."

"How do I do that?" shouted Mayor.

"Touch the button on your mic when you want to talk. It's on your helmet. Release it to listen. You'll hear everything through your earphones."

"This is Mayor. This is Mayor, Mary Crane and Flying Eddie. Come in, Sheriff John."

With a scratch and hiss –

"Read you loud and clear. Come in, Mayor. This is Sheriff John."

Mayor about had a heart attack. But it weren't long before he got the hang of it all and the confidence along with it that he needed to help get the job done.

The moon shined off the propeller blades like icicles cutting through the sky. The whine of the engine was steady, the pistons sparking like a snare drum leading a parade.

Mary looked through the spinning prop and thought of Amelia Earhart flying alone across the Atlantic in 1928.

"Sheriff John, we are air born," shouted Mayor. "I'll give you coordinates to where the campfire is when we find it. Over."

"We'll wait - over," scratched Sheriff John through the ear-phones. "Be careful."

Mary looked over the side for a landmark she would recognize.

There it was, Pompey Hollow Road.

She decided to take Mayor's advice. The area was the most wooded to the east of it. If that didn't work she would have the plane circle around and look over the second falls at Big Mike's place. She signalled ten o'clock, grabbed the windscreen and Eddie obliged, banking the plane a slight left.

"Hang on!" yelled Eddie.

The plane would first tilt and then angle weightless in the sky.

Once over the road, Mary signalled twelve o'clock level. The plane rolled back and over the middle of the Pompey Hollow Road they flew, two thousand feet up. It was just past spinster Nettie's when Mary thought she saw a glow off to the right and down. She turned her head around and got Eddie's attention by pointing down to the glow of a fire. Eddie nodded he could see.

"Hang on!"

He banked the plane into a slight dive to go take a closer look. Sure enough it was a campfire.

Ole Charlie here couldn't have been prouder.

Eddie circled around twice to be certain it was Marty's camp. There it surely was, a campfire, a wagon and two horses looking a bit nervous with the sounds overhead. Eddie banked back out and waited for Mary's next signal to start finding coordinates.

"This is Mayor calling Sheriff John. Mayor calling Sheriff John - come in please."

"Sheriff John, here. Come back."

"We've found the camp, Sheriff John. Spread out a map and I'll send coordinates for you to rule in."

"Roger and over."

There were scratching noises in Mayor's ears.

Mary signalled three o'clock and the plane banked to the right. More comfortable with the motion she leaned with the plane like it was a flying bicycle. She then pointed twelve o'clock forward and it levelled off. As soon as she could make out a farm and silo below she turned her head and shouted.

"Mayor, whose farm is that? That one down there."

"Barbers'," he shouted.

Mary signalled that their barn would be the first coordinate. She then signalled to Eddie to fly straight from the farm back up over the campfire and then to keep going up the tall hill.

"Come in, Sheriff John. Come in Sheriff John."

"Come in, Mayor."

"First coordinate is Barber's farm. Come back."

"Roger that. Barbers' farm."

The engine roared as they flew, climbing up the steeply graded hill over heavy, tall, wooded areas…passing over the camp fire until over the top of the hill they were coming into the lights of Cazenovia sparkling under a full moon. Mary signalled back to Eddie he could turn around.

"Hang on!" Eddie shouted.

The plane banked into a turn.

"Brae Loch Inn," Mary shouted back to Mayor.

He gave her a thumbs-up, hearing her.

"Sheriff John, this is Mayor."

"Come in, Mayor - Sheriff John here."

"Barber's farm up to the Brae Loch Inn is the first coordinate, Sheriff John."

"Roger that, Mayor. Barbers' farm and Brae Loch Inn. Over."

As the plane banked around right Mary signalled and pointed the plane over to and around the second falls at Big Mike's. The waterfalls glistened under the moon. Looking down at the falls, Mary got her bearings and signalled another bank toward the campfire - looking straight down for another landmark. Sighting one she turned her head toward Mayor and pointed down.

Mayor nodded and pushed the button on his mic.

"This is Mayor, Mary Crane, and Flying Eddie. Come in, Sheriff John."

"Sheriff John here - come back."

"Burlingame Road and the Cobb Hill Road connection, Sheriff John. Do you read me?"

"Corner of Burlingame Road and Cobb Hill Road. Have it. I read you loud and clear. Come back."

Mary gave a thumbs-up and pointed the plane straight towards and over the campfire glow again. Soon after it she reached a final coordinate – one she recognized. She pointed down at it getting Mayor's attention.

"Sheriff John. The crossing of Oran Delphi and Cherry Valley. Do you read me? The crossing of Oran Delphi and Cherry Valley!"

"Read you loud and clear. Burlingame Road and Cobb Hill Road over to Oran Delphi and Cherry Valley. We know exactly where the camp is now. Good job all of you. Fly safe. Sheriff John signing off. Over and out."

Mary signalled Eddie to bank a left and turn up the Oran Delphi heading for Delphi Falls, and then the hayfield back home.

"Hang on!" shouted Eddie. "We're going home."

The moon's reflection rested on the screen visor. Mary had a contented smile on her face looking up at the bright stars, her hair flowing behind her. A job well done.

Mayor rubbed his hands together briskly to warm them in the cold night air. He thought of the boys in the War who flew planes in the dark over Germany. He thought of the paratroopers like Eddie who jumped from high in the night into enemy gunfire. He looked up at the heavens enjoying this adventure of a lifetime while Eddie watched Mary for a signal…that below was the lantern in the distance.

Eddie was shivering in the cold – but warmed by the thought of getting his money back and flying back to Binghamton and his family. He steadied the stick between his knees, briskly rubbed his hands together and looked up at the full moon feeling the wind on his face. He thought of missing his wife and girls and seeing them tomorrow. Mary turned around, caught his eye and gave him a thumbs-up.

He looked down next to his seat, looked back up at Mary, and with two hands near his mouth shouted:

"Mary, is there a lake near here?"

"A lake?" she shouted back. "Water?"

"Yes," Eddie nodded his head yes.

Mary gave the twelve o'clock sign to fly straight and follow Oran Delphi Road to the water. A mile or so past Gooseville Corners would be DeRuyter Lake – a fishing and swimming reservoir popular in the summer.

As the moon glistened from the still water of the lake, Eddie banked the plane left and circled the lake bringing it down to about a thousand feet.

"What are you doing?" shouted Mary.

Mayor looked around, eyes as big as quarters wondering what was going on as well.

"This!" shouted Eddie.

He held the unopened bottle of whiskey he had next to his seat in the air. As the plane glided over the middle of the lake he threw the bottle over.

"Won't need that anymore," he shouted as the bottle hurled down and splashed into the middle of the lake.

Mary grinned and gave him a thumbs-up.

"Proud of you, Eddie!" she shouted.

"Well, turn around, Mary, and find us that lantern at the end of that field," shouted Eddie. "So we can land this thing."

Mary turned to the front and pointed to one o'clock and hung onto the windscreen for a bank right.

CHAPTER TWENTY TWO
THE JIG IS UP

Young'uns' can be angels when they're sleeping.

Duba was just that. Conked out the way he was. He'd been in a deep sleep like he finished a good book ever since sunset. His jowl pressed up against the side window of his pickup – his lower lip wrigglin' with each breath he took. A fog would cloud the window over his nostrils with every exhale.

Pickpocket rapped his knuckles on the window. Duba startled and about sprained his neck waking up.

"Are you for hire?" asked pickpocket in a loud enough tone to be heard through the window.

Duba rose to the occasion, sitting up with a, "Huh?"

"I noticed the taxi sign in the back of your truck, mate. Are you for hire at this hour?"

"For hire?" mumbled Duba, wiping drool from his chin.

"I need a lift," said pickpocket.

"Sure, - for hire – that's right - for hire - jump in," snorted Duba – shaking his sleep off.

Pickpocket stepped around in front of the pickup carrying a large satchel as Duba pulled the headlights on. Carnation, beret and all, the scoundrel made it around to the passenger side door when Duba realized he still had Sheriff John's copy of the map in his hand. A dead giveaway, if pickpocket ever saw it. He bolted - crumpled it up and stuck it down the front of his pants as the door opened.

"You can put the bag in the back, if you want, it won't go anywhere."

"I'd rather keep it with me, if is all the same to you, Gov."

"No matter to me."

Duba realized it was probably filled with money.

"Thank you."

Pickpocket climbed in and rested the satchel on the floor between his legs. Duba started the truck and put it in gear ready to back into the Lincklean House drive, to turn around.

"It won't take long, fella," said Duba. "You'll be there in no time at all."

"Be there? Be where? My good man, won't you need to know where I might be going first?"

"Well ah - yes, ah ya, I meant to say when you tell me where you need to go, after that, I'll get you there. Fast – ya' see. I mean..."

Duba shook his head, stretched his eyelids rolling his eyes in circles and slapped on his cheek to wake up.

"I have a map of instructions," said pickpocket. "I can't quite make it out. If you know the area you might be able to read it."

Duba stepped on the brake in the middle of the driveway and took Pickpocket's map from the envelope and unfolded it. He did best he could to look as if he was studying it. He held it up close to his eyes examining the paper, its authenticity. Lad was overacting now that he almost blew his cover before, as might be said.

"See that X there? Right here on the map. See it? I know where that spot is," said Duba. "It's a popular campsite for people traveling through. Apple farms all about it."

The pickup finished backing into the Lincklaen House driveway to turn around and head to Albany Street.

This is when Duba began his small talk.

"In town on business, are ya?"

Pickpocket didn't answer.

Actually Duba was a bundle of nerves knowing he had failed to get the map to Sheriff John – having slept through it all after four sandwiches, a bag of Wise potato chips, two Nehi orange pops and a setting sun.

"What time is it anyway?" asked Duba.

Pickpocket pulled a pocket watch from his vest pocket and held it up to the dashboard to read.

"It's eight o'clock," said pickpocket.

"Right on time," mumbled Duba.

"Pardon me? What did you mean – "right on time?" We're you expecting me?"

"Huh?" grunted Duba. "Right – what did you say..." on time?" No - I said right - on Albany Street – then left down at the end... "right" was for Albany Street..."

"I beg your pardon, Gov. It's been a long day and I've been hearing things lately."

"In town on business, are you?" asked Duba – beads of perspiration gathering on his forehead.

"I'm with a traveling troupe of theatre players. I play Sherlock Holmes in The Final Adventure. It's a stage play. Are you a Doyle or Sherlock Holmes fan, I have tickets if you are."

"Oh, I've read a Sherlock Holmes book once – about the dogs..."

"The Hound of the Baskervilles, it's a marvellous intrigue," said pickpocket.

"I liked it," said Duba. "Lots of dogs and stuff. I liked him – that Sherlock Holmes guy and his doctor friend."

"Doctor Watson. Indeed, yes."

Still waking up, Duba was dazed but somehow star struck.

"So you're thee Sherlock Holmes?"

"At your service," snapped Sherlock Holmes.

The pickup turned right on Cherry Valley and started the steep climb to the top and then down twice as far towards the Pompey Hollow Road turnoff.

"Lots of fog in England, is there?" asked Duba.

"We're surrounded by water, ya' see," said Sherlock Holmes.

"Like Long Island, I guess," said Duba.

Sherlock Holmes looked over, puzzled, trying to make the connection of Long Island and England.

"That's where our potatoes come from mostly," said Duba.

"I see," said Sherlock Holmes.

Sherlock did a double take.

"Oh, I see now – it's an island, like Great Britain. I get your point."

About this time Duba was slowing down to turn left on Pompey Hollow Road.

Completely at a loss for what to do (thinking Sheriff John was in the dark about where the camp was) - Duba tried to invent some solutions on his own.

"Do you want me to wait?"

"Yes, please," said Sherlock Holmes. "It shouldn't be long. Would you mind terribly?"

Duba slowed down before spinster Nettie's house and cautiously turned in on the dirt path that would lead back to Marty's camp. He was about fifty yards in when they could hear the low gravelled whinny of the horses. Another fifty yards and they could see the glow of a fire lighting up the canvas covered wagon.

Ole Charlie here rose up and rested on a maple tree branch over the wagon, behind the camp fire to watch over my flock.

The horses were tied up to the right of the wagon and Marty and Jerry were sitting by the campfire staring into it – cool as cucumbers - pretending to make no notice of Duba's pickup driving in. The truck pulled to a stop. The headlights turned off. Duba sat in the truck sweating the worst while Sherlock Holmes stepped out carrying his satchel. He walked towards the campfire.

"Lovely night," said Sherlock Holmes.

"It surely is," mumbled Marty holding his coffee tin with both hands for warmth.

Marty and Jerry sat there sipping coffee, looking at the fire. Jerry pretending he liked the taste.

"I'm here to do business," said Sherlock Holmes.

"Need some water, do you?" asked Marty.

"No water, I'm here….."

"What are you doing here, then? Sorry, we don't have enough food cooked to share," blurted Marty. "We pretty much ate it all."

"Thank you, no – I ate with the troupe earlier?"

"Troop?" You a soldier, are ya?"

"Oh my, no, it's an acting troupe. Easy enough mistake. I'm Sherlock Holmes, don't ya' see, in town New Woodstock tomorrow."

"Sherlock Holmes, eh," said Marty. "So why are you here in the woods, Sherlock?"

"I don't quite understand," said Sherlock. "I brought my money to exchange for your counterfeit, just as we said."

"Don't know what you're talking about. I find water for people – a séance now and then if need be."

Sitting there listening to this bantering, Jerry was about to have a heart attack. He bit on his lip.

"Oh, right," said Sherlock. "I get it now - Séance. The lady gave me the clue. I'm supposed to say I'm here for the Séance."

"Could have saved a lot of time," said Marty. "How much did you bring?"

Sherlock opened his satchel and tipped it so Marty and Jerry could look inside. It had a pile of wallets and loose cash.

Relieved that he finally connected, Sherlock stood up, patted the palm of his hand on his chest, took a deep breath and sighed.

"Oh my, I brought enough, I'm sure. I believe we were talking one thousand American for five thousand of yours."

"None of my business, but where's a guy like you get all those wallets and all that money? Not that I care."

"Lots of folk daydreaming about the fair's Midway distractions, not paying attention to business. Carnivals are ripe too. I pay attention to my business a little better," smirked Sherlock.

"…and your business is?" asked Marty.

"Oh, I'm an actor by trade, but its thin pickings, acting is, mate. Lifting a pocket or two pays the lights, shall we say?"

"You mean stealing," said Marty.

"I like to call it removing blokes from the temptations of sin. You know those horrific sideshows – naked trollops – and such. The buggers may go home broke but they can go home to the Mrs. with clear consciences."

"Pretty smart. Most people, even thieves work to earn their money to buy my product. You got no cost or sweat in your money at all, stealing it to begin with."

"So we can do business, mate?"

"Your counterfeit money is in the back of the wagon. It's a package wrapped with twine in the big trunk. The lock's open. Count it carefully. Make sure it's all there, and you're happy. I don't make refunds. Pay me after you count it."

"Should I leave my satchel with you?"

"No, take it with you. I don't want to take chances of anyone seeing all those wallets. 'Sides, you ain't going to run off anywhere until I get my money," said Marty. "We know the woods better."

Sherlock looked at Marty, then over at Duba sitting behind the wheel of the truck.

"You mean he's?..." asked Sherlock.

"Yep. He works for me," said Marty. "Now go count your money. Make sure it's five thousand and you're happy. Then come back and pay me the thousand you owe me."

Sherlock Holmes smiled at the well thought through organization Marty had. It actually gave him confidence that Marty was on the level, and that his counterfeit bills would be high quality. He saluted, tipping his brow, took two steps back and turned looking at the horses munching the broken hay bales. He found his way around to the back side of the wagon and lifted the canvas tarp curtain.

Just then a flashlight beamed in his face startling him.

"Don't move and put your hands up, Mr. Sherlock Holmes!" barked Sheriff John from inside the wagon. "You're under arrest! Put both hands in the air, now."

He was pointing his pistol at pickpocket.

With the crook's arms raised in the air, Sheriff John crawled to the back end of the wagon, stepped down and whistled.

Out from behind trees and other hiding places in the woods came Holbrook, Randy, Dick, Minneapolis Moline Conway, and Dwyer. Alice was sitting in Conway's car.

Sheriff John handcuffed Sherlock and walked him around to the campfire.

"It's not a fair cop, Gov," barked Sherlock. "You can't arrest me for buying counterfeit. No money exchanged hands. I'll get a solicitor."

"I'm not arresting you for counterfeiting. I'm arresting you for theft. You're a pickpocket – we can prove that. You just admitted it. I heard the whole thing from the wagon. That's the same as a confession and that's grand larceny."

"None of those wallets will have more than a few dollars. That's not grand larceny, Gov. You'll never get me on grand larceny for a couple of quid," snarled Sherlock.

"Maybe only a few dollars in each of those wallets, but honest and hard-earned dollars, and they'll all have names in them – the owner's names. Why some of those wallets are heirlooms, I have a feeling. All they have to do is press charges."

Sheriff John opened the pickpocket's satchel. He lifted out a manila envelope and tore it open.

"Hmmm – looks like six hundred and forty dollars in this envelope alone. Unless you have a good reason for this six hundred and forty dollars, this makes it grand larceny."

"That's my money, Gov. Ahhh…er…it's the ticket money for the Sherlock Holmes Players performance tomorrow. Everything in that envelope was my money.

Sheriff reached deeper into the same manila envelope and lifted out a smaller envelope that was sealed inside.

"Well look what we have here. These are torn coupon ticket receipts for airplane rides," said Sheriff John. "Looks like a few dozen of them. Doesn't say anything about any Sherlock Holmes' play on them. I'm supposing you can show me where you park your airplane for plane rides, can you?"

Sherlock dropped his head in defeat.

Ole Charlie here was so proud of the flock!

It was a few minutes when Barber drove Sheriff John's car into the open. Three other cars came out of the woods to the campfire. Sheriff John walked pickpocket over to his car.

"After you, Sherlock…" he said, locking the crook in the back seat. "…and watch your head."

He was about to take the scoundrel to a lockup.

As he was putting the evidence (the satchel) into his trunk he paused. He walked over to Marty.

"Marty, I believe this manila envelope – money and coupons - belong to Eddie. No need to do paperwork – the proof's pretty strong it's all his. See to it he gets it, will you?"

"Sure will, Sheriff John. I'll be more than happy to."

"And thank everybody for everything. You all were very good at pulling this off. Oh, and thank Eddie, Mayor and Mary for getting the coordinates to me at the last minute like they did. We'd have been lost without them."

"What do you mean? Didn't you get the map I left?"

"It wasn't there," said Sheriff John.

Duba walked up carrying his handmade 'taxi' sign.

Lifting the harnesses, Marty looked over at Duba as Dick stepped in to help.

"I wonder what ever happened to Sheriff John's map – the one he needed to find the camp," said Dick.

Duba swallowed a gulp and threw the taxi sign into the campfire setting it ablaze.

"Beats me," said Duba, "I'll have to ask around – up at the hotel."

With that Duba turned his back to everyone, pulled the crumpled envelope and map from the front of his pants and dropped them on the fire, blocking their view until they were ablaze. The lad wasn't one to keep secrets from Dick, but now was not the time. It would be too complicated to tell in one sitting.

Marty hitched up the horses. He and Jerry doused the campfire with coffee, a jug of water, some dirt and climbed on the wagon. Following Minneapolis Moline Conway's taillights they drove the team out of the woods, left onto Pompey Hollow Road and back towards Farmer Parker's farm.

"Sheriff John," said Dick. "Pickpocket has three hundred of Big Mike's and Mike Shea's money. Doc Webb's too. Can we get it?"

"They'll get it back. I have some paperwork to fill out, but they'll get it all back. Did you mark the bills like you did for the store burglars?"

"We were afraid to," said Dick. If we got him thinking it was counterfeit, he might have inspected the bills close up and seen a mark."

"That was smart," said Sheriff John.

"What if there's a reward?" asked Holbrook.

"The Pompey Hollow Book Club will get it, of course," said Sheriff John.

In single file each car made their way through the winding dirt road around trees and out of the woods slowly down to Pompey Hollow Road following the horses and wagon up ahead. No one was in any particular hurry. It was a parade of cars, everyone with windows open – laughing and cheering and singing. There were lots of smiles glowing in the moonlight celebrating another victory for the Pompey Hollow Book Club.

CHAPTER TWENTY THREE

SIGN FROM ABOVE

This was about when the moonstruck happened - first time ever, for ole Charlie here.

I had decided to stay and sit a spell on the maple branch over Marty's camp. The fire was out but I had the full moon to reflect on. I wanted time to reflect – angels do that sort of thing - count our blessin's as be said.

Sheriff John drove out of the camp and turned right down Pompey Hollow Road. He was on his way to locking up the young lad overnight in Cazenovia...moving him to county jail next day to wait for a judge. Unfortunate as it was for the nefarious actor scoundrel, his undoing was at the cost of a perfect performance for my flock under the glow of this moon. It made me as proud as an orange-red sunset of an Indian summer.

It was when Sheriff John was making his turn onto Cherry Valley that I first saw it...

...the full moon flickered twice.

Can you imagine?

Not just a blink, mind you, the whole moon – turnin' on and off like a kitchen light bulb. It sure enough flickered full out, twice.

So you won't be in the dark, you should know the only body that could see a flickering of the moon like that aren't bodies at all – they're Guardian Angels…

…but to be clear, not every Guardian Angel can see the flickering, neither.

Moon flickering is calling a special Angel Congress, sure enough, but only for the angels who could see it. That'd be me tonight, no telling who else. It was signalling an Angel Congress on top of Big Mike's barn garage roof.

Oh, I've called Angel Congresses before but callers don't see the flicker. Beings this was my first time ever, my being called to one - I thought I'd pause, savor the moment, taking it all in.

Those above had a different timetable, it appeared.

It was about when I made the 'savor and take it all in' decision that a third flicker happened, and I somehow almost magically appeared on top of Big Mike's barn garage that quick.

"You have a valiant flock, Charlie" said Angel Arnold. "Teddy Roosevelt would be proud. I'll let your pap know you're doing well."

"I appreciate that, Arnold. Tell him I think about him. I'm just gettin' the hang of this whole angel thing. Do you know what this Congress is about…

…and why aren't there any angels here ceptin' you and me?"

"Not me for long, neither, Charlie. They moon-blinked me in, asked my opinions. I said my piece, and they excused me. I stayed to say good-bye to you. You're important to us tonight, my friend. Someone had a notion they should pick you to help save a soul. I seconded their notion."

"Who had the notion?"

"Why don't you go to the other side of the roof and see for yourself? God speed, my friend."

With that Angel Arnold disappeared.

Floating up the front side of the roof, I could see across the way - the horses and wagon, the cars one by one pulling into Farmer Parkers. About to be celebrating with Eddie. They deserved to have a good time. By the looks of all the lights on in the house, it glowed like Christmas candles. I reckoned Mrs. Parker would have some hot chocolate and a late night breakfast for some happy souls.

On the other side of the roof it was darker, damp, with the moon to our backs. The white rock high on the cliff across the creek seemed to reflect a glow.

He was sitting there all prim and proper studying his pocket watch glass off a beam of the moon. Waiting for me was none other than Sir Arthur Conan Doyle. My mentor on subjects once foreign to me – now my friend in these few days I've gotten to know him here in the Crown. I couldn't believe an angel of his stature and renown was actually asking for ole Charlie.

As a courtesy I waited for him to speak first.

He caught my eye. Then he looked at the white rock up on the cliff across the creek aglow under the moon.

"The lad's name is Dudley Smythe. He was born on Bond Street in London, not all that far from me; a decent, respectable, proper family.

Seems young Dudley had just turned fifteen, when he, his sister, mother, and father all took cover in a 1942 blackout. The sirens were wailing. They hurried down to the basement under their three-story London flat when the German U2 bombs dropped from the sky and destroyed his family home, shattering two adjacent homes and a school just across the park. The house foundation dislodged, and a falling wooden beam timber killed his parents instantly. His sister lost her left arm from a tetanus infection she got cutting herself on a metal piece of shrapnel she fell onto in the basement."

I was stunned.

Sir Doyle continued.

"Times were not easy in London all throughout the War. Orphaned, Dudley and his sister were separated and shuffled about from home to home. Food was scarce. The boy loved to read, but he was belligerent, incorrigible, kept running away whenever he could. He became a roustabout, picking up odd jobs, quitting school, stealing books, sleeping in alleys and parks. He's never come to grips with losing his parents the way he did. He won't forgive anyone for his sister, as he sarcastically puts it, "losing her wedding ring finger to a trash barrel."

"Above wants you to be his Guardian Angel now, don't they, Sir Doyle? I have that feeling."

"I will be the very second you take me to him, Charlie. He appeared in your kingdom first – how do you put it, the Crown? Above has given you the power to transition him to me."

Now it's not like ole Charlie here to get all persnickety like I was about to, but I felt I had to hold my ground.

"I'm humbled, Sir. I'll gladly do it but I have a condition, if I might."

"'Condition', Charlie? Are you in any position to…

… what might the 'condition' be, my friend?"

"That you be the guardian angel for his sister too, is all. I don't know where she is nor what's her state, but the poor girl, needs you as well, I'm thinking."

Sir Doyle smiled at me.

He looked up at the glowing white rock on the cliff across the creek. That's when I looked up. Mysteriously it flickered from its bright reflection of the moon to black, twice. That was a sign. Above approved Sir Doyle being the sister's guardian angel as well.

Doyle tightened his lips and looked down pensively.

"It was a magician doing card tricks on the streets of London that found him. Young Dudley would stand beside his sidewalk table, watch his every move. He could always tell which card the pea was under. The magician took the lad under his wing. Oh a scoundrel he was! He taught young Dudley how to lift pockets with the best of them. He gave him books to keep him happy, tailor-clothed him to look the part of a gentleman, and gave him a bed, and one meal a day. When the lad was to his liking he put him on the better streets of London from dawn until sunset to line his own pockets with Dudley's daily take. Oh, he'd slap the lad soundly, he would, even hold his supper from him if he didn't bring enough booty each day.

On the back street bars and alleys away from the upper-class parts of London he was called – 'Dudley the Dipper'."

"Poor lad," I said. "I thought he was an actor."

"He is, and a decent one. He picked it up while he was lifting the pockets of theatre-goers. He'd read Sherlock Holmes novels over and over to see if he could learn how to get around the law – be above it. Reading so many stories he literally became Sherlock Holmes gone awry."

"Can you save him, Sir Doyle?"

"Only he can save himself, Charlie. He looks to the Sherlock Holmes players as his family, now. Maybe they can help. I can watch over him, and must. Having a guardian angel gives the soul ballast, conscience. We'll see. Time will tell."

"I'll help you any way I can, Sir. Bless you for helping me through the week."

"I may have questions for you about the systems and procedures here in America, Charlie. Can I ask you to take me to where he might be, transition him and stay with me through the ordeal until I am acclimated?"

"Of course, you can, my friend. Let's go."

With that, ole Charlie here seemed to know what to do, don't ask me how. I raised my arm and without having to think about it both Sir Arthur Conan Doyle and I appeared in the center office of the Cazenovia courthouse and jail. Sheriff John was sitting on one side of the wooden table; Dudley Smythe was sitting on the other side smoking a cigarette.

We each sat on top of a filing cabinet to observe.

Sheriff John was making a point, "This will go a lot easier on you if you cooperate, young man. What's your name?"

"Yer the copper, Gov - find it yer own self. Why should I make it cushy for you?"

"I have twenty five wallets, four ladies purses," said Sheriff John. "We're looking at four hundred and thirty dollars here, plus the six hundred and forty you stole from the airplane ride pilot. Grand larceny in this state is two to twenty-one years."

"I found that satchel with all of them in it, I'll swear to it. You can't prove otherwise. I don't know why you're holding me. You got no case, Gov. Nobody can prove I took anything. I was about to turn them in."

"I have a witness, son. Remember the lady in the wheelchair?"
"So?"

"She's a fourth grade school teacher, and also a good actor. How many days do you think she was watching you - picking pockets on the Midway?"

Pickpocket nervously lit another cigarette.

It was here when Sir Doyle nudged Sheriff John by stirring up a breeze that shuffled some papers on a side desk. The sheriff stood and lifted a paperweight to set on the papers when he noticed handwriting of earlier notes about the pickpocket. The notes said he first spoke in a French accent, pretending he was Vichy. The sheriff turned, tweaked his chin with his thumb and finger – thinking. He lifted his leg and placed his foot on his chair, looking down and across the table at Sherlock.

"Here's what's going to happen now, Mr. Sherlock Holmes," said Sheriff John.

Feeling the jig may be coming to a boil - pickpocket raised his eyes looking up at the sheriff.

"Or would you prefer to be called "Monsieur Holmes?""

Pickpocket was jolted. He stiffened his back. Sheriff John saw the squirm. He tried again.

"I'm sure you have a mother and a father somewhere who will worry about you when you're locked up. Most likely some sisters and brothers," Sheriff John prodded. "I'm going to lock you in a cell so you can think about them, and what you're doing to their name. While you think about it I'm going to walk over to the Lincklean House and ask your actor friends about you. I'm sure they'll tell me everything I need to know."

Pickpocket stared down blankly at the table top.

Seeing his angst, Sheriff John tried again.

"Want to tell me your father's name so we can contact him?"

"What does your mother like to cook for holidays?

Do you have a sister? Is she married?

...any brothers?"

"Okay, okay, Sheriff, enough. I'll spill it - I'll tell you everything – just ask me. I'll tell you straight – anything you want to know. Please leave the actors out of this."

Ole Charlie here looked over at Sir Arthur Conan Doyle. He had his cheeks resting in the palms of his hands. His fingers were toying with his sideburns. He looked over at me, nodded his head and then he looked back at his Dudley Smythe.

"Let's start at the beginning," said Sheriff John. "Are you French Vichy or British? We have to report non-citizen arrests."

"My name is Smythe, Dudley Smythe. I'm British, Gov. I only pretended I was French Vichy so no one would get wise and connect me to my English acting troupe company. They're a good lot, they are."

"You pretended to be French, what - to cover your tracks?"

"Yeah, that's right, Gov, but not French – French Vichy – the Vichy were those Hitler-loving bastards."

Sheriff John sat down resting his forearms on the table. He waited for pickpocket to make the next move.

Slowly, methodically, nearly as if he were in a trance, Dudley Smythe stared down at the table top and began telling the story of how he could remember hearing the bombs from the Blitz every night, and the ground in all of London shaking under their quake beginning in 1939 and all through the War, until 1945. He told of his family hiding in the basement during a blackout and seeing the beam coming ajar and crushing his mother and father as he watched, helpless. He spoke of having to wait in the hospital hallway and hearing his sister screaming as they took her in to cut off her arm. He told of the homes he was in, the many beatings, running away. He told of the magician and the lifting of pockets and the books he had read, and finally running away from him.

"I lifted the wallets, Gov. Every one of 'em."

It was then when Sir Doyle rustled the air loosening more desktop papers.

Sheriff John got up, turned and stepped over to catch them. He paged through. One was the billboard poster for the Sherlock Holmes Players' performance in New Woodstock set for tomorrow.

"Starring Dudley Smythe as Sherlock Holmes and his 'family' of players," it said.

Sheriff John set the poster down, under the weight and stepped back to the table thinking.

"And the players had no part in any of your thefts?"

"Not a lick. I swear. They've been like a family to me – the lot of them."

Sir Doyle smiled, knowing the sheriff was thinking this through. The clue of the simple word 'family' was helping everything come together – to make sense to him.

"Okay, in the cell you go," the sheriff barked, "I have some thinking to do."

"I told you the truth, Gov. Honest I did. Every word."

Sheriff John took Dudley by the elbow and led him into a cell, locking the door.

"I'll get you some food. You must be hungry."

"I'm sorry I got cheeky with you, Gov. You're a good bloke."

Sheriff John pulled on his jacket and walked out of the court-house jail, locking the door behind him. He stepped off the curb and, looking both ways, he crossed Albany Street. He turned up the sidewalk and into the lobby of the Lincklean House. At the front desk he slapped on the bell two times.

She had come from the dining room next to the lobby from putting linens on tables preparing for tomorrow.

"May I help you, Sheriff?" came a voice from the night clerk lady.

"You have some actors here from England – the Sherlock Holmes actors?"

"We do," said the clerk.

"I need to see them all. How about in the back room - the one behind the dining area fireplace? That should be secluded enough."

"Is there any trouble, Sheriff?" asked the clerk.

"I just need to talk with those folks. Can you call them down?"

"Yes, of course. I'll call their rooms and send them in. They're all sharing two rooms. If they're not there I'll check the Seven Stone Steps pub below."

"I'll go in there and wait," said Sheriff John. "Thank you."

At the Parkers, lights beamed out from all the ground floor windows. Laughter and merriment was the order of the night. Eddie's satchel was on display in the middle of the table, as a prize.

"Can somebody pass the syrup," said Mayor.

"What time you taking off tomorrow, Eddie?" asked Marty.

"Mid-morning I think," said Eddie. "I could use some sun, flying in this cold air."

"Your little girls are going to be so happy," said Mary. "They'll get to see their daddy."

"Eddie," said Farmer Parker, "you're welcome to crank the phone and call them tonight. Or in the morning, if you'd care to let them know you're coming."

"I thought about it, Farmer Parker. I think I want to wait and surprise them."

"You're nervous," said Mary. "Don't forget what I told you about daddy's little girls. There's no need to be nervous."

"I bet pickpocket is nervous," said Holbrook. "I wonder if he's in jail or are they grilling him, making him sweat and confess under hot lights."

"You mean, Sherlock Holmes," said Barber.

"I wonder what could have happened to the map I left for him," said Marty. "It was marked to 'Messenger' I remember seeing it. The girl had three of them — mine and another two. I wonder what happened to Sheriff John's."

"Mrs. Parker can I have more pancakes, please?" asked Duba, avoiding the subject altogether.

"Honey, you can have all you want," said Mrs. Parker. "Plain or buckwheat, dear."

"Either one is fine."

"Mayor and I got to fly around tonight," said Mary. "It was so amazing flying low - it felt like we could reach out and touch the trees."

"Eddie is such a great pilot - I'll say!" said Mayor.

"We saw you buzzing the camp," said Marty.

"Yeah," said Jerry. We weren't sure if pickpocket was walking in and could see us so we pretended not to notice while you were doing it."

Big Mike and Missus stepped up to the back door. He rapped his knuckles on the window, opening it, and they both walked in.

"Hi, folks," said Big Mike. "Not here to spoil the party. Myrtie told us all the news. What an adventure it must have been! Well done, gang…

…wanted you to know, folks are planning celebration and a going-away party for you tomorrow, Eddie. Eleven o'clock – our place. Sheriff John will be there with some words to say. Now we've called each of your parents; they said you can all stay over tonight. Tomorrow being Sunday, all of them were okay with it. Mary, your dad said to tell you he'll deliver your papers."

Ole Charlie here invited Sir Doyle to join me at the party. It'd be a thank-you and a send-off party for Eddie, all rolled into one. Ain't nothing will let 'younguns' sleep better than knowing there's a new venture to dream about behind them and a social coming about wakeup time. Churchgoers would even let 'em sleep in, look the other way, tomorrow being Sunday. They figured the Pompey Hollow Book Club earned the right to sleep in this Sabbath with the good they'd done tonight.

That pretty much settled it. The club was staying over. Eddie was about to have a party before he took off. Wasn't a soul there not in favor of it, including Eddie.

"Eddie, are you crying?" asked Mary. "Don't cry, Eddie, be happy. We got your money back, just like we promised. It's going to be a great Christmas."

Eddie tightened his lip, looked up at the ceiling – shaking his head yes at Mary. It was his thank-you.

Jerry interrupted with a toast tapping on his glass with a spoon:
"After all, we ARE…

…the Pompey Hollow Book Club!"

"Here! Here!" said Dick raising his glass of milk in a toast. The SOS boys and the club just kicked some butt and took some names."

"Quit hogging the bacon," said Barber.

"Randy, grab the bacon plate away from Bases. Pass it over here, will ya?"

CHAPTER TWENTY FOUR

A RIGHT PROPER TAKE-OFF

Big Mike brought more boxes of warm glazed donuts from the bakery than ole Charlie here had ever seen. All lined up around the dining room table for the taking they were – and with large pots of hot chocolate with ladles in them and a big urn of coffee he borrowed from Leonard's Coffee Shop in Homer. Sugar piled high in a bowl for spoonin' and rich cream in glass quart bottles for the pouring. There was enough of everything for three helpings all around, sure enough, and then some.

Everybody inside the house was smiling and lickin' their lips smelling the honey glaze and fresh roast coffee in the air waiting for the festivities to start.

Outside was a different matter.

Cars and pickups were puttering in from the front gate like a Memorial Day parade, parking every which way – must be about twenty or so.

"I wonder who's coming," said Big Mike with a grin. The look on his face was a hint he was in on a secret.

It was Mike Shea from Shea's Store and the sheriff they let in first. Most everybody behind them edged their own way in smelling the coffee and donuts. They all gathered about, most removed their hats and waited for proper introduction and invite.

In the background, Sheriff John looked out the front window to the end of the long drive where he could see Dick driving in with his Willys car; then Duba drove behind him in the pickup; and then Conway in his Chevy.

"Here they come," he said.

They each parked in front of the barn garage and a group of gents and two young ladies crawled out of their vehicles and followed the lads into the house.

As they came in, Sheriff John said, "Would you please all stand over there for a second, if you will?"

He pointed toward the upright piano against the wall.

Little did he or anyone else know ole Charlie here and none other than Sir Arthur Conan Doyle were setting up on top of the upright taking it all in.

Big Mike got everyone's attention and had them turn – he had a sense Sheriff John was ready and had something important to say.

"Thank you all for being here," said Sheriff John. "You may not know each other, but many of you folks are here because you were pickpocketed at the State Fair this year. Some of you came because you helped us catch the culprit…and, yes, he is behind bars today…but I'll let Mike Shea take it from here."

Big Mike interjected, "Farmer and Mrs. Parker are here to join with everyone to say good bye to our new friend, Flying Eddie – but we hope it's only until next year when we see him again. We think the Parkers want to adopt the young man."

Mike Shea stepped up.

"I'm happy to report that every person who was robbed at the state fair has received their money and wallets or their purses back. I know most of you, and it pleases me to see you came for some fellowship and glazed donuts, compliments of Big Mike and Missus."

"Already?" asked Mary.

"Already what, Mary?" asked Mike Shea.

"Did everybody get their money back already?" Mary asked.

"Yes," said Mike Shea. "Well, they either have it or they know we got it and will get it to them. Fortunately we were able to identify all the owners of the wallets and purses and most of them were at home last night."

Pointing to the young people standing by the piano he added:

"Those nice young folks over there by the piano are all performers in the Sherlock Holmes Play that is going on this afternoon and tonight up in New Woodstock. They knew nothing of the pickpocket's shenanigans. They were most surprised. He was an actor with them and they were very disappointed to hear what he had done."

"So he really was Sherlock Holmes?" asked Duba.

"The best," said one of the actors.

"He was their lead actor," said Mike Shea. "But they have what's called an understudy who can play his part. What I would like you to know is - it was those actors standing over there that called you folks last night or drove to your homes and returned the wallets and purses before midnight and apologised for their friend's error in his ways."

"Was it hard finding the places, you being from England and all?" asked Holbrook.

The eldest Sherlock Holmes player spoke up:

"Someone who knew the area went with each of us, mate. Hardest part was driving on the proper side of the road. We do it backwards back home."

"Thievery it was," mumbled one farmer.

"It certainly was," said Mike Shea. "And as you should, and had every right to - several pressed charges against the scoundrel last night. I can't blame you one bit for being upset."

"Being as there were charges pressed," said Sheriff John, "I called Mike Shea to see if we could get a court date set. The law says the young man had to go before a judge."

"Folks," said Mike Shea. "I called Judge Munson, in Syracuse late last night. I woke him up, in fact. I thought it best not to talk about going fishing at that hour. I straight out told him the situation we had and asked him about setting a court date, given the extenuating circumstance that the pickpocket isn't a citizen and all."

"We wanted to take his confessing into consideration," said Sheriff John. "The fact he wanted to make restitution."

Mike Shea added, "I told Judge Munson about the acting company calling everyone and apologizing on behalf of their friend – and of their getting every wallet and purse they could, back to their owners – one even being as far away as Schenectady."

"He needs to pay for his crime," came a voice.

"And he will," said Sheriff John.

Mike Shea stepped in.

"Judge Munson met us in the courthouse at three this morning. His bailiff came in his pajamas – the court reporter came in hair curlers. But we sure enough had a court. The young man pled guilty – no question about it - he didn't try to hide behind any excuses."

"We told the judge how the money was returned or the owners notified – and that's all we told him, I assure you," said Sheriff John. "It wasn't our intent to go light on him."

"Judge Munson gave him ninety days, at which time he's deported and has to leave the country," said Sheriff John. "He's letting him serve his time in Cazenovia city jail."

"Good," said a voice from the crowd.

"Serves him right," said another.

With that, and the air cleared about the capture and punishment of the notorious pickpocket – Big Mike called Eddie up to the table for the first glazed donut and cup of coffee.

"Eddie," said Big Mike, "we are proud to make your acquaintance. You've only been here a week but you graced us with a week we'll be talking about for a long time. You gave us an adventure we'll never forget. Thank you for it from all of us and special thanks for your service to our country, especially on D-Day. You'll always have many friends here, Eddie."

Oh it was a buzz after that. Everyone going about socializing and catching up with each other while licking the glaze chips from ofn' their lip and sipping their coffee or hot chocolate. It was a time…

Round about the second cup for everyone Big Mike took Eddie aside and told him to call a Mr. Spaulding when he got back to Binghamton. Mr. Spaulding owned a bakery in Binghamton and was a friend of Big Mikes. Said he would give Eddie a job – any job he wanted – and he'd let him off to give plane rides at the State Fair, as well.

Eddie then stepped over and asked Barber to gather the book club around for some last words. Most came in no time at all with a warm glazed donut in their hand.

"I don't know what to say to all of you other than you're the best friends a body could have. I'm sorry I was such a mess when I got here. Thank you for helping me through it…and I hope you always think of me as a friend."

"We will, not to worry," was pretty much the sentiment he heard back.

"And I promise I'll bring the wife and kids up sometime before the end of the year so they can meet my new friends."

"Eddie, said Mary, "When you land in Binghamton, park that plane fast and run hug everybody the longest hug ever. Hug them for us too."

Marty piped in, "Now, Eddie, don't be landing on top of any hayfield hills or too close to barns. We'll want to see you back here in one piece."

Mayor saluted Eddie.

"Thanks for the ride in your plane, Eddie."

Then he teared up and turned away.

It was just before the third cup, the Sherlock Holmes Players let it slip they had free tickets for everyone there – for anyone who wanted to go to the show. It became the buzz of the donut clutch.

"Well, what good would a play about Sherlock Holmes be without Sherlock Holmes in it?" asked Farmer Skeele from up Fabius hill way.

"Farmer Skeele, the young man is in jail serving time at the moment," said Sheriff John. "He can't very well be in the play."

"Well, what good would a Sherlock Holmes play be without Sherlock Holmes being in it?" repeated Farmer Skeele.

"Farmer Skeele, what are you saying – are you saying they shouldn't have the play? They have a substitute actor for the Sherlock Holmes role." said Mike Shea.

"No, I'm suggesting just because he inconvenienced us once ain't no reason he should be allowed to get away with inconveniencing us agin' by not acting in the play that people like us paid good money to see, is all," argued Farmer Skeele. "We didn't pay all that money just to see a substitute."

"Farmer Skeele…well…Duane, you didn't have to pay for tickets. Actually the tickets have been given to you free of charge," said Mike Shea.

"Makes no never mind," insisted Farmer Skeele. "A play just ain't a play of any quality without, well, you know – the players."

"Farmer Skeele, might I remind you, you were one of the three people who pressed charges against the lad."

"Well, what's that got to do with a play?"

"Yeah!" Chorused the second and third persons who pressed charges against the pickpocket. "What's that got to do with the play?"

"I say give him back some of his own medicine. He took something that didn't belong to him. Make him give us something that does – a free performance."

Farmer Skeele's proposition was a most compelling conflict in juris prudence was how Sir Arthur Conan Doyle put it to ole Charlie here.

Mrs. Skeele interrupted, hoping to put it all to rest. "You're not going to win, Sheriff. Duane's pretty much made up his mind. His favorite book – one he keeps at the bedside is Sherlock Holmes. Only reason he pressed charges was the rapscallion besmirched the name of Sherlock Holmes. Weren't no other reason t'all. Herbert Duane Skeele, you tell the sheriff like it is now."

Farmer Skeele stood stiff and tight-mouthed. His lips were sealed.

"Show of hands," said Sheriff. "How many here want to see the Sherlock Holmes play with Sherlock Holmes in it?"

Every hand went up.

"...and how many will watch it without resorting to the temptations of booing or hissing or throwing grapefruits or rotten tomatoes," asked Mike Shea.

Every hand but Farmer Skeele's stayed up.

"Duane, you're objecting?" asked Sheriff, befuddled.

"When will his ninety days start, yesterday, today or tomorrow after the show?"

"How about tomorrow," said Sheriff John. "After the shows this afternoon and tonight. Will that suit you?"

Skeele's arm went full up.

Pots and urns emptied, donuts gone, everyone walked together down the driveway and to the field just beyond the alfalfa field.

"Farmer Parker, Mrs. Parker," whispered Eddie. "When I get her in the air, watch for my wave. It'll be just for you. I'm sorry I was such a nuisance. Thank you both for everything. I'll bring the family by soon, I promise."

The book club followed Eddie across the field to his plane.

"We're standing here at the end of the runway so we can wave when you take off and fly over us," said Mary.

Flying Eddie started her up, moved the chocks and taxied down the length of the field. Everyone but the book club lined up along the road.

From the distance you could hear the engine roaring as he turned it around to take off, the propeller slicing through the air, pistons pounding. The biplane rolled and bumped along the length of the field, faster and faster she came.

Just before it jumped off the ground and into the air, Eddie looked out the side of his cockpit, caught Mary Crane's eye, pointed to her, saluted and off he flew.

Up it climbed, over the trees next to the creek – climbing up Farmer Parker's side pasture hill over Buddy's grave. The plane disappeared over the hill...

It was just as people started milling about when the plane reappeared, going the wrong way. Engine whining as it sliced the air flying fighter plane fast at about a low thousand feet to the Maxwell place down on the corner. Once there it banked a sweeping U turn and sped back, straight as an arrow up Cardner Road...

Farmer and Mrs. Parker were in the middle of the road waving at the lad. At just the right moment the wings of the plane did a sharp tip down to the right and up and then a sharp tip down to the left and up.

It was an Air Force salute to the Parkers, Flying Eddie's new friends.

The plane climbed...disappearing into a cloud in the horizon, on its way home to Binghamton...

EPILOGUE

Economists say globalization had its roots around the millennium. I think it started back in 1939, with the advent of the first and only world War this planet has ever known. If the youth of today take the care and remember this War and the times - study them, not bury them, we just might learn all over again how to coexist. If you look closely - at the largest War in history that ripped our world apart – it was our ability to coexist during those horrendous years that enabled the world – the globe - to prevail and win the War. If we don't keep a lamp burning on that one simple fact and retain this history for other generations to study – the Hitler's will ultimately win and the world will lose. JMA

www.ingramcontent.com/pod-product-compliance
Lightning Source LLC
Chambersburg PA
CBHW031230120726
47905CB00002B/534